RABBIT HEART

BOOK 1 OF THE TERRAFOLK TRILOGY

FRANCESCA CRISPO

IBSN: 979-8-9885719-0-2

Cover illustration by Melissa Hudson - www.mhudson-illustration.com

Editing and proofreading by Three Fates Editing - www.threefatesediting.com

Formatting by Nezhda Seyfulova - www.nezhformatting.org

CONTENTS

To my husband, for a love story more magical than any fantasy novel.

AUTUMN

CHAPTER ONE

*I*magine if one day, deep in the middle of what seemed like nowhere, you stumbled upon a hidden, completely untouched society. What's more, you realized the creatures of this society had complicated rituals and social structures... and yet they were so familiar, so *human*. When you stumbled upon this hidden society, perhaps you would gently, respectfully, and reluctantly attempt to study it. You'd observe. You'd listen and watch and breathe their air. You'd probably be amazed, full of wonder; at least, I hope that you would approach this opportunity with naive excitement like I would. If you were like me, maybe you'd try to experience the world from many points of view: you'd lie on your belly in the dirt, look through the holes of leaves, and watch your crawling step as you explored their domain, careful not to disrupt or damage anything around you. That's how I feel about humans.

Although my people, a race of elemental beings called terrafolk, have always known about human existence, we often spoke of your kind as if you were something out of a story. You probably feel the same about us. What would the humans call us, if they'd discovered us, I wonder? Forest spirits? Elves? It's hard to say, but I suppose any name would make sense except for "fairies," which is considered a slur among our people. I couldn't tell you why, other than the fact that it associated us with glittery little wisps with wings and fragility – an image that our kind don't like to be associated with.

Because my kind look so much like yours, it was quite easy for me to blend in, at least physically. Living in the forest also teaches you how to move gracefully, how to blend into your surroundings, and how to adapt; this was helpful in my transition between worlds, though I didn't always understand human behavior. Animals felt more intuitive in comparison. Do humans ever feel confused by the behavior of their own kind? If you do, you must be better at hiding it than I am.

After venturing out from home and my people with no specific return date in mind, I found a small, somewhat cramped – and yet, outrageously expensive – apartment above the bar and restaurant I'd somehow acquired a job at. Both my job and new home were right in the heart of Seattle because that was the major city closest to Yannava, the forest where I'd spent the past several hundred years. I was in the middle of watering the tangle of plants that lined the balcony and sliding glass door when my fully human roommate, Zara, came home from work. It seemed like people were constantly bringing us plants in need of rehabilitation, and our home had quickly become a miniature jungle that was thriving in my care despite the rapidly cooling temperatures of fall. I wasn't sure how the word got out, but we became known as the house of green thumbs, which is curious because Seattle was going through a period of booming plant sales citywide. Apparently, however, folks were quickly realizing that they had no clue how to care for the rare and shockingly expensive – yes, your entire paycheck kind of expensive – plants that they'd acquired as part of the trend. How could people put a price on a leaf? I wasn't sure.

My preoccupation with the plants and my tendency to become easily consumed by whatever I was working on meant that I hadn't bothered to see if Zara was still nearby or if she'd gone to her room to relax. As I emptied the remainder of my watering can and watched the parched soil of a new plant thirstily gulp each drop of water, I smiled to myself. Then, of course, I dipped my fingertips into the cold, new mud with a sigh. Small red and white mushrooms sprouted from the holes I'd made with my fingers, and the plant, the newest addition to our home, seemed to perk up immediately with the added attention. Despite my magick with plants, it seemed to me that people just lacked basic knowledge on what most plants needed: water, light, and positive thoughts. It turns out most people would probably benefit from the same.

On the ledge of our balcony, my familiar, Mazus, watched me with curious eyes. Maz, as I often called him, was a small crow with glistening black feathers. He chattered noisily as I worked with the plant and made comments about my behavior that only I could hear: *Are those the kind of mushrooms you can eat? Can I eat one? No?*

"I wouldn't," I murmured aloud, tracing the cap of one of the mushrooms with a damp fingertip. Without thinking, I sunk my fingers further until they were deep in the pot and, when I withdrew them, smeared the slick, chilled soil over my cheeks. For me, nothing compared to the scent of wet soil. I was immediately transported home, where the scent of the damp ground drying after a rain was the most divine intoxicant to me. I imagined lying on it as the animals stayed holed up in their homes and smiled, inhaling the scent of wet earth.

You look ridiculous, the crow told me with a chitter that sounded a lot like laughter.

Before I could respond, my roommate chimed in, "Oh my gosh, did you go to LUSH without me?"

I raised an eyebrow, hastily wiping my muddy hands on my pants, and stared at my roommate in confusion as a glob of mud dripped onto my shirt with a splat. She was standing at the breakfast bar between our kitchen and living room, work backpack still slung over her shoulder. I'd been around humans long enough to know that my gardening adventures often weren't acceptable behavior, but sometimes my wild side just took hold of me and I failed to consider what my audience might be. "Huh?" I had no idea what lush was, but had found that vague confusion was the easiest way to learn things from humans. They always wanted to talk about themselves and their interests and their, er, lush.

"Your mud mask! That looks so, like, *nourishing*, you know? I bet it does wonders for your skin. Your skin always looks so fresh and dewy..." she mumbled before dropping her bag onto one of the bar stools in our kitchen and opening the fridge. "I'm kind of jealous."

Mud *is* nourishing, I thought.

Zara was a short, slender, and fiery young Black woman who was the age I likely appeared to be in human years – probably late twenties or early thirties. She wore her hair cropped close to her skull except for the top and back, where it was fashioned into a mohawk of tight curls, and she was covered in tattoos, even on the sides of her head. I loved the way she decorated herself, even though part of that decoration extended to our apartment, which seemed to be in constant disarray. Somehow she still knew how to find exactly what she was looking for, though. Looking for a pen? Zara could probably describe its coordinates down to the inch even if that meant you'd find it in the top right corner of her room, under her bed, and behind three boxes and a box of tissues.

So what's lush? the crow chirped curiously, his words forming in my mind. Mazus kept me feeling sane when the human world confused me.

"No clue, Maz." I returned to my gardening, tuning out the sound of cars buzzing past on the street below. We lived on a side street, but were still pretty far downtown Seattle proper, so the air around us was constantly buzzing with human noise. I plucked a red flower from a nearby plant and stuck it behind my ear as I worked on pruning, watering, and generally sending kind thoughts to the plants on our balcony.

"Michelle? Michelle!" That was what Zara called me since the day we'd met; I had introduced myself and she'd misheard my actual name, Mycel, for this, apparently common, human name. I've been Michelle to the humans ever since; that's the name on my name tag at work, on my apartment lease, and every other important human document. I'd met other Michelles, so I imagined it worked just fine as a human name. Some research taught me that this name has something to do with God, which is a thing that humans believe in as well, so it checked all the boxes for me.

"Nice to meet you, Michelle," she'd said, shaking my hand with a grip that was firmer than I'd expected. I wondered if she used her strength to compensate for her small stature. The look on her face seemed friendly and curious.

"Michelle?"

Just like now, it seemed that Zara had a knack for ignoring my quirks and keeping the ball rolling when others might have found my behavior suspicious or off-putting. "You know, my brother's wife's cousin is named Michelle. She's pretty alright, I guess. You seem cooler."

When I finally looked up, my roommate gestured to a small white box on the counter bearing the logo of the restaurant and bar that we both worked at – a P&P with a peach behind it. "Brought you a snack, made it myself. Make sure to eat before work this time! I'm going to take a nap."

"I will, I promise." I smiled, crossing my heart with a muddy finger and waving her off. We worked opposite shifts, and she always brought extra desserts home from her work as a pastry chef, though I wasn't sure if it was because they were going to get thrown in the trash or because she was worried about my forgetfulness when it came to feeding myself. While human food was truly one of my favorite things about living in Seattle, I often found myself so caught up in the day-to-day experiences of human life that eating slipped my mind; I just wanted to soak up every last bit of my time here.

Once Zara disappeared to her room, I wandered over to the box and unwrapped it with care. Inside was a small fruit tart with purplish filling and edible flowers on top. I scarfed it down in two bites, licked my fingers clean ignoring the lingering taste of potting soil, tossed the box, and made my way to the bathroom to prepare for work.

Moments later I was mud-free and dressed in what Zara had taught me was appropriate attire for a bartending job; high-waisted black jeans with a loose black blouse tucked into them. I had one pair of black leather boots that I wore nearly all the time because they were the only attire from home that actually blended into the human world; in fact, I'd made them myself and knew that they'd stand up to any terrain and wear-and-tear I sent their way. My boots also had a little slit in one of the heels where I kept a small blade. I mostly used it for opening packages and slicing up apples to share with Maz on the balcony, but I couldn't get over the habit of keeping it nearby just in case. After all, Seattle was supposedly full of shady characters like most big cities, and I'd been encouraged to keep protection on me at all times. I tied my wild mane up into a messy bun and glanced in the mirror briefly.

Whereas Zara was short and thin, I was tall and thick. At just under six feet tall, I found myself to be among the tallest of female humans I'd encountered, and for whatever reason, many of my traits appeared to spark a lack of confidence in humans that embodied them as well. That felt strange to me because I found myself marveling at any women I encountered that were bigger or taller than me. I had wide hips, a soft middle, muscular thighs and arms, and a strong, but less-than-bountiful chest. My body was made for running through the forest barefoot, climbing trees, and lifting boulders to explore beneath them. I loved those things about myself, just as I loved the bodies of the people I'd encountered so far: all wondrous in their own ways. Perhaps one day soon, I'd understand why humans seemed dead-set on finding reasons to be at war with themselves.

Zara popped her head out of her room as I grabbed my bag and went for the door. "Forgot to tell you, sprout – there's a big event at the restaurant tonight," she told me with a yawn, probably exhausted from preparing for it. She looked set for sleep in a pair of plaid pajama pants and a tank top, though I could still see smudges of decorating chocolate on her now sleeveless forearms, where they accented her various tattoos. I stifled a chuckle when I noticed that it looked like the flaming skull on one arm was licking the chocolate. "I bet it'll be a good night for tips... and phone numbers." She winked and retreated before I could say anything else. Then, almost as if on cue, the phone in my back pocket buzzed with a message.

TEXT FROM ANALA

Hey M. Miss you. Any chance we can link up tonite? ;)

Sorry – big party @ work. Maybe another time!

I was really bad at turning people down. Anala had been fun, but I didn't feel like we had anything long-term, much like I felt with most humans I encountered. That was okay with me. Part of the appeal of adventure for me was the fleeting excitement and promise of encountering so many new people and experiences over such a short period of time. I headed to work without a second thought about Anala. Maz followed, hopping from tree to tree above me, until I ducked into the restaurant for my shift. Although the little bird had been my familiar since I was a baby and he was a hatchling, we both respected that we had our own lives and places in the universe; we'd meet up again at the end of the night and marvel over the strangeness of humans together.

CHAPTER TWO

a big city like Seattle might seem an odd place to venture into when being around humans isn't your forte, but it's the closest large city to the Olympic Rainforest where I'm from. That's what you call it, at least; my people call our kingdom in the woods Yannava. Though there are terrafolk from every ecosystem of the earth, my people are blessed with magick from the forest. Although it's vastly different from living solely in the woods, Seattle's similar climate had helped me acclimate a bit to life in the city. I found the city to be dirty, confusing, and incredible. It was the first place I'd ever encountered a pigeon, also, which had proven to be one of my favorite new creatures aside from the humans. It felt unfortunate that my two new favorite groups seemed constantly at war with each other, but the pigeons were not very forthcoming in their explanation of what had started the human-pigeon war.

Maz was also wary of the pigeons.

I slipped my phone into my back pocket again just as I arrived downstairs for work. Peach & Port was just like any other hip bar and restaurant in Seattle, boasting local alcohol and "farm-to-table" food. I'd originally been very confused by the concept of "farm-to-table" until I'd learned about factory farming, which was a completely foreign concept to me. P&P drew in all sorts of folks, from grungy locals swinging by for a drink, to couples out on a date night, to people negotiating business affairs over expensive dinners.

Zara was right; the restaurant and consequently, the bar were bustling. It seemed primarily occupied by a large party of men who were already engaged in a business meeting, but there was also the regular bustle of patrons finding their way in as they usually did on Friday evenings. I didn't really focus on them too much as I grabbed an apron, clocked in, and headed back to the bar.

The bartender role, although difficult for me to learn at first, was the perfect fit for me; it allowed me to mingle with the humans, but also gave me the perfect spot for observation and learning without being too obvious. It's incredible the things you overhear while people are chatting with each other, especially when alcohol is involved. Bartending also appealed to me because mixing drinks felt a bit like concocting a magic potion, which was endlessly amusing to me.

The evening went on as they normally do for me, and a few regulars filtered in in addition to the business party, which eventually dispersed, leaving a few men at the table by themselves. Before I could take a good look at them, my attention was yanked away again. The constant change in direction that day had me feeling a bit disoriented. Despite my time in the human world, I found I still longed for the unique chaos of the forest. I understood how everything worked there and exactly where I fit in, even if it would've seemed disorienting to an outsider.

"Hey stranger," purred a voice to my right. Anala, a stunning young Indian woman, was leaning on her forearms over the bar.

She had long, catlike nails that she tapped on the bartop to get my attention; the sound made my brain feel like it was buzzing. Her gold-eyed gaze was heavy-lidded, and if I didn't already know her to be the flirt she was, I'd assume she'd been drinking already. Her dark hair tumbled over one of her shoulders in waves and nearly grazed the counter thanks to its length. She was a truly captivating woman, and anyone who encountered her would likely agree that she was attractive... until they got to know her better. Beautiful, yes, but also quite overpowering. Anala was like an overly fragrant flower or a straight shot of strong liquor.

"Anala, hi," I replied, putting on the customer service voice I'd learned for this setting. I didn't particularly like it when I told someone I wasn't available and they then proceeded to show up at my work, of all places. Fortunately, this was more public and more appropriate than her showing up at my apartment, which she also knew the location of. I knew that my coworkers would be likely to comment on her hovering and my boss would want to ensure that I wasn't screwing around on the clock. That concern itself still felt a bit foreign to me. Adjusting to living on someone else's schedule and for a meager wage was definitely a big change for me; the service part, meanwhile, didn't faze me. "What can I get for you?" I flipped the glass I'd been cleaning up in the air and caught it, then placed it on the counter and locked eyes with her.

"I mean, I'd really like the chance to walk you home tonight." Whew! She really wasted no time in attempting to put on the charm. "We had a fun time last week, didn't we?"

"It's not a far walk, Anala. I think I can handle it." Um, it was literally one flight of stairs above the restaurant. I understood that she was looking for any excuse to get into my bed and pants, but sometimes I used my natural, oblivious thought process as a defense mechanism; I knew she wouldn't come out and say that she was trying to hook up.

"You know what I mean." She giggled, an over-the-top sound meant to make her seem submissive and feminine, brushing her raven hair behind her ear and looking me over with her glimmering, soulful eyes. She ran her tongue over her shapely lips, which were painted an eggplant color. They were nice, I admit, and she had been a good kisser. "But for now, I guess my usual will do."

I forced a half-smile and nodded before turning to make her "usual": a Moscow Mule with extra ginger. I busied myself by spending extra time cooling a copper cup for her beverage.

When she took a sip, she winked at me. "Perfect, you know exactly how I like it." I shrugged a little, unsure of how it could be possible to screw up what I'd learned to be a very simple drink and slightly annoyed at her attempt to continue flirting with me. I wasn't interested, and even though we'd had fun, her pushiness was becoming more and more of a turn-off. "So, I'm guessing you're off in a couple of hours... What are my chances of going home with you?"

I gritted my teeth and forced an apologetic smile, irritated by her persistence. "Low," I snipped. "I'm sorry. It's really busy tonight and I'll probably end up staying late..."

As if on cue, the edge of Anala's sleeve shifted and a small red newt – the woman's familiar – skittered its way out onto the bar top. It tilted its head to the side, looking up at me with beady eyes, then turned back to Anala. "I don't think she's interested anymore, Ember," she told the lizard with a dramatic frown.

Trying my best not to crush the small creature, I clasped my hand over the top of it. "It's not that. This just isn't very discreet," I muttered, voice low as I placed the lizard back into Anala's open palm. I lowered my voice even more and whispered, "Humans aren't used to having animals all over the place."

Much to my dismay, Anala simply took her familiar and

plopped it into a half-full glass of water on the bar, where it swam happily.

It was then that a cheer from the large table of businessmen stole my attention once more. "To ocean conservation! And a fruitful partnership!" one of them said loudly, raising his glass to make a toast. The others joined in, and I used that as an excuse to leave my current charge. "Excuse me," I told her, flagging down a waitress nearby with a small wave. Anala rolled her eyes, but turned away in the bar stool and sipped her drink. "What's going on there?" I asked Rachel, a younger girl who'd just recently started with us. She was thin and tall, a few inches shorter than me, with curly blond hair and sparkling blue eyes.

"They're celebrating some big business deal." She shrugged, then scooted past me with a tray of food expertly balanced in one hand. "Expect more drink orders soon, I'm guessing... some of those guys are a little *too* in the mood for celebration, if you know what I mean. They better be good tippers..." Rachel looked annoyed, but dutifully carried her tray toward the table.

I nodded and gave her a look that said 'let me know if any of them get too friendly' before turning back toward the bar. Soon enough, I forgot all about them and Anala and fell into my routine, chatting up regulars and getting to know new patrons. It was nice. Fun. Easy for me now that I had a handle on how humans operated and what they liked. I liked thinking that they liked me and what I had to offer; I liked feeling like I was fulfilling all of my duties in this position. At one point, a particularly happy member of the business party made his way to the bar to order another drink and bought me a shot while he was at it. It certainly seemed celebratory, so I assumed he'd come out on a favorable end of their deal. I tossed the shot back and flashed them a goofy smile, as if potato water had any effect on me. It didn't. It was cute to watch what alcohol could do to humans, though more often than not I

found myself concerned about their lack of control and self-preservation when under the influence. Besides, there are way tastier
uses for a potato and things way more intoxicating to distill than a
grain... I'd brewed concoctions that made me feel like I was
exploring an alien planet or walking on the sky.

Just as I tilted my chin down and licked my lips clean, someone
at the table of the large party caught my eye. It was simple, really.
He just happened to be looking my way when I was looking at him
and that was it – he caught my eye. It wasn't quite like what I had
seen happen in movies. Time didn't slow, my pupils didn't turn
into hearts, and I didn't trip and fall due to my distraction. I caught
myself trapped in this man's stare from far away, though, and it
felt beyond my control. From where I stood, I could tell that his
eyes were light, a stunning blue-green, and his lips were pressed
into a hard line, as if he was concerned. The harshness of the
expression was beautiful on him. This wasn't an entirely new
feeling for me, though... I have a tendency to fall in love with little
bits of people without even knowing them, like the way their
perfume smells while passing me or the pace of their walk.

I still remember every detail about the first human I became
enamored with. I was walking through the city, absolutely lost and
unsure of where I was going, when I bumped into a young punk
kid dressed in tattered clothes, adorned with spikes, and sporting a
foot-high mohawk. Something about the smell of his obviously
less-than-clean clothing, hair gel, and the cigarette he was smoking
caused me to turn back and look at him after we'd collided. In
response, he looked back and sneered, though there was a mischie-
vous glint in his green eyes when he hollered, "Take a picture, lady,
it'll last longer!" and flipped me off. It was charming. Oddly,
though, that brief moment made me feel seen in a way I hadn't
quite yet by the humans.

And now, I found my breath caught in my throat when the bar

patron tore his gaze away from mine and looked back to his business partners to mutter something. He forced a smile following his comment. I listened intently, confused by the entire ordeal, and I tried to focus on both their conversation and the very tipsy man at my counter. "Yes, of course. They'll be pleased to hear that our alliance is coming together so smoothly and for the benefit of so many," the man with the blue-green eyes said, though his enthusiasm didn't reach his voice either; not only that, but he was much calmer than his colleagues despite the positive content of his commentary. He tucked a lock of his golden mane behind his ear, then twirled his glass of water so that the ice cubes hit the sides while he nodded along to whatever his colleagues were talking about. Perhaps he masked his true self like I did, though he didn't seem quite as happy as I was to be doing so. For the most part, my mask benefited me, gave me access to things I desired. It had downsides, yes, like ignoring many of my basic instincts and attempting to suppress my quirks unless I was around Zara, who conveniently just didn't notice them. From what I could tell, this wasn't the same for the man at the table.

I wasn't expecting, however, to turn around from making another drink for a patron and find the mystery man now standing at the bar. "Oh!" The drink slipped from my hands, but somehow I caught it before it hit the counter; my reflexes have always been pretty good as someone who has spent centuries blending in to the sometimes-dangerous forest and balancing on tree branches or mountain ledges, but I rarely had to use them like this in the human world. I swallowed hard, then set the drink down on the counter, wiping up the droplets I'd spilled before addressing the green-eyed man. I fiddled with the bar rag, using the texture of the fibers as a mild distraction. "Sorry, I didn't see... you, um, uh... can I get you something?" I forced a smile, but the act itself confused me. I was happy to be speaking to him, but for some reason my face wasn't catching up with my brain. Something about his demeanor made it seem like he was safer to admire from afar rather than risk mingling with up close. Perhaps he was dangerous. Many predators are beautiful, after all… and my, was he stunning: a sculpted jawline, slight chin cleft, and pristine, crisp clothing. It didn't look like there was a crease to be found anywhere on him, and his face, while not clean shaven, seemed to have the exactly perfect amount of stubble on it to look just care-free enough. Had he forgotten to shave for a day or was it just as calculated as the rest of the front he put up?

Before he could answer, though, his partner in business and now in celebration elbowed him in the side. "How 'bout a Sex on the Beach, champ?" he suggested. His comment was followed by one of those god-awful drunken laughs, as if he was so proud of his joke and expected applause for it, picking up the additional drink I'd given him. "I'd say ya earned it!" The balding, middle-aged man grinned at his colleague, leaning heavily on the counter as he tried to steady himself. A sheen of sweat was forming on his upper lip, and he seemed to be out of breath even though he was standing in one spot. It was beyond time to cut this man off. I cursed myself mentally for letting him drink so much and promised that I'd keep an eye on him for the evening. Unfortu-nately, I'd let him become my responsibility because I'd been too careless to give him more of my attention.

Somehow, the masked man didn't miss a beat. "I think I'll pass on that for tonight, Matthews," he told the man with a good-natured chuckle. I wondered how long he'd worked to become that effortlessly charismatic; any outsider could see that he was humoring this man and yet Matthews seemed as pleased as ever. Was it possible that some people were just like that? Just effort-lessly smooth? That must've been nice. "I'm just here to make sure you're not harassing our host. Wouldn't want you giving the Salt and Earth Alliance a bad name... I'd like to return to this restaurant in the future." He glanced at me as he made the last comment, his eyes glittering and attentive. I basked in his gaze and didn't bother to stifle the smile that spread across my face.

"Bah, bet you would! You're no fun..." The businessman waved him off before grabbing his drink and then turning to chat up Anala, who was still sitting at the bar. She was nothing if not persistent. I'd have to keep an eye on them while I worked, not because I was feeling possessive of the young woman, but because I didn't want any harm coming to her even if she had been annoying the ever-loving shit out of me. When I finally looked back toward the taller man, I didn't thank him; keeping other men in check was the least human males could do to protect their female counterparts.

"Nothing for you, then?" I asked on an exhale.

"I'm not a big drinker," he confessed as if it was an oddity – it was, especially for someone at a bar on a Friday night in Seattle – and leaned on the bar on his palms. His fingers strummed the surface idly while his forearms bulged under his clean dress shirt, threatening to tear the fabric. The vein running from his hands into the cuffs of his shirt caught my eye. I felt heat rise in my cheeks. "But I wouldn't mind trying something new if you have a suggestion." Oh hell, could I be the "something new"? I found myself flustered as his eyes bored into mine; perhaps I'd gotten far too used to bar patrons flirting with me and thought that I could will this man to be just like everyone else. My mind began to wander away from me as I imagined straddling his waist while sitting on the bar. I could envision exactly how the fabric of his fine shirt would feel under my fingers, the way his breath would smell, and the way those green-blue eyes might twinkle up close.

We settled on a Tom Collins without much conversation, and when he grabbed it from the bar, I stifled a sigh of relief knowing that he would be gone soon. Leave. Come back. Leave. Come closer. God, please. While I knew to add his drink to the party's tab, he leaned over to stuff a crisp twenty-dollar bill into my tip jar before walking back to the table he'd been at moments before. Prior to tasting his drink, he raised the glass at me in imaginary cheers. I nodded in response, unable to muster a smile for all of my flustered bewilderment, and returned to my work, exhaling again as I turned away. For whatever reason, I couldn't wait for my shift to be over. I turned away from the bar, flushed, to take a break and check the clock: twenty minutes left.

CHAPTER THREE

After hastily wrapping up my shift and clocking out, I stepped out of the restaurant into the crisp late-fall air, leaves crunching under my boots. It was dark and had been for quite some time. My pocket contained a larger-than-usual amount of tips, which was nice, and I wondered what I might buy with that extra cash; the human world was full of little treasures that I'd never be able to find back home. The rest of my people would've called these tendencies materialistic or consumerist, but I didn't care. I gave a lot to nature and took very little in return. The least I could ask for was a candle or piece of clothing that I'd never find in my homeland. Maz, too, enjoyed collecting special objects from the human world. His favorite seemed to be small beads, strings, and scraps of fabric that he'd find in the streets of the city. In fact, the windowsill of my bedroom was littered with his tiny treasures.

The leaves distracted me again. That was one of my favorite sounds. It seemed that Seattleites loved the feel of fall as well. I was even beginning to acquire a taste for the infamous "pumpkin spice latte," though it tasted absolutely nothing like pumpkin. I knew pumpkin. I'd grown and harvested and fashioned homes for squirrels out of pumpkin. That was not pumpkin. Zara had tried a million times to explain to me that it was pumpkin-pie-*spice* that the beverage was modeled after, not the gourd itself. Nevertheless, the acquired taste was part of my mask and I diligently purchased at least one pumpkin spice latte each fall season in the city.

The restaurant and bar didn't close for a couple more hours, so I had left hoping I could make my way back home without encountering many departing patrons. Unfortunately for me, the door behind me suddenly opened. I tried to ignore the conversation between those who exited it and turned the corner toward the stairwell that took me back to our apartment, feeling hopeful that my quiet sanctuary was so close by.

I had barely made it a couple of steps when I noticed the very tipsy middle-aged man from earlier attempting to wave down a taxi where there weren't any. Matthews, was it? Maz let out a startled cry from a nearby tree, one that no one else would've noticed, but that I'd home in on anywhere. We didn't see a lot of taxis on that street, but unfortunately for Matthews, one had made its way down the road toward him, and he was literally in the street. I sighed, feeling oddly responsible for this drunken idiot, and headed toward the road. Just as my foot left the sidewalk and my hand closed around the moron's coat sleeve, the blinding light of another car's headlights hit the side of my face. I squinted, realizing what was about to happen, and had to make the split-second decision of what to do. I shoved the drunk man farther into the road and knocked both of us from the path of the swerving car, annoyed that we were now both face down in the middle of a side road in the city. The street was dirty, littered with trash and scattered with puddles. My body ached momentarily, then returned to its normal state of uninjured comfort. Meanwhile, the man on the ground next to me groaned; he would feel that for a lot longer than

I would, but hurt was better than dead. I'd managed to avoid the police this long, and I didn't want my first interaction with them to involve paperwork regarding a dead human. That would be a bad look.

"Get up, Matthews," I heard a newly familiar voice order as I was hauled up off the ground by a man's hands. Blue-green-eyes-sandy-hair stood there with his free hand extended toward the groaning man. The next thing I knew, I was pressed up against him while he pulled his business partner up out of the road and directed both of us onto the sidewalk. My surroundings spun a bit, which was a new sensation for me; not much frazzled me in the way of physical experiences, and I gripped the taller man's shirt without realizing it. I stayed glued to him without thinking until he'd directed Matthews into a rideshare and sent him on his way. He grumbled to himself about idiocy and then looked down at me, where I was still nestled against him like a scared child. What on earth was I doing? Somehow I felt small against this man who made my six feet of height seem average. This was a novelty. "Are you alright?" he asked finally, looking down at me. He raised an eyebrow in questioning. The movement shifted his golden hair and stirred up what must have been body wash or cologne: a mix of cypress and bergamot and his own flesh that I had the sudden urge to lap up as if he were the only water in the Saharan desert.

"Fine, really," I murmured in response, my mouth dry and thirsty.

He chuckled good-naturedly. "It doesn't seem like it. You've got a death-grip on my shirt."

I let go and embarrassment washed over me. "Oh, ugh, I'm so sorry," I muttered, failing at my attempt to straighten out his shirt before wiping my sweaty palms on my jeans. I was slightly ashamed at the blush that rose to my cheeks as I desperately tried to rearrange the fabric of his clothing and inadvertently ran my hands over his chest as I did so. In the brief seconds I'd touched him, I could tell that his chest was thick and firm. "Sorry, I wasn't... thinking straight."

"I'll say," he replied with a smile; it was soft, warm, and open, in complete contrast to what I'd seen between him and his colleagues. "You nearly got hit by a car trying to corral my drunken business partner. Let's get you home before we have any more near-death experiences. Are you nearby or should I get us a car?"

"No, really, it's okay. I'll be—" And just like that, as if the universe had deemed me unable to make my own decisions, I stepped into a puddle on the sidewalk and found myself flailing as I slipped. Again. "Fine," I squeaked as I fell. I'd been left with no choice but to submit to gravity and release what little grace I had left in my body.

This time he grabbed me before I hit the ground and looked at me in a way that suggested he no longer trusted my judgment. He propped me upright, but kept a guiding hand out as if he thought I might topple again at any moment. Certainly I was not building a great reputation.

"It's around the corner." I sighed, surrendering as he held out an arm to me. I linked mine in his without another word. This had truly been an evening of firsts. Was this what being drunk felt like? I knew I wasn't, but my disorientation felt inexplicable and other-worldly – strange. The heat from being so close to this man and being in a jacket that I normally would have skipped had I not been tired of the constant commentary from humans about how I "must-be-so-cold" had a few droplets of sweat running down my back. Not only that, but the walk seemed to be taking longer than usual. "I'm Michelle, by the way," I added after several silent steps, unsure of how to fill the sudden dead space between us.

"I know." The man nodded, letting go of my arm so that I could lead him up the stairs. He kept a gentle hand on my back, I assumed as a way to keep me upright if I started to fall backward. The small gesture caused my heart to race even more. His hands were large, his palm splaying across my lower back, and I wondered how dexterous those fingers were. "You're quite popular with your regulars. I'm Earwyn."

We made it to my door, and I turned with even less grace than usual to face him. It occurred to me then that his clothing was completely dry, whereas mine was spattered with not only the sludge of a Seattle side street, but the scattering of a light rain that had been falling during our walk. "Well, thanks, Earwyn, for catching me. Twice. I promise I'm generally more coordinated and less flustered than this." The latter was a lie. I offered a sheepish smile and put my hand on the doorknob, fumbling to unlock it. I tried to internally blame my stumbling on the fact that the building and, in turn, the door and lock were old. If the universe could bless me with one freaking graceful moment in front of this man, that would've been nice. The door still refused to open, so I turned away from the man so I could focus on the very simple task at hand. "I hope you had a nice night with your partners and that you make it back—" When I turned to face him, I was silenced by the nonexistent space between us as he pulled me into an unexpected kiss. It was so unexpected, in fact, that it took me a moment to register what was happening and respond.

The sensation of his lips against mine was like fireworks: an explosion of soft, serendipitous pleasure. His lips were sweet and gentle but searching; the taste of gin and lemon juice lingered on them. I couldn't control the whimper that left me when his fingers pushed into my hair, effectively freeing it from its elastic bonds. The hair tie flew somewhere in the hallway, and I immediately decided I didn't really care. In fact, I wished he would do away with my clothing as quickly as he'd undone my mane. When

Earwyn finally pulled away, I saw stars. Whether because of the potency of our interaction or the lack of oxygen, I wasn't sure, but at that moment I was certain I wanted Earwyn-induced stars in my vision until I was reabsorbed into the earth.

My clearing vision eventually revealed that Earwyn was back against the wall on the opposite side of the hallway, breathing hard. He looked surprised, almost as if he hadn't been the one to initiate our interaction and instead, the universe had shoved us together like a small child playing with dolls. For a moment I even doubted what the reality of the situation was; maybe I'd put the moves on him? "I'm sorry, I... don't know what came over me," he said following a sudden exhale, looking ashamed, confused. It seemed that his ultra-confident and suave disposition had vanished the moment he'd pulled away.

"Likely the same thing that came over me." I smirked, feeling a little devious and triumphant after having embarrassed myself so thoroughly before. Apparently I hadn't fully put him off yet. Thank you, universe. "Do you want to come in?" The sudden distance between us confused me, however, and I wasn't sure if I was allowed to close the gap or not. When I realized that he may be regretting his actions, I shook my head a little. "Sorry, I didn't mean to assume. Are you okay?"

"Yeah... yes, I'm just..." He cleared his throat finally and straightened his shirt a little, as if he were trying to reset his smooth-talking exterior. It looked awkward and unfamiliar to him. "I just can't go any further, I'm afraid." He offered me a soft half-smile, as if he pitied me, and my stomach sank. "Thank you, though... for that," he murmured in reference to the kiss that he'd stolen; in his defense, though, it wasn't as if I had protested in the slightest. "And the invitation, of course." There was the charm and, consequently, the facade returning.

"Oh, right, of course. I didn't mean to assume, you're probably…" I struggled to find the right words, desperately not wanting to shame or push him away. I really didn't want to push him away. I also wasn't a fan of being self-deprecating, so I steered away from suggesting that he wasn't interested; he obviously was. The sudden loss of contact from our separation was almost painful, and the intensity of my desperation for him startled me. I liked sex and connection. Men. Women. Other folks. Different shapes and sizes and backgrounds and abilities. Beautiful beings of all sorts. Somehow, this was different. My head swam as I tried to compose myself. Oh man, I really hoped he wasn't married; I knew that unions like that deserved respect and would've hated to push myself in the middle of that when it wasn't welcome. Still, he'd started it… I stifled a sigh of relief when I looked for and didn't register a wedding band.

"It's not about virtue, Michelle," Earwyn assured me aloud, an amused smile crossing his lips. "I'd really like to." He shifted his stance as if he were trying to hide the very obvious bulge straining against his slacks. I thought then that I wouldn't mind feeling that bulge against me literally anywhere. God, what would it feel like to bury my face in his crotch? When he noticed my wandering gaze, he cleared his throat a little as if to say "my eyes are up here." My face flushed immediately.

"You're smiling…" I flipped through my mental encyclopedia of human behavior, which often felt similar to mine, but on other days felt like a foreign language. His smile and the physical evidence of his arousal did not align with the farewell he was trying to commit to. Surely, his words were much more important than anything else, but I was struggling to understand the situation. What did this stranger want? The same interaction with any other human would've likely ended with us in bed if I was interested, so why was it so difficult to see the trajectory here?

"I mean it. I'd like to have that with you, but I can't. It's complicated."

"That's okay, I can appreciate the complexities of other people," I told him honestly, unhurt, but curious. I pulled the shoulder of my shirt back up from where it had been slid down by his hungry, seeking hands, and straightened the fabric. As much as my body suddenly ached for his, I would never be one to force another into, well, anything. Nothing was quite as exciting as being fully wanted by someone else whom you also desperately wanted. "I mean, if you want to share yours?"

He licked his lips. "Maybe one day," he told me seriously, his stormy gaze penetrating mine. Why was my mouth watering? "This is where I have to leave you tonight, though." He must've noticed some disappointment in my expression because he laughed a little and added, "I can't leave my brother alone in the bar for too long. He's liable to start making bad decisions and I'll have to clean up the mess... Besides, drinks at your bar aren't exactly cheap, and Firth's a big guy. He'll have us broke within the hour."

"When? You said 'one day.' When? Not because I'm trying to seduce you, I just... I'd like to know."

"I don't think you need to try." The man sighed as if he was ashamed of the fact, running a hand loosely through his sandy locks. "I'm not from here. I only visit every once in a while for business, so I really can't say when I might be lucky enough to see you again." It was also difficult for me to understand why the tone of our encounter had gotten so serious so fast... One moment he was escorting my clumsy ass back home, taking my breath away with a kiss, and the next he seemed intent on vanishing with no explanation; the latter seemed like something neither of us wanted, so why?

Before I could respond, Zara poked her head around the edge

of the doorframe and snorted. She looked Earwyn up and down, narrowing her gaze as she took him in. "Is that why you've been at the restaurant the past four nights in a row? Business?" She smirked a little, muttered to herself, "the business of getting some ass, maybe," and then went back to whatever she'd been doing while eavesdropping. She tended to be quite feisty upon waking from her post-work sleep.

I couldn't help but chuckle.

"Um, I don't know that I should answer that and incriminate myself any further..."

"Then stay. Go get your brother and hang out with us." People said that, right? "We'll order food and watch a movie, then you can get back to business whenever you want. We'd love to know more about the business you do... and why you've been at the restaurant so much. After all, there are plenty of other places to eat and drink in Seattle," I commented with a smirk, turning to finally walk into the apartment.

* * *

I HADN'T QUITE REALIZED THE EXTENT OF FIRTH'S SIZE UNTIL HE HAD to duck his head to get into our tiny, ancient doorway. At nearly seven feet tall, his width was equally impressive; his broad shoulders barely cleared the doorway sideways, and he grumbled a little as he entered, his heavy boots thudding on the old flooring of our apartment. For being Earwyn's brother, he looked very little like him, but still managed to dazzle me with a smile when he shook my hand. His dark, almost black hair was buzzed short and tight to his skull, and his face was clean shaven. It was hard to distinguish the color of his deep-set eyes – perhaps a dark blue or maybe a similar green to his brother's – because of the shadow his heavy brow cast over them. He had a large, hawklike nose, and thin, but shapely lips. Everything about him appeared typically masculine and soldierly, bordering on brutish. When we introduced ourselves, I learned that Firth was Deaf and Zara quickly used the opportunity to claim him as a friend. "I know some ASL!" she announced, grabbing him by a massive hand and leading him to the couch, where they quickly fell into conversation about what we should order for dinner. Leave it to Zara, in all of her petite mightiness, to approach the human version of a lion. I mean, I liked the idea of lions, but I'd probably steer clear of them in the wild because I was fond of being alive.

"He doesn't—" Earwyn attempted to call after her, but before he could explain that he and Firth didn't use American Sign Language and rather sign language from their home, he'd lost them. I knew enough about sign language to know that different languages had their own version, but that there were also different dialects... Perhaps he was from a region that had its own, but as for where "home" was, he didn't let me in on that detail. I hoped desperately that this wasn't my only chance to learn more intimate details about him. Meanwhile, I felt pleased that Firth had ended up here, with Zara, who was an expert at making people feel welcome and understood. It was no shock that she knew ASL because she seemed to know a ton of different languages and had even started teaching me Igbo words and phrases. I'd learned early on in our friendship that her mother was from Nigeria: a big point of pride for her. In fact, Zara's full name was Ozaram Uzochukwu.

"It's close enough!" Zara hollered, giggling as she chatted with a less-than-enthused Firth. Still, he seemed comfortable in our home, and it was clear that they understood each other well enough. "And we want Chinese!"

I couldn't help but crack a smile as I led Earwyn over to where they were relaxing and pulled out my phone to order food. Phones were another human contraption that I found myself constantly marveling at. It was bizarre and exciting to me that you could talk into a tiny electronic box and sometime later, a person would appear in your home with hot food. Incredible. "What do you like, Firth?" I asked, looking directly at him because I was unsure if he could read lips or if someone could interpret for us. I felt like I was learning to speak "human" all over again, but I was in the majority with my hearing abilities, so I tried not to focus on myself. I wondered if Firth was the only Deaf person in his family or if he'd grown up in a tight-knit community that supported his differences. Were their parents Deaf?

"Kung Pao shrimp," he replied effortlessly in a voice that was a little different from most I'd heard, but deep and charming nonetheless. "And crab rangoon."

"A seafood fan, I see." I smiled.

Once I'd entered the number for our favorite Chinese place in my phone, Earwyn held out a hand from his spot on the couch opposite of his brother and next to me. Having a favorite Chinese place felt very human to me. "May I?" I surrendered the phone easily and attempted to ignore the spark that occurred when his fingertips brushed mine. It made my stomach flutter. He ordered and paid with the elegance of someone far more graceful than myself, and soon enough we were all seated in the living room, an old Western movie playing with subtitles, and mouths full of really good Chinese food. I looked over at Firth and Zara in my attempt to stifle the staring I wanted to do at Earwyn and wondered how I could ask the giant brother if he liked his food without making him read my lips.

As if reading my mind, Earwyn grabbed my hand with both of his after setting his food on the arm of our couch, and helped me arrange my fingers into shapes I soon learned to mean "taste - good - ?" I found my breath hitched in my throat as I watched Firth for his response, which was an enthusiastic and greasy-fingered "yes." Meanwhile, Earwyn ate in a manner so clean and refined, he might as well have been royalty. I couldn't compete and licked my fingers clean after scarfing a crab rangoon that Firth tossed me across the room; Earwyn had already seen me fall multiple times, so being realistic about my eating habits seemed the least of my worries.

"Alright," I murmured between bites of another crab rangoon. I didn't think I'd ever tire of human food. Who had decided that a little edible wrapper filled with cream cheese and crab would be so delightful? "Time to confess."

Earwyn looked genuinely shocked that I'd been so blunt at first, but then laughed a little and wiped his mouth with a napkin. "That was part of the deal, I suppose."

The other two eyed us from their spot on the couch, but ultimately returned to chatting and half-watching the movie. "Business," Earwyn mused, turning his body away from the television and toward me. Suddenly receiving all of his attention made me nervous and excited. He sat his empty takeout box on the arm of the couch, and to my surprise, it balanced there easily. How many times had I tried that just for it to topple right off? Was this dude a freaking wizard or what? "I work with an organization that focuses on ocean conservation." I saw his gaze flit from me to his brother and back. That seemed innocent enough... My nature-loving heart couldn't help but be a bit enamored.

"Huh, cool. Where are you visiting from?"

"San Clemente, California," he told me with a smile. I could easily imagine him on a warm beach, his hair in saltwater-drenched waves. The picture made perfect sense. "Good place for an ocean enthusiast."

"And your... organization... has had meetings at P&P four nights in a row? I hadn't noticed any large groups until this evening."

"No." Earwyn chuckled, looking at me curiously as though he hoped I wouldn't be bold enough to ask him for clarification again. "Just tonight."

"Well, go on then. There's no way you think that's a good enough explanation." I definitely didn't.

A blush rose to the man's cheeks, and he looked away for a moment, rubbing the back of his neck. His embarrassment was charming and made my heart race a little. "I dropped in a few nights ago to scope out the restaurant for this evening's meeting. It's my job to find places that everyone will enjoy. The food and drinks were great, then I saw you working and..."

"You thought you might enjoy the staff as well?" I mused aloud, teasing him gently. My commentary may have come across as cocky or at least confident to others, but the truth was that I assumed people were being genuine and allowed myself to enjoy the truthfulness of situations; the idea that this man had visited my work just to sneak a glance at me was charming and flattering. This was probably only true because I was attracted to him, but I *was* attracted to him, so I allowed myself to enjoy the moment and take his actions as a compliment.

"I did. I have... and I'd like to continue to, if that's alright with you."

I wanted to ask why he hadn't spoken to me prior to that night, but reasoned that not everyone was as forward as myself or Anala or Zara. Instead, I just smiled, popped one last bite of food into my mouth, and leaned back on the couch to watch the rest of the movie. I could feel Earwyn's presence and steady breathing next to me, and that was enough; he lulled me deeper into the couch cushions with breaths that rocked me like the sounds of the ocean.

CHAPTER FOUR

That night, I dreamt of the sea, probably because of Earwyn's line of work and the deep storminess of his aquamarine eyes. Despite Seattle's proximity to the ocean, I hadn't really ventured to the beach since my arrival; in fact, I had a tendency to avoid bodies of water in general. In my dream, I imagined lying on a beach, warm waves crashing over my bare body. Surely this dream wasn't happening in the Pacific Ocean; I knew the water there to be frigid and unforgiving. Nevertheless, I was enamored by this dreamscape even though deep down I had a healthy fear of the sinking depths of the sea, where creatures beyond anyone's wildest imagination hid from sight. I walked along the sandy shore, loving the way the soft sand between my toes reminded me of walking through moss or grass at home. It smelled different here, though: like salt and brine and a fresh breeze carrying it all off the water.

I wandered into the water, which was something I'd never do in real life. As I ventured farther out, I found that I appreciated the way the sand washed over my feet and back out again with the tide. Fish swam in a clear pool beneath me, exploring my ankles and then darting away with each step I took. The sensations in the water tickled, and I couldn't help but smile. Suddenly, the sky darkened, and foreboding clouds rolled in above me, where they threatened to dump a storm at any moment. I sat myself in the shallow water and watched as the world turned gloomy around me and droplets splashed onto my flesh; there had been a time when I'd loved storms. Here, in my dreamscape, it seemed I fancied them again.

Before I knew it, I felt the presence of someone else near me, emerging from the ocean with salt-doused locks: Earwyn. He crouched before me and tangled his fingers into my hair, crushing our lips together as if his life depended on it. My body bloomed alight with fire immediately, and I leaned into his touch with no resistance. He pressed his body, hard and wet and heavy, against mine until we were lying in the wet sand in the storm. Every inch of me ached for him, and I could sense his desperation as well. I wanted to strip him bare of his sopping wet clothing right there and ride him in the rain. When he pulled back to look at me, lightning shone in his gaze. I craved his closeness and reached out for him in eagerness only to find him backing into the water.

No, not backing. He was being pulled.

The look on his face rapidly changed from sensual curiosity to genuine fear. His fingers reached for mine, brushing my fingertips as he was pulled farther into the water, mouth open in a silent scream. Water from the crashing, stormy waves sloshed into his mouth, and he choked, spit, and sputtered before disappearing into the tide. Lightning reflected off the surface of the water, and it became violent in its splashing. I ventured a few extra steps forward and sank to my knees, where I tried to feel around in the dark, shallow water to no avail. He had been pulled farther in than I could reach, and I just couldn't will myself to go any deeper. In the distance, another flash of lightning illuminated the horizon, and I caught sight of a hand popping out of the water, grasping in desperation.

I woke with a gasp to find my mind and body at war with each other; part of me was on fire, aching with need, while the other was mortified by my dream-turned-nightmare. On the opposite side of the couch was a sleeping, wild-maned man. He slept soundly with his lips slightly parted, and I wished I knew what he might be dreaming about. For a moment, his brows furrowed into a scowl, and I hoped that it wasn't in response to a dream similar to mine. I let my eyes close and my head tip back so I could calm my racing heart and clear my head. Zara and Firth were draped over each other on the other couch, looking as though they'd known one another forever and couldn't be more comfortable. When I looked back to Earwyn to check that he was still resting, I finally steadied myself to stand and retrieve two blankets. Once our guests and my roommate were sufficiently tucked in, I cast one last glance at my dinner partner and dragged myself off to my own bedroom, which was very un-beach-like and severely lacking Earwyn. Despite my disappointment, I reminded myself Earwyn had drawn a line between us and, while I didn't know why that was, I had to respect it. As much as I wanted to recreate part of my dream right there in our living room, I also feared the threat that was intertwined with the second half of my dream. Even though he lay there in front of me, sound asleep, the memory of him being dragged away in my dream left me with a sense of dread.

CHAPTER FIVE

*W*hen I woke the next morning, Earwyn and Firth were no longer in our living room. It took me a while to leave the bed when I found that someone had covered me in the blanket that I'd draped over Earwyn the night before. If I hadn't remembered the color of the blanket, I would've known it was his by the scent of it alone. I looked at it longingly before I finally left the room and promised myself – and the blanket – that I'd be back soon. Zara would be in the bathroom getting ready for work; I'd memorized her schedule.

"Hey, when did they leave?" I asked, trying not to seem desperate for information as I rubbed my sleep-filled eyes. I could still smell Earwyn on my shirt, too, and the thought of being close enough to smell him in real time again sent a chill through my body. I tried to shake the sensation, but the hardened points of my nipples grazed the fabric of the oversized t-shirt I'd finally fallen asleep in the night before. Smell had always been the sense to have the strongest effect on me, whether it be sparking memories or desire, but this was unparalleled.

"I'm not sure, but Firth put his number in my phone." Zara smiled, waving her cell phone in the air before putting it back down on the counter and resuming her makeup routine; somehow she always looked ready for a runway or rave even when she was about to spend the day in a kitchen making pastries. That day it looked like the theme for her makeup was every shade of red. "We're gonna play video games tonight after work!"

I gave her a contented smile and nod before heading back to my own room to figure out what I'd do with the day, but before I closed my door I heard her holler, "Don't worry, I told him to bring Earwyn, too!" I couldn't help but laugh to myself at how easily she read the true me even when she ignored so many of my weird eccentricities... or maybe that was just her really, truly knowing me and knowing well enough that I was actively trying to hide those parts of me. My bond with Zara was a type of friendship I'd never really had back home.

I had the day off, so I tried to do something I knew would occupy my mind instead of letting myself stew over whether or not I'd see Earwyn again that evening. Goodness, since when did I even care that much about seeing some man again?

Some time before, Zara and I had pooled our money to buy a clunker of an old car: a beat-up silver 2007 Ford Taurus that was being held together with a lick and a promise and a little too much duct tape. We rarely used it because most of our daily activities were within walking or bus distance, but she let me take it when I needed some "forest time" as we'd come to call it. Zara didn't question how often or not that was. The car faithfully, although loudly, brought me to the nearest clearing of uninterrupted woods, where I found a space with no trails and no people. Before exiting the vehicle, I removed my boots and socks to chuck them in the passenger footwell. So much time being "human" had made my feet soft and tender – useless for adventuring in the wilderness – so

I relished any chance I got to be barefoot in nature. Despite the changing seasons and subsequent chill in the air as I got out, I couldn't help but breathe in the crispness of fall. It was different in the woods. The trees were a vibrant explosion of autumnal colors, and the occasional chittering and chirping of forest animals, like grouse and squirrels, fluttered into my ears as I ventured out. My heart rate seemed to slow as I ventured farther into the trees and my body suddenly felt more aligned, more regulated, as my toes sunk into the earth. There was something very centering about being back in nature.

While part of my magick ability involved skills that could seem grand or showy at times, what I loved most was the way I always felt connected to Mother Earth. With every step I took, I somehow knew which way to position my footing so that not even the smallest insect was harmed... and the moment my stomach grumbled, it was as if my gaze knew exactly where to spot a patch of berries or an edible mushroom. Without much thought, I packed away some of those treats in my bag for Zara, who had shown me many different ways to prepare them at home; while I could stomach raw almost-anything, I'd learned that humans had to cook quite a few things to consume them without experiencing... well, side effects. Maz had hopped into my passenger seat before I left the city and followed me along for this outing, so I tossed a couple of berries his way before packing away the rest.

It also seemed that the other creatures of the forest were drawn to and understood me, and in turn, I understood them. I had just popped another blackberry in my mouth when the sound of crunching leaves to my left drew my attention. I found a young black bear with a similar plan for foraging, munching on forest fruits to prepare for winter. I couldn't help but giggle at the sight, and when the young bear looked at me, snorting a little in the cold fall air, I gestured to her to let her pass as if to say "after you." She obliged and we went our separate ways, though there'd always been part of me that was curious about a black bear's abilities as a wrestling partner. As a child, I'd spent a lot of time romping with forest critters. They made great playmates! Another time, I told myself, knowing that this creature had a full schedule with winter right around the corner; self-preservation was much more important than play when it came to being wild.

Of course, as a member of the Yannavi race, there were other perks to being equipped with elemental forest magick. First and foremost was likely our blessing of having very long lives. In fact, most days I couldn't recall how many years I'd been walking the earth in much the same way I was during that outing. Was it two hundred? Three hundred years? That wasn't to say they'd been monotonous or blended together, but we didn't celebrate birthdays in the way that humans did. It felt a bit silly to think that each and every creature's birth was worthy of a party every single year. Was each person and animal important? Yes. But we demonstrated that gratitude and acknowledged their meaning in the grand scheme of things on a daily basis, rather than annually. Terrafolk weren't immortal nor invincible, but less prone to injury and quicker to heal. I imagined if we were frequently faced with danger, we'd likely find ourselves hard to kill as well. Despite how clumsy I was, I hadn't accrued many scars in my very long lifetime… I did have one particularly dark scar on my knee, though, from a time I had blindly fallen off a cliff as a child. Anyone who knew me would insist that my gracefulness hadn't improved too much since then, however. It wasn't until my forties or fifties that I'd learned to harness enough of my magick to catch myself when falling those great distances or understood my place in the forest well enough to avoid big falls like that to begin with.

When I finally took a break from my exploring, I wasn't sure quite how far from my car I'd wandered, but I propped myself up at the bottom of a Douglas fir and pulled a mushroom from my pocket to eat. Maz landed on my knee, helping himself to a bit of the mushroom that I offered up and then flying off again to explore. "Yep, anytime," I murmured, watching his blue-black feathers in the sunlight as he flitted into the trees above me. I supposed another thing about being from the forest meant that it was easy for me to traverse; my muscles didn't really tire when walking in the dirt, and I could easily cover twenty to thirty miles a day without much of a fuss. I tilted my head back and chewed thoughtfully, just in time to see a red squirrel make its way down the trunk of the massive tree toward my head. I said nothing as the creature gave me a quick sniff, then began rummaging in my hair.

"I don't have anything in there, little one," I told him, trying hard not to laugh out loud at the feel of the animal's tiny paws on my scalp. I guess I had my mushroom and maybe some berries in my bag, but I could go find some for the squirrel if he wanted his own. Seconds later, though, I realized he wasn't looking to take, but rather trying to find the perfect hiding spot for an acorn. I rolled my eyes a little as he finally became satisfied with his work, leaving me with a messy nest of hair that now housed a tiny animal's treasure. "Um, thanks?"

I left it, not wanting to break the animal's heart, and closed my eyes to disconnect a little bit. This wasn't *my* forest, but I felt connected to it just as well. The only difference here is that I wasn't near my Yannavi family, but considering the fact that I'd left to explore, I supposed I didn't feel too lonely without them. There was a lot of chaos that came from living in a kingdom of any sort. Even though the human world had rules and hierarchies all the same, they weren't mine, so they didn't bother me nearly as much. I don't think I even knew who the president was at that point.

Yannava was the central or primary forest-folk kingdom in all of North America. There were beings like me all throughout the country – and world – of course, and they had their own communities and civilizations, but everyone knew of Yannava and generally took guidance from its leadership, which used to be two married female forest-folk. These two stewardesses ruled the kingdom somewhat temporarily, as the natural born heir to the throne had abandoned her post and had not been heard from in quite some time. It was likely several decades that the heir had been missing. That may seem like a long time in human years, but since our kind lived for an unprecedented amount of time, it really wasn't too long in the grand scheme of things. The High Court structure of Yannava also didn't really matter unless you're a big part of it. That was how I felt about most royalty, in fact; it was pretty silly and full of useless formality, responsibility, and most of all, drama. It also felt like proof that all societies, no matter how idealistic, eventually fall into some hierarchical ruling pattern.

In addition to Yannava, other kingdoms rule different parts of the world having to do with their elements, terrains, and ecosystems. While all of the domains of our people are different, we are obviously united by our connection to nature and its bountiful, but finite resources. That is one thing that puts us at odds philosophically with the humans, or would if they knew we existed. The truth is that humans cross our paths every day, every minute, and have no idea. I didn't know if it was me or if many of us felt this way, but I found the human world charming and genuinely believe they aren't malicious, just uninformed. We thought of you the way you likely think of your pets; cute, amusing, but maybe not the brightest when it comes to important things. Like animals believe you'll care for and feed them to any end, so humans believe that the earth will provide regardless of how it's treated. Some of you are passionate about being kind to that which provides you with so much, but since those are such a minority, the impact of their good deeds is negligible at best.

It felt strange at times, knowing that the humans had been so close, just beyond the edge of the forest for as long as I'd been alive. If humans had ever come across Yannava, however, they probably wouldn't know what to think of it; it's more of another world than just a section of woodlands.

When I returned home a bit dirtier but beyond invigorated, the apartment was alive with the sounds of laughter and a video game I didn't recognize. That didn't mean anything, though, because I couldn't keep them all straight if I tried. I was quite fond of one game that involved creating a neighborhood for cute little animal characters – very "up my alley."

Firth and Zara sat next to each other on the same couch facing the television. Zara was more crouching than sitting, though, because she really got into her games. When I realized that they were the only two at home, I gave them a little wave and went to the kitchen for some tea. Their round played through, and Firth looked up at me to wave and asked, "How are you?"

"Good, how about you?" I signed, and when he responded, I tried to ask a follow-up question. "Where is E-A-R-W-Y-N?" My fingerspelling was sluggish and embarrassing, but Firth was ever-patient. That certainly seemed like a shared trait between the brothers. It was then that I promised myself I'd learn more ASL from Zara so that I could communicate with Firth when he was over; based on how comfortable they seemed, we'd likely be seeing more of him. He gave me a good-natured laugh and then explained to me that Earwyn had a much easier sign-name, which was a relief because I was fairly certain I'd called his brother Marvyn. It was then that I realized I still had a mass of tangled hair on top of my head, and I reached up to undo the acorn while watching Firth closely; he didn't seem to think much of it, and Zara was busy equipping her game character with the new weapons she'd acquired.

"Like this," he said vocally, then made the shape of an "E" with his fingers while making the sign for "straight-faced," as Zara explained it to me with a giggle. I'd seen Earwyn smile quite a bit, but perhaps that wasn't the norm for him. I copied it, and he nodded, but his answer to my question was disappointing. "I'm not sure," he said with a frown. "I think he's working." I didn't know Firth well enough to decipher if he was telling the truth or not, so I just thanked him and assured him that it was okay. Earwyn hadn't accepted the invite, left me a number, or made an attempt to reach out in any way; I could take a hint. Maybe I should text Anala after all. If anything, she'd be a good distraction...

I tried not to look like a sad sack as I made my way back to my bedroom, tea in hand, and flopped onto my bed. The tea sloshed a little and spilled onto my shirt, and I groaned, leaning back against my headboard. What little grace I'd had had really gone out the window the night before. It had been nowhere to be found since and had apparently been replaced by desperation and some sort of lovesickness. God, was that what a "crush" felt like? I sipped my tea and finally convinced my frantic brain to let me close my eyes. I found myself grateful that I hadn't worked that evening because the thought of being at the bar and realizing Earwyn wouldn't be felt torturous. The minutes would've undoubtedly crawled by. Why was that? I'd always been one to look ahead excitedly, but that evening found me very reflective of the night before... and longing for a repeat minus the drowning-themed nightmare. I considered swinging by the bar just to see if I'd run into him and then immediately talked myself out of it.

Maz perched on my windowsill, having just set down a new piece of treasure. I had left the window permanently cracked since I'd moved in, regardless of the weather, so that he could come and go as he pleased. *I've never seen you this worked up over a human*, he told me, puffing up his feathers and settling into a small ball on the sill. He eyed me curiously.

Consciousness left me in time, and I found myself face down on my bed sometime later with a puddle of drool on my sheets as proof. Thankfully I'd remembered to put my drink down on my nightstand before passing out, but the buzzing from my cell phone buried deep in my blankets woke me with a start. I normally slept like I was hibernating, but something about that week had me feeling on edge and more alert than usual.

TEXT FROM UNSAVED NUMBER

I'm sorry I missed video game night.

The smile that burst onto my face was probably ridiculous and I caught myself grinning, tried to stifle it, then let it take over again. Thankfully, Maz was asleep and therefore unable to pick on me for my childish reaction to hearing from Earwyn. I understood then why humans called it having "butterflies in your stomach" – this was exciting! Fun! Terrifying! How could I feel so many things for a man I'd only met once? I chastised myself, still smiling, then responded.

Who is this? We have a lot of people over for video games and I don't have this number saved in my phone.

I deserve that, especially after how kind you were to us last night.

You DID vanish without a word. At least Zara got Firth's #.

> Well, now you have mine. And an apology… I'm sorry I didn't show and that it took me this long to reach out to you, I was busy with work and admittedly, nervous.

I raised an eyebrow as if he could see my face. What was there to be nervous about? I couldn't think of a more welcoming household, and Firth obviously didn't feel that way. Human interactions were very confusing for me at times, but I knew for a fact that I'd been very friendly and accommodating the night before. Was it the blanket? Had I been talking in my sleep during our very passionate dream interaction? Oh no…

> About what?

> I'm not sure. I don't usually care what people think of me, but…

I waited a few moments for a response, then felt the need to reassure him. Why was he doubting himself?

> If it's any consolation, my blanket smells like you and I'm lying under it right now.

> :(

> ?

> I don't have anything that smells like you.

Another stupid smile.

> When can we remedy that?

I'd asked that eagerly, unabashedly, when Earwyn had

expressed his distaste for not having anything that smelled like me. When I bundled myself up in the blanket and waddled my way into the living room, however, I was shocked to hear a familiar voice that snapped me from my lovesick reverie.

"Hey you! Noticed you were off tonight so I thought I'd swing by – I didn't know it was video game night," Anala practically shouted, perched casually on the couch opposite Firth and Zara. She looked so at home in our apartment that I wondered if I hadn't been clear about my lack of interest; it certainly wasn't my intent to lead her on, but perhaps I had been without realizing? Either that or our relationship was so casual that she intended to be a fixture in our household even if we weren't actively sleeping together. Based on my knowledge of human relationship dynamics, this had the potential to make it difficult for me to get close to Earwyn. I couldn't just collect lovers in my apartment...

Zara shrugged a little and shot me a look that said "what the hell was I supposed to do?" I didn't blame her, though; Anala could be very pushy even when she wasn't particularly persuasive, and it did seem a bit rude to suddenly deny her entry into our home when she'd been a frequent guest over the past month or so.

I sighed, annoyed that I was being pulled away from my phone, where a less-than-riveting content-wise but endlessly exciting emotion-wise conversation was waiting for me. For a moment, I considered sending Maz in to try to eat Ember... That might be one way to get Anala to leave, but then I'd have to explain to my roommate why I was unfazed by animals chasing each other through our apartment. I knew I couldn't leave the unexpected guest with my friends, so I draped my blanket over the back of a bar stool in the kitchen, to keep anyone else's scent from mingling with Earwyn's, and plopped myself down next to Anala on the couch. Every now and then, I cast a glance at the blanket to make sure it hadn't moved.

The evening trickled by, and when Anala noticed I was simply being polite and not indulging in her attempts at flirting, she eventually tried her hand at roping Zara and Firth in with her casual wooing. They were too distracted with the game and each other and didn't buy it. I miraculously found a way to escort her to the door sooner than I'd anticipated and anxiously sprinted back to my room to return to my conversation with Earwyn, whom I hoped I hadn't lost due to my lapse in responding.

TEXT FROM EARWYN (1 HOUR 50 MINUTES AGO)

Soon, I hope.

> Well, you know where I live… and work. Maybe one day I'll get to learn more about you?

Maybe, Michelle. Sweet dreams.

> Dream of me.

Once I hit send, I set my phone down on my nightstand fully prepared to crash for the evening, only to find it vibrating seconds later. I was startled to see a phone call incoming – despite that supposedly being the primary function of phones, I had learned that most humans did not prefer telephone calls – and even more surprised at who was on the other line. "Earwyn?"

"Michelle," he said, breathing as if… was he flustered? Had I done that to him?

"Is everything okay?"

"You want me to dream of you."

His statement caused me to second-guess myself a bit, but I bit back any self-doubt and answered him confidently. "Yes."

"I've dreamt of nothing else since I first saw you."

Goosebumps spread across my flesh like wildfire, and I found myself instantly wishing that he was next to me, wishing that he didn't have to dream about me and could have the real thing instead. I bit my lip hard. "Is that so? Then it should be an easy task."

CHAPTER SIX

"You often refer to yourself as part of another species, some sort of magical being from another realm. Is that your way of creating a boundary between yourself and your peers?" Dr. Eline Jansen pushed her round glasses up the bridge of her nose as she spoke to me during our biweekly therapy session. When she'd informed me of doctor-patient confidentiality, I'd let slip my true identity, and ever since then, she was dead-set on the idea that we were working within some sort of metaphor that would lead her to diagnose me with a complex human condition. Humans certainly seemed hell bent on finding things wrong with themselves. Oddly enough, attending therapy was something I'd done to better fit in with my human counterparts, and yet here I was trying to discover why I couldn't quite swing it as a human. Everyone else I knew who attended therapy, however, said it had really helped them discover who they were. I knew who I was. The whole ordeal was very confusing to me.

"Um, no, I don't think so. I just come from a different place with different customs, you know? So sometimes navigating human life can feel a little alienating." I picked at the knee of my jeans, feeling very put under a microscope in this doctor's presence. We'd revisited the idea of this metaphor many, many times.

"So you're saying you feel like an alien around other humans?"

"I... um," I stammered, all of my feigned confidence disappearing. The setting of this woman's book-lined office, complete with row upon row of framed diploma, credential, and photograph of her speaking at psychologist events was a stark contrast from the dark, veiling climate of the bar at Peach and Port. It almost seemed too transparent, too out-in-the-open for such intimate conversations. Her wild, gray-streaked hair stood out in every image on the walls, and I struggled to direct my attention back from them to her; humans certainly expected you to look directly at them when you spoke – otherwise they'd accuse you of not listening. Meanwhile, the intense eye contact often left me feeling like I couldn't focus on what they were actually saying. I shifted in my seat, then took a deep breath to steady myself and met her gaze again. "Yes, sometimes, I guess. But lately..."

The glasses came down then and hung around Eline's neck by a thin gold chain. She leaned forward, resting her thin, manicured fingers on the notepad in her lap and attempted to gaze into my soul with her dull brown eyes. "I'm listening." Yes, Eline, that's why I'm here, scraping together my pitiful bartender paycheck to sit on your leather couch every other week. You should be listening.

"I met someone recently... and it just feels like we might be more alike than... I don't know, I feel like he gets me somehow."

"I thought Zara 'got you,' too?"

"She does!" I exclaimed, anxious to make sure I wasn't being misunderstood; Zara meant so much to me that the thought of anyone – even someone who'd never speak to her – thinking otherwise deeply upset me. It felt like an injustice toward Zara. "But so far, it's just been her, so this new connection has kind of surprised me even though we barely know each other."

"Based on what I know about you, *wanting* to know this person better, to let them into your life in the way that you have with Zara, is significant for you."

I found myself chewing my lip and scraping my pointer finger-nail over my thumb as I thought through her words. "Yes, it's significant."

"What would it mean for you to let them in?"

"To let them in? Like, fully?"

"Yes."

"I don't know yet, and that's both terrifying and…"

"Yes?"

"Exhilarating."

"Could it be that this new person—"

"Earwyn." The name itself caused my stomach to flutter.

Dr. Jansen jotted the name down on her notepad, her pen scratching in a soothing, repetitive manner. I traced the movement of her hand and pen with my eyes. "Could it be that Earwyn 'gets you' because he's similar to you? Because he reminds you of your home and your people?" Even though Dr. Jansen had assured me that she believed my "homeland" and my time in the "human world" were simply metaphors, she committed to them so well that I often forgot I was speaking with someone who'd never been to Yannava or met more of my kind. She was good about really getting into the moment with me.

I opened my mouth to speak, but stopped myself. After thinking on the question for a few seconds, I asked, "In what way?"

"Well, I'm not sure. I don't know enough about your… forest realm—"

"Yannava."

"Yannava." She jotted the name down again. "I don't know enough about Yannava to begin to suggest similarities, nor do I know enough about Earwyn, since this is the first time you've mentioned him. Why don't we backtrack a little bit?" When I nodded, she continued, "You've mentioned Yannava during many of our sessions so far, but you have yet to explain to me why you left. When you speak of your homeland, you do so with such fondness... it's easy to see that you hold it dear to your heart, so why leave? Why come into the human world if your home is so full of wonder? I haven't even heard you mention visiting your home despite how long you've been living with us here in Seattle."

"I..." Again, I found myself struggling to formulate sentences. I picked at the edge of my sleeve absentmindedly as I thought of the day I'd decided to leave Yannava. My throat went dry and painful in an instant. "I left Yannava because..." My heart raced.

"Did something happen there?"

"No! I mean, no, no," I said through forced laughter, trying to lighten the tone of our conversation in panic. "I just left to explore. To see new places, you know? For an adventure, that's all."

Eline eyed me curiously, then scribbled again in her notebook. "Mhmm."

Silence hung heavily in her office. It seemed like she was waiting for me to fill it, but I didn't. Instead, I distracted myself with the way Dr. Jansen's hair looked like thin tree branches reaching for the sky.

"Let's go back to Earwyn."

"Alright."

"Let's say you get to know him well enough that you decide to fully let him in, like you said earlier. We know this is significant for you, but you're excited at the prospect," the doctor recounted, pulling me from my momentary franticness back to a topic that made me happy. Then, of course, she bundled them together. "If you got that close to him, would you tell him about Yannava?"

"I'm not sure. Maybe. Humans aren't really supposed to know about us. The last time that happened was hundreds of years ago, and we convinced them that they were hallucinating. Can you believe they thought we were fairies? Our realm is so far out in the woods that it would take a lot for them to stumble upon it, plus we have protective—"

"Logistics aside."

"Yes, maybe."

"And would you tell him why you left?"

I swallowed hard. I gritted my teeth. "Sure, it's not a big deal, like I told you. I just wanted to explore."

CHAPTER SEVEN

Several days later I stumbled out of my front door for work and right into a pot of flowers that had been delivered on the doormat; it was bursting with blooms of rust and burgundy complemented by stunning sage greenery. Whoever had sent this surely knew the way to my heart – plants! Flowers! Things that grow! The front of the pot had a gold bow. I stopped for a moment to appreciate how much the plant screamed "autumn" before carefully picking it up to take a closer look. For some reason I'd become clumsier as of late, so I made sure to handle the delicate container with care. Perhaps it was the fact that I hadn't been sleeping much; it seemed that I was either talking to Earwyn on the phone late into the evening or kept awake by restless – but lovely – dreams of him each night. They had continued with the theme of both painfully steamy interactions and deeply unsettling oceanic chaos. I glanced at my phone for the time and, deciding that I was heading out way too early anyway, brought the flowers inside while reading the attached card. Maz hopped back in behind me stealthily enough that Zara didn't notice. Then, he soared toward the balcony's open door and perched himself outside to wait for me.

"Ooooh, I wonder who those might be from," Zara teased as she sat at the kitchen counter, licking yogurt off a spoon. She smirked at me, and I felt giddy inside. It was hard to stifle a giggle, and I felt my face screw up in confusion after the sound burst out of me against my will.

The card was printed on heavy black stock with gold detailed text and decor and read:

> *You've been cordially invited to the*
> *Salt & Earth Alliance*
> *Gala and Charity Event*
> *benefiting ocean and sea life conservation efforts.*
> *— black tie —*

The date beneath it was that evening's and in, what I assumed was, Earwyn's handwriting, there was an additional note:

> *Sorry for the late notice, but will you join me? I can pick you up at 6pm. - E.*

I stared at the card for a while and ran my thumb over Earwyn's handwriting, savoring the way the indents in the card-stock felt from the weight of his pen; he had written this while thinking of me. Had his hand trembled at all? His writing seemed heavy, as if he put a lot of pressure on his pen. I wondered if he always wrote like that or perhaps he'd been thinking of our shared kiss and gripped his pen a little tighter. What a gift. I chewed my lower lip and considered the possibilities.

"Um, you can't just stand there looking all gaga and not explain what's going on. What is it? You two getting married? Is he moving in? Did we win the lottery?"

"Huh? Sorry... no lottery..." I murmured, glancing from the card to Zara, who looked like she was itching for the inside scoop. I set Earwyn's gift on the counter and absentmindedly traced the petals of a burgundy dahlia, which perked up at my touch as if it were a cat being petted. I admired the dips and peaks of each tiny petal and how dark and deep the reddish color got within them. "No marriage or moving either, I promise. Um, Zara... what's a gala?"

"It's like a really fancy party," Zara explained as she scraped the rest of her yogurt out of the bowl in a few too many strokes. The sound made my eye twitch. "Rich people dress up and get drunk and dance and sometimes they give their money to charity... there's usually fancy food and each seat costs, like, thousands of dollars."

"Why are the chairs so expensive? Seems like they should just put that money toward the charity, don't you think?"

"Not the actual chairs." Zara laughed, shaking her head a little at what I then realized was a ridiculous question. "It costs that much to attend."

I didn't even have thousands of dollars in my bank account, let alone floating around to spend on the entry to a big party. I couldn't imagine someone spending that on me when I knew how much work went into earning a single dollar, at least for myself and Zara. However, for a moment I imagined dressing up with Earwyn and dancing with him in a room full of beautiful people. Maybe he'd give me his arm as we entered the room; perhaps behaving like royalty wouldn't be all that bad after all, and maybe I'd just had an unfortunate experience with it back home. I wondered what my date would wear... Suddenly, I snapped out of my reverie and palmed my forehead in frustration. "Ugh, I can't go, Zara. I'm supposed to be going to work in a couple of hours!" And, just my luck, I wouldn't be off of work until the guests of the gala were wasted and dancing the night away. I pulled my phone out of my pocket and opened a message to Earwyn, bracing myself to put my rejection as kindly as possible. I truly wanted to go, so I hoped he would understand that. Perhaps we could see each other afterward? I sighed a little, knowing it wouldn't be the same at all; I'd never been to a big human party like this before, and the idea of attending it with Earwyn had briefly gotten my heart racing.

"Wait, wait, wait," Zara insisted. She hopped off her seat and put a hand on my phone to stop me from texting. My gaze flicked from her to the empty bowl on the counter and back to her again, feeling a little overwhelmed by her directness. "There is no way you're going to miss this, girl. Just call out. Say you're sick."

I gasped. I'd never done such a thing… and to call out of work for *a man* of all things? Of course, I'd also never been sick. As if reading my mind, Zara added, "You've, like, never called out. It's just one time… It'll be worth it, I can tell." It took some more conversation, but eventually Zara convinced me, and I managed a sick-sounding phone call to my boss. Somehow, he didn't question me at all. I'd probably pay for it later guilt-wise, but for that moment, I had a gala to get ready for.

> What does black tie mean?

It's code for "really fancy and maybe kinda stuck up." Does this mean you're coming?

> I'd love to.

:)

> But I don't know if I have anything that fits the dress code... I don't really go to big parties.

Don't worry about that. Dress however you like – I want you to be comfortable.

Before I could thank him for the sweet, but less than reassuring comment, Zara had snatched my phone out of my hands and was texting Earwyn. I instinctively reached to get it back, but ultimately surrendered because she knew way more than I did when it came to fancy outings based on what I'd learned in our brief conversation about them.

> Give us a color to work with - I'm doing her makeup. - Zara

"You are?" I asked aloud after reading over her shoulder. I let out a sigh of relief; that took some of the stress off my shoulders at least.

TEXT FROM EARWYN

Hi Zara

Gold should do it.

"Ooh, gold... fancy. Alright, say goodbye to your lover boy. We have some preparing to do!" Before I could protest, Zara was dragging me toward the bathroom. I scrambled to type out one last message to Earwyn before I submitted to her loving, but firm guidance:

> See you soon.

I parked myself in the bathroom while Zara rummaged through my closet, no doubt underwhelmed by my modest selection of clothing; there was a fashionista in our home, and it definitely wasn't me. I knew for a fact that nothing in there was appropriate for a gala even though I'd never been to one. When she returned, she held a soft gold wrap dress that I didn't remember buying. My roommate held up the gown for me to examine, hoisting it above her head so it wouldn't drag on the floor. "This will work!" she said from behind the fabric.

"How do you know exactly what to do? Have you been to one of these before?"

"Kind of... well, not as a guest, but I've done catering for them before... fancy ass pastries and stuff, you know..." Zara explained, a bobby pin perched between her lips as she styled my hair. Somehow her creativity spanned so many different formats: pastries, art, makeup, she could do it all. "Always wondered what it would be like to show up on the arm of some rich dude, though. Free drinks. Fancy food. Rich people talking about rich people things, probably crap I'll never actually care about, but... could be nice to pretend for one night." She shrugged, then pinned back a few more locks of my hair before examining her work in the bathroom mirror. "Mmm, yes, dah-ling," she commented in a mock-posh accent. "You look positively radiant." The resulting style was a half-updo with waves that cascaded down my back. I'd never really considered that Zara might lust after a wealthier lifestyle; we lived on the far end of cheap and had to work for every penny we earned, but I enjoyed it. Perhaps it was different when you had to do that your entire life and weren't just doing it field-trip style like I was. At any point, I could leave this life behind and return to my home, where nature provided for me abundantly and with only the request for respect in return; Zara didn't have that luxury.

When I finally tried the dress on, I understood Zara's choice of smoky eyeshadow with glittering gold accents. She lined my lips, then filled them with a smoky orchid colored lipstick that made them look even fuller.

"Wow…" I mused as she fastened the wrap around my waist. The fabric felt divine against my skin. Perhaps that was why I'd purchased this dress however long ago. But what on earth was I supposed to do about shoes? There was no way I also magically had matching footwear hiding in my closet. I groaned, then looked back to Zara in distress. "I don't have any shoes that will go with this!"

"Oh come on, sure you do!" Seconds later found us back at my closet, at which point Zara confessed, "Okay, maybe you don't."

When I reached down to grab my boots, I could sense her getting ready to protest. "I'm wearing these," I said sternly as I turned to face her. "I can't just go barefoot, Zara. Besides, no one will notice!" I gestured at the edge of the dress, which fully covered my bare feet. If I walked carefully enough, the boots would stay hidden. They had to; it was my only option at that point.

"I just have to… tread lightly," I murmured as I pulled the footwear on and reemerged in the hallway once more. After lacing them up, I took a deep breath and straightened myself, taking a moment to really feel myself within my body and ignore my surroundings. If I could pretend I was barefoot, running through the woods, balancing on boulders and fallen trees, I could make this work. I had just gotten the hang of striding in a way that kept my feet covered when 5:58 rolled around and Earwyn was knocking at the door. I glanced back at Zara, "Well… how do I look?"

"Stunning. A little weird, but that's just how I like ya." Zara smiled, tossing the lipstick tube that she had been fiddling with back onto the bathroom counter. I'd have to remember to put that away later. Before I could dwell on it too much, she was ushering me to the door. She plucked a flower from the arrangement, tucked it behind my ear, then disappeared into her room; I'd forgotten that she was normally napping at this hour. I smiled to myself, grateful for her friendship. Not once had she asked if Firth would be attending the gala since he and Earwyn worked together, nor did she do anything but center me and my experience. I'd have to ask Earwyn about his brother, I thought, since it had completely slipped my mind until that moment. Perhaps he wasn't going. It often seemed like Earwyn was out working a lot more than Firth was, so maybe he just wasn't part of this particular event.

The way Earwyn's breath seemed to catch in his throat when I opened the door sent a thrill coursing through my entire body. It made me feel powerful. His gaze wandered from my face down my dress, then back up to my painted lips, where he chewed his own in response. My face flushed at his intense attention. "Michelle," he breathed finally.

"Thanks for the flowers…" I told him with a smile. I reached for the coat rack near the door and pulled down a light wrap that Zara had assured me would go with this over-the-top ensemble. "And the invitation… I've never been to a gala before." I debated letting him in on my shoe-secret to see if he'd be put off, but decided against it.

"I… well, no need to thank me," he said finally. I wasn't used to seeing him quite so flustered. "You're doing me a favor, after all, and on such short notice. Wow…"

"Everything okay?"

"Yes, I just… you look incredible."

"You can thank Zara's expert makeup skills." I laughed,

offering him a goofy wink. I'd probably used both eyes by accident.

"It's not the makeup," Earwyn said seriously, his greenish-blue gaze boring into mine. The tone of our conversation had changed in an instant.

"Well, what is it then?"

"Mm, where to begin," my date mused aloud, searching my face. "Your eyes... that green, so dark and deep, like an ancient forest. What have they seen, I wonder? And those lips... soft, supple... I've thought about them quite a bit since we first met. I'm convinced anything that comes from them must be sweet like honey."

My face flushed.

"I'm afraid there isn't enough time for everything else I'd like to say. The line of your collarbone, the curve of your neck... those alone would take the rest of the night." He seemed to snap himself from his daze momentarily to look at his watch, a gold Rolex, then offered me his arm. "Shall we?" He contrasted and complemented my attire perfectly with an all-black suit, the lapels of which shimmered with satin. One of them was adorned with a gold brooch that looked to be an abstract figure of a fish, fitting for the evening's theme. The ocean sure did seem like a big part of his identity, but I had no room to judge, not when I left mushrooms in my wake if I walked barefoot. Meanwhile, his hair was smooth and shiny, tumbling over his shoulder in sandy waves. He looked great. I could see the appeal of dressing in luxury, but I wondered how much of this was truly him and how much was just keeping up appearances for work. He even smelled rich and was obviously wearing a cologne that was different from the first night we met. It smelled nice, but I found myself missing the scent that had soaked into my blanket; it had seemed more uniquely him and less wealthy Seattleite.

He was what I'd seen described as "a perfect gentleman" in movies and led my flustered, lovestruck self down to the limousine that was waiting near P&P with careful grace. Maz eyed us curiously from the large maple tree near my apartment building's stairs: the same ones that Earwyn had led me up during our first encounter. I couldn't speak to the crow around other people, so I just gave him an assuring nod and hoped that he had as good a feeling about this man as I did. His look in response said he'd peck the man's eyes out if there were any missteps. *I mean it*, he told me as I got into the car.

The drive to our destination, a waterfront restaurant called Pacifica, was brief. We fell into small talk effortlessly. Our time texting had, no doubt, helped grow our comfort levels with each other. From what I knew about Pacifica, it was a seafood restaurant, which seemed a bit backward for an ocean conservation event but what did I know? Perhaps it was spot on for how humans liked to do things; in theory it looked good, but they'd likely be responsible for decreasing the population of the ocean in that one night alone. It seemed like Earwyn's thoughts were elsewhere, but every time he looked over at me, he offered me a soft smile. We'd been traveling in silence for a few moments when he calmly reached over to take my hand in his and put our linked fingers onto one of his legs. My heart raced; his hands were large and vascular with calloused fingertips that I imagined exploring my body. I noticed that his free hand rested on his other knee, where he rolled the fabric of his slacks between his fingers so subtly that I almost missed it. Was he nervous?

"I hope you'll enjoy yourself."

"I'm sure I will. I imagine you have to mingle?" Admittedly, I wasn't completely sure what that night would entail besides what Zara had explained to me earlier: small talk, rich people dancing, money, food. Let's go. This would just be another page in my internal encyclopedia of human behavior.

"Yes, unfortunately. It's all a bit stuffy," Earwyn said with a sigh, clearly not looking forward to that part of the event. "I'd love it if you mingled with me, though. I wouldn't want the sharks to get you, looking like that."

"I think I can fend them off," I chuckled.

"I know you can," Earwyn nodded, giving my hand a little squeeze as he glanced out the window. The restaurant pulled into view, and its entrance was bustling with beautiful, overdressed, and likely disgustingly wealthy Seattleites. "That won't stop me from keeping you close."

The heat in the car was stifling and, in an attempt to keep my cool, I asked, "Doesn't Firth work with your company? Will he be there?"

"Yes." Earwyn nodded, moving his free hand to the door handle as we pulled to a stop. Before he could open it, however, it swung out without any effort on his end, and standing there in a tuxedo was Firth. I raised an eyebrow but didn't ask any more about it.

Firth escorted us through the crowd and into the restaurant, which was decorated as extravagantly as everyone was dressed. Half of the building was adorned with floor-to-ceiling windows that looked over the ocean; despite my healthy fear of the sea, I was still in awe of it. As we navigated the crowd with Earwyn charismatically greeting people left and right, he never let go of my hand. He also wasted no time in introducing me to each guest as "Michelle, who has blessed me with her presence tonight" or "the woman I'm so fortunate to have on my arm tonight, Michelle," or "my lovely date, Michelle." I came along, nodded and smiled pleasantly at each introduction, and tried my best to combat the overwhelm I was feeling in the crowded room. Much of my focus went into shuffling the right way so my boots wouldn't stick out of the bottom of my dress. The lighting, the mix of perfumes and colognes, and my increased heart rate just from being near Earwyn left me with my head spinning. I felt entirely out of place. At one point, I was positive I saw a familiar face in the crowd – a blur of stark raven hair and golden eyes. But before I could greet her or attempt to hide, I was pulled back into the fray. Meanwhile, I occasionally noticed Firth out of the corner of my eye. He seemed to be keeping up with us just barely, a few feet between him and ourselves at all times, but he wasn't mingling quite as emphatically as Earwyn was. It occurred to me then that I'd never learned what exactly Firth's role was at the Salt and Earth Alliance, though that evening he certainly seemed like Earwyn's bodyguard. Guarding from what, however, I couldn't be sure.

At one point, a stunning young redhead in a tight black cocktail dress nearly threw herself at Earwyn during their introduction. He offered her a courteous, masked smile and released my hand just to place his own on my hip and pull me closer to him as they spoke. My breath left me in a rush, and I forced myself to remain composed. I wasn't jealous or concerned, but I certainly wouldn't turn down the opportunity to be closer to him. God, he smelled good.

My date must have noticed how saturated my brain was by our surroundings because I soon found us out on the waterfront balcony, which was empty by comparison. I took a few deep breaths as Earwyn led me to the railing.

"I'm sorry," Earwyn confessed, the first statement he'd directed at me since we'd arrived at the restaurant. "I know that was tedious."

I leaned back against the railing, a little sad at the loss of contact now that Earwyn had let go of me, but glad to have a moment to gather my senses. "You're a busy man with plenty of people relying on you for appearances. I don't mind." I took a deep breath and stared up at the night sky for a moment before turning my gaze to my date.

"I do." Earwyn smiled a little, but it was warm and deep, unlike the grin he'd been sharing in the restaurant. The contrast was stark. I wondered how he switched between the two so fluidly. Part of me wanted to ask him for tips while the other wanted to take him somewhere he could leave the mask off forever.

"Really? It all seemed pretty natural to you."

Earwyn leaned on the railing on his elbows and looked from me down to the inky water below. The lights from Pacifica's windows reflected off its dark surface, bending and warping with each ripple. "It's an act... except for anything I said about you, of course. The rest has to seem natural."

I searched his expression as well as I could from our contrasting positions and realized that he must've been right; the Earwyn I saw before me had changed drastically once he'd stepped out onto the dock. "At least you know that about yourself," I offered, trying to look at the situation through an optimistic lens. "Most people are still figuring themselves out."

"It's a recent development," he admitted with a small chuckle. "... a recent understanding I have with myself."

"Well, test it out. Show me a bit of the real Earwyn right here, right now. Maybe it'll tide you over for the rest of your appearances this evening."

"The real Earwyn..." He sighed, laughing a little at what seemed like a preposterous suggestion. He ran a hand loosely through his hair as he glanced around the dock at the couple of other guests who were chatting. They all seemed preoccupied. The noise of the conversation, toasting, music, and laughter poured out of the open door leading back into the restaurant, and it seemed just loud enough to ensure no one nearby could hear our conversation. A slight breeze blew off the water, and I inhaled it deeply, forever grateful for anything that helped me feel closer to the earth despite my discomfort with open water. "You've probably guessed that I love the ocean," he told me, meeting my gaze before looking out onto the water again. I listened quietly, not wanting to stifle his expression, but strongly aware of our differences on that front. "We have a complicated relationship, but I'm mesmerized by her wonder. Look there," he instructed, voice barely above a whisper as he pointed out onto the darkened surface of the water on the horizon. Then, almost as if on cue, I saw a large fin glide out of the water, followed by another, then another: a pod of orca whales. It wasn't a rare sighting in the Puget Sound, but so close and almost as if on-demand, it was surprising to say the least. "Incredible, don't you think?" Earwyn looked enamored by the sight.

"Wow," I breathed, focusing on the whales as their dorsal fins cruised along the horizon. They looked like a show of shadow puppets, their dark appendages gliding across the night sky, which was illuminated slightly by stars and city lights. I felt a sudden ache in my heart at its vastness; I'd always felt small in comparison to the earth and its creatures, but there was something so colossal about the depth of the ocean and those who inhabited it. I wondered what it would be like to fall into the sea and sink to the bottom or get carried away by a current. Perhaps that was why Earwyn loved it so; it was mysterious and dangerous, but undoubtedly beautiful.

"The real Earwyn," he began again, and to my surprise, moved much closer to me. Before I could respond, he was watching the whales over my shoulder, his hands on the railing on either side of me effectively trapping me in place. His chest was pressed against my back as we stood there overlooking the pier. I could feel his breath against my neck, and it sent a thrill through my body. Between his smell, his voice, the breeze of the ocean, the fabric of my gown, I was overwhelmed by pleasant sensations from all angles. His voice was soft and tender when he explained, lips brushing my ear as he spoke. "Well, he would dive in and be consumed by her in a heartbeat... be swallowed up in her depths without question."

A splash in the distance stole my chance to respond and halted my wandering thoughts; the orca whales were breaching the surface of the water almost as if in a display of synchronized swimming. Their sheer beauty consumed me, but our special moment was effectively stolen from us when the other gala attendees on the dock noticed them. Normally I was happy when humans could appreciate the natural wonder of the earth, but disappointment hung over me at our stolen time together. He'd been opening up like I'd wanted him to that first night on the couch and suddenly, it was over. Gone. While I appreciated his stoicism to some extent, I wanted to dig in and learn more about him. The average human I'd encountered was rarely quite so mysterious.

"Oh my God, whales!"

They swarmed to the railing almost as if we weren't there, one woman even bumping into me as she claimed a spot to view the creatures.

"Hey, get a video of me with them in the background! I need this for my TikTok!"

"So cool! Wow, did they hire them for this event? They're definitely getting my money now!"

"I bet this will get you a ton of followers!"

I stifled a laugh at the strangeness of humans and how they seemed to believe in owning everything; of course they'd think you could snap your fingers and order a pod of orca whales for gala entertainment. My date didn't seem to view them that way, though, nor did he find our interruption to be humorous in the slightest. He grabbed my hand and led me back toward the restaurant. He nodded at Firth, who had been standing near the door, watching us. Again, I wondered what he was protecting us, or at least Earwyn, from.

"Wait." I stopped in my tracks and tightened my grip on his hand so he'd stop with me.

"Michelle?"

"What's stopping you? From letting her consume you?" *From letting me consume you,* I added internally, secretly wishing he'd say "nothing" and press me up against the building for a kiss.

"Obligations." Earwyn sighed. He flexed his fingers against mine and gave me a look that said "back to business" as his mask slipped back into place. "Let me get you a drink."

Sometime later I found myself seated at a table with a few of Earwyn's partners from the Salt and Earth Alliance, as indicated by the place cards in front of each of our plates. I had inspected them while being seated so I had some chance at remembering a name or two; I always found that challenging when it came to my relationships with humans. Their names were strange, after all… How many Dans and Marks and Ashleys had I met? Goodness, how many Michelles? I swished my drink in its glass thoughtlessly, enjoying the clinking of the ice cubes against the glass, and nodded as one of the partners talked at me about the cost of each plate of food. Apparently it was quite the point of pride for them. I didn't mention how weird it was to be eating seafood at an ocean conservation event. They would, no doubt, argue about ethical fishing practices, insist that this was different, and I'd have to stop myself from letting my eyes roll back into my head. Earwyn, meanwhile, was approaching a podium at one end of the room where he was likely preparing to give a rousing speech that would encourage these people to donate their money to his company's cause. I couldn't focus on either.

When Earwyn talked about waves crashing to the shore, all I could see were the waves of his golden mane and think about how I desperately wanted to tangle my fingers in them, to tug on them gently while in the throes of passion. His gaze reminded me of sea glass. I thought about swimming naked in the ocean with him. He spoke with such tormented passion about the sea that I was certain she was an old lover, not a body of water, and I wanted nothing more than for him to speak about me that way.

"All of that, my friends, is possible, but not without your support. I truly hope you'll consider giving during tonight's charity auction event. Without further ado, please enjoy the evening!" He completed his speech with an impassive nod, almost as if he hadn't realized his confession of love for the ocean had been public until it was over.

I waited in my seat anxiously, joining the crowd in applause, and was disappointed to see Earwyn pulled aside as he left the podium. Music played, and some guests meandered onto a dance floor, while others stayed seated, chatting and eating their over-priced meals as other facilitators of the gala set up the podium for the auction. One of the men who had been sitting near me, a man I'd learned was named Garrett Miller, extended a hand across the table. "Care to dance?"

"How'd you end up here?" the man asked as he led me out to the dance floor. He was average height, which made him shorter than me, and was probably in his late 30s. I was getting good at guessing ages after practicing with Zara during a people-watching session at Green Lake Park. Garrett had slicked-back dark brown hair with a meticulously groomed mid-length beard and thick rimmed glasses – a "look" that I saw often around Seattle.

"I'm a friend of Earwyn's."

"No, yeah, I know that... but how? Do you work in conservation?" I wasn't sure why, but his prying had me on edge. I couldn't imagine how my occupation had any value to him.

"No, I work at—"

Before I could reply, Firth's looming figure was cutting in. He gave the gentleman a stern look, and I was released without argument. There was something comforting about Firth's presence, so we fell into the dance together without effort. I could see why Zara liked him so much; he was like a big bear, and I felt safe to be myself around him, much like I did around her.

"What's up, Firth?" I looked up at him so that he could see my lips clearly when I spoke.

"Earwyn told me to keep an eye on you."

"Huh… how come? Does he think I'm itching to cause trouble at his fancy event?"

"He doesn't really trust this group."

"Oh. Aren't they *his* group?"

"Not really. That's just me." Firth winked. "How is Zara?"

"Missing you, I'm sure." I smiled. "I'll make sure to tell her how nice you look in a tuxedo."

"He does look nice, doesn't he?" Earwyn interjected, causing us to pause our dancing. "Mind if I cut in?" Before taking his brother's place, the two continued their conversation in sign; something Firth said caused Earwyn to scowl and glance in the direction of his partner, but ultimately he thanked him and resumed the dance with me. I couldn't help but be curious about some of the signs they used. I didn't know ASL, and what they used was slightly different, but it turned out to be pretty intuitive, so when a sign looked completely foreign to me, I couldn't help but feel nosy. It was strange to feel left out of a conversation that was happening directly in front of me, though that was probably how Firth often felt. Again, I made a mental note to ask Zara for any new signs she wanted to share once I got home. If I remembered the ones I'd just seen, I'd try to replicate them for her.

"How are you?" I asked curiously, trying hard to get a read on him. That seemed to be a common trend when we were together in person – I wanted to know what he was thinking, and it seemed that he wanted the exact opposite aside from tiny doses that left me starving for more. I was selfish in that sense.

"Fine."

I had a hard time masking my skepticism. "And how is the real Earwyn? Is there a code word I need to say to get him to come out? The coast is clear."

"Feeling a bit 'over' the charade… and as much as I'm enjoying this moment, I'd rather spend time with you alone, away from the obligations of this event," he admitted, sounding suddenly vulnerable in his admission. In his true stoic fashion, he ignored my joke. His hand squeezed mine gently as we continued to glide through the crowd of other dancers, almost as if we were in water. Everyone else faded from view. I could tell he was working hard to maintain appearances for the sake of the setting and the people he was being forced to interact with while balancing the tenderness he wanted to show me in our interactions. While I was grateful for his effort, I wanted nothing more than for him to feel as comfortable around me as I did him and Firth.

"Then let's leave… You've done your speech, you mingled… Let's go somewhere else. Let him out to breathe," I pleaded through a sigh, then placed a hand on his chest where I toyed with the buttons of his shirt. I could feel his heartbeat quicken under my fingertips.

It didn't take much to convince the real Earwyn to abandon his post as entertainer, entrepreneur, and charity auctioneer to climb into the back of the limo with me. It dropped us off not too far away, near the shore of the beach that we had seen from the restaurant's pier. I kicked off my boots in the sand, completely forgetting that I was exposing my lack of fashion sense, and waded out into the water with my dress hiked up around my thighs. "It's freezing!"

"It's November!" Earwyn laughed. The sound was full and hearty; it felt genuine. I couldn't help but laugh in response. *This* was the human experience I'd been craving.

"That shouldn't deter a true man-of-the-sea like yourself!" I snorted, gesturing for him to join me. I didn't leave my spot in the water, though, and instead stared up at the night sky where a bright yellow moon was peeking through some rapidly moving clouds. It was beautiful. A breeze came off the water and washed over me again. I closed my eyes and inhaled it.

"It would take a lot more than some cold water to keep me away from you."

Once again, Earwyn surprised me by appearing at my side. I looked down and realized that he hadn't taken off his shoes or socks and instead was standing in knee-deep water that was soaking into his fine suit. Before I could comment, the tide pulled out again, this time farther than it had since I'd entered the water. Earwyn bent down in front of me to pluck something from the sand, and when he stood again, he was holding out a conch shell. It was shimmering and opalescent, and he offered it to me with such genuine eagerness. As I took the piece of sea treasure, something about the way the moon reflected in his eyes caused my heart to swell; he was painfully beautiful and so obviously, painfully stretched between his obligations and his heart's desires. I couldn't help myself when I slid my free hand through his hair to rest on the side of his neck and leaned in to press my lips to his. His hand soon found mine, pressing it firmly against his neck almost as if he were trying to hold it captive, to ensure that it wouldn't wander. My focus on each detail of our interaction was overpowered by the sensation of him being so close to me. I could taste bourbon on his lips, could smell his cologne, could feel him melding into me when his tongue swept into my mouth...

"What would it take?" I panted, pulling away from the kiss momentarily to suck on his lower lip.

"Hellfire, Michelle... or your word."

CHAPTER EIGHT

Firth continued to be a seemingly permanent fixture in our apartment, though I couldn't quite suss out the extent of his relationship with Zara. It really wasn't my business, I just liked to observe and muse about how people might interact with each other; at the end of the day, all that mattered was that they had a lot of fun together. I was always pleased to see him in our living room. Sometimes I'd walk in to find them playing video games or in the midst of a food fight that had likely started as a baking lesson. Other times, I only knew they were home by the sound of their conversations and other activities drifting from Zara's room. No matter how often Firth was over, however, Zara never forgot to ask me if I wanted to hang out with them, nor did she stop making sure I ate each day. Admittedly, the dessert that she and Firth made together was the least delectable thing I'd tasted from her, probably because they had gotten distracted and let it burn. I didn't care. I ate it all, smiling at how pleased they seemed to be with each other and simultaneously wiping whipped cream off the cabinet doors.

Earwyn, unfortunately, didn't grace the apartment with his presence nearly as often, and as much as I tried to glean from Firth or from texts, I still felt like I knew very little about him and his whereabouts. Nevertheless, with every text, phone call, and snippet of time that we got together, I felt my attachment to him growing out of my control.

It seemed to blossom into something else when he showed up at my door on my day off and asked to accompany me on "forest time." I had not ever mentioned that activity to him, so I wondered how he'd learned about it; perhaps Zara had been generous with her sharing information about me. Or maybe she'd mentioned it to Firth, who'd then mentioned it to Earwyn. It was strange to me that others might be speaking about me when I wasn't around and exciting to me that those people might involve Earwyn. I tried to dismiss my slight paranoia at the idea that Zara might have brought it up in a "weird things my roommate does" sort of way. It was then that I realized I'd never really taken anyone else on my forest adventures with me.

Since Earwyn didn't know how to drive – not totally uncommon for people in Seattle, who often relied on walking or riding the bus – we settled on taking the clunker because I didn't want to be responsible for their luxury car, which Firth typically drove. I just couldn't wrap my head around the value of such a thing and didn't know how to conduct myself in a manner that showed enough respect for the automobile. Instead, I drove us out to Deception Pass, a strait in northwest Washington, where we wandered off a hiking trail together, much against Earwyn's better judgment. I kept my shoes on for the sake of appearances, which felt strange but necessary. Earwyn, much like he had been every other time I'd been around him, was dressed perfectly for the occasion by human standards. He wore khaki-colored pants, hiking boots, and a zip-up windbreaker; all of it seemed brand new, as if he'd raided an outdoor apparel store prior to our outing. My standards wanted him stark naked and rolling around with me in a patch of clover, but alas, I'd settle for just his presence in any form.

"Are you sure you'll know how to get back?" Earwyn asked, surveying the trees as we trekked farther into the woods. The forest was alive with the sounds of bird chatter and buzzing insects. Ah, perfection. Fall leaves crunched harmoniously under our feet. Maz, if he could, would've probably rolled his eyes as he flew overhead, no doubt eavesdropping. I was certain I'd hear about "wasting time with a guy that doesn't know his way around the woods" once we were back home, chatting about the day.

I chuckled a little. "I haven't gotten lost yet, but then again, they say there's a first time for everything... Are you afraid you'll end up lost in the woods with me?" I glanced back at him briefly and kept walking without looking ahead of me, navigating my natural habitat with ease. Humans were always afraid of getting stuck out in nature as if their species had popped up in the middle of civilization, luxury sports cars and all. "What will we do for food?" I gasped, teasing him. I flung the back of my hand over my eyes in mock-distress. "We may have to eat each other! Oh, what a tragedy!"

I saw a glint in Earwyn's eye at the mention of one of us being eaten, and he licked his lips briefly. "Tsk tsk, Michelle. It's not nice to tease." His expression was flirtatious, and despite his attempt to be domineering, he let slip that he was a bit goofy at heart. "As much as I'd love to taste you, I'd rather it not happen in the context of cannibalism..."

I was about to quip back at him again when I noticed that he was stopped in his tracks. I halted too, and as the sound of our crunching footsteps vanished, I tuned into the forest. "What do you hear?" Then, it sounded again: a whimpering squeal nearby. It was coming from a small creature... It sounded injured. I stood silent for another second, then both of us homed in on its source in an instant and turned to look at a nearby pile of brush. Maz, who had been following us rather discreetly, landed on a nearby tree branch and watched us curiously, tilting his head toward the sound. *I wonder what happened.*

I sank to the forest floor and gently moved the brush where the sound was coming from. We pushed pine needles and twigs and leaves aside to find a small juvenile wild rabbit on its side, breathing erratically. It squeaked again as we approached, its small beady eyes watching us in fear. It seemed a shame that the only animal I could directly communicate with was my familiar, but I hoped that this small creature could sense my intentions. I'd asked Maz time and time again if he could communicate with other animals for me, but he always seemed offended. "Shhh," I told the rabbit, reaching out slowly to pet its petite head with a few gentle fingertips. The creature closed its eyes and let me rub its ears without further protest, and soon, I had it in my arms. I marveled at the softness of its gray-brown fur and the way its rose-lined ears twitched toward every sound in the forest. They were like tiny satellites, scanning restlessly in order to keep him safe. It watched me closely as I turned to look up at my travel companion. Would today be the day that I outed myself for using magick around a human? For healing an animal? Saving a life would be worth the risk, I decided then.

"Michelle, what are you doing?" Earwyn asked, looking put-off for a moment. Eventually, however, he joined me on the forest floor on his knees and sat only a couple of feet from me. He glanced from me to the rabbit and back again. "What's wrong with him? Why was he screaming?" He looked confused and concerned, which sent a rush of relief through me; I'd have been startled if someone so passionate about sea life couldn't see the value in this tiny being. That would have, no doubt, been the end of the road for the two of us.

"He's hurt. I'm not sure how…" I mumbled mindlessly, cradling the rabbit as if it was now my charge. I could fix this. I could help him; after all, he had called out for us. I had to help. I inspected my new friend carefully, gently moving his small limbs to see if I could identify an injury. There was no blood on his body, but eventually, when I moved one of his paws, he let out a small squeak of pain. I immediately stopped, gently holding the paw in one of my hands. "His foot, I think it's broken. We have to help him." I looked from the rabbit to my partner in adventure, a silent plea in my gaze. Maz chittered above us, trying to warn me against outing the both of us: *This isn't a good idea. What's going to happen if he sees who you really are?*

"Why save it? All creatures must die eventually, Michelle. Who's to say that it isn't his time? Why give it more of yours?"

I sighed, looking down at the tiny, soft creature in my lap. Who would protect it if not me? And who was I to say that any creature didn't deserve more time on Earth? "It's not his time…" I told him honestly, feeling that it was the truth deep in my bones. "And if it is, he shouldn't die alone." I stroked his small chest with my thumb, then met Earwyn's gaze again.

"We all die alone."

Maz let out a judgment squawk from his post in the tree nearby: *Pessimist! Yikes!*

"No. We're all connected," I told him earnestly, taking a free hand to reach for his chest. I believed in every word I said, but it certainly felt like I was trying to convince him of it. My fingertips grazed the fabric of his shirt, where he grabbed my hand and pressed my palm against him tightly. "The same heart beats through all of nature… through you and I… just like it does through this little rabbit and through every being in this forest."

Earwyn's breath hitched in his throat as he looked at me, but I felt his heartbeat quicken under my fingertips. I wanted desperately to fall into him, to bare my soul to this man, but this was as close as I could get for now. I held the rabbit a little tighter to me and closed my eyes, willing it to heal and breathe in the life of the forest again. I was exposing myself a little, being vulnerable, but I had to. I couldn't let this innocent creature's life be cut short for the sake of convenience. "You'll be okay, little one," I told the animal, stroking its soft ears after I removed my hand from Earwyn's shirt. When its small nose twitched and wiggled, I breathed a sigh of relief. I moved its once injured paw again, and the rabbit let me without any protest. "See? Not bad…"

"How did you…"

I shrugged. "He just needed some rest, some nurturing, what we all need at one point or another… and for someone to believe it wasn't his time. He has a lot of life left to live. Don't you, little one?" I folded my legs underneath me and set the creature in my lap where he flopped down comfortably to rest, then I dug through the forest foliage nearby for an empty acorn. Its small base was the perfect vessel for my next request. "Can you fill this with water?" When Earwyn complied, not without raising an eyebrow, I exhaled in relief. He swung his bag off his shoulder and opened it, filling my makeshift cup with water from a water bottle he'd packed; I'd told him he wouldn't need anything, and yet, he looked like a bona fide Seattleite with his wide-mouth water bottle covered in stickers from local shops. I'd have to get one of those! I could've sworn his water bottle had been empty when I watched him pack it that morning, but perhaps he'd filled it in a creek during our hike and I hadn't noticed. Nevertheless, I took the water with thanks and held the acorn up to the rabbit, who sipped at it sweetly while eyeing us, though less nervously than he had before. I hoped this man would believe that the rabbit and I had just gotten lucky, but our situation certainly looked suspicious – broken limbs didn't just heal themselves, not in the human world. Both my curiosity and my need to distract him from my use of magick fueled my question. "When did you fill your water bottle?"

Earwyn froze momentarily, then resumed screwing the lid onto his bottle. He didn't look at me when he spoke. "There was a water fountain at the trailhead." There wasn't. I would've remembered that.

We spent the rest of the afternoon ensuring that the rabbit was okay. When it was finally time to let the little creature go back into the forest and to its den, Earwyn looked at me curiously and asked, "Don't you want to keep it?" Something in his tone suggested that this was a pop quiz question and not a suggestion. Why he was quizzing me, though, I wasn't sure.

"Keep it… how?"

"You know, like a pet." There was a glint of amusement in his eyes.

Somewhere, up in the trees, Maz chittered with a curious annoyance I'd never heard from him before: *What the hell is a pet?*

It came out more harshly than I intended, but I responded with a curt, "No." I'd seen pets in other peoples' homes and while cats and dogs seemed mostly okay with the arrangement, I couldn't fathom taking a creature from its home and sticking it in mine for my entertainment. Besides, humans kept rabbits in cages! The thought alone made me uncomfortable. "He's not mine to keep," I explained, reminding myself that if I was going to live among humans, I'd need to humor them and when given the chance, educate them a little bit just like they did me. "Nor is any creature of the earth. Would you put your orcas in a fishbowl?" I raised an eyebrow at him in curiosity and anxiously awaited his response; it seemed once again, we were approaching a potential deal-breaker. It saddened me a little to think that the man I'd been daydreaming about for so long might not be as perfect as I'd made him out to be, but I had to stand by my convictions.

"Some might." Earwyn smiled, seemingly pleased with my answer. I tried to ignore the straightness of his gleaming white teeth.

I set my jaw, determined not to show my cards. His response mattered to me, and I wouldn't be swayed by the fact that he was disgustingly gorgeous. "And you?"

"I wouldn't dream of it." Before I could acknowledge his answer, Earwyn's face fell, and he continued. "I know what it's like to be held captive." As quickly as he'd let me in, he shut me out again by clearing his throat and returning his expression to neutral once more. Boy, this man was a tough nut to crack.

"Well, we can rejoice in this creature's freedom... together," I told him honestly, then got to my feet with the rabbit in my arms. I held the little bunny out to him with an encouraging smile. "Go on then, send him on his way. Maybe it'll be cathartic for you." I marveled at the tenderness with which Earwyn took the rabbit, after some hesitation, and set it back near the brush in which we'd found him. Briefly I wondered if he utilized that same tenderness elsewhere; would he stroke my hair as if it were the downy fur of a small woodland creature? Would he regard me as fragile, break-able? Or would he be a conqueror, a captor hellbent on getting revenge for whatever wrongdoings he'd experienced? Would he be soft and sweet or brutal... unrestrained?

When the small creature hopped off toward its home and family, joy filled me. I was grateful for our period of rest, too, because most magick required some energy on my part; big magick, like healing an injury, could leave me feeling rather depleted, more so than, say, reviving a plant. Thankfully, the rabbit was small, and his injury was too, so I was able to bounce back faster than if it were something more serious. Eventually, it was time to return to our car. We had been walking in silence for a few moments when I caught Earwyn's gaze out of the corner of my eye and turned to face him. "What is it?"

"Has that crow been following us?" He gestured to Maz, who had indeed been hopping from tree to tree as we walked.

I feigned ignorance. "Huh? Nah, this forest is filled with crows... Besides, I tend to attract critters, if you haven't noticed." I glanced up at Maz as if to say 'get lost!'

He cawed in annoyance, then flew out of sight.

The filtered light of a fall evening shone through the canopy of trees and cast shadows on Earwyn's handsome face as we stood there, trying to feel each other out without admitting it. Was he really worried about Maz, or had he just been looking for an excuse to stop and talk again? I sincerely hoped it was the latter. He ran a hand through his hair and sighed as if he were at his wit's end, and suddenly, as if he'd been fighting himself for longer than I knew, he said, "I need to kiss you." When I nodded in agreement, stifling an overly pleased grin, he took me in his arms and kissed me softly. The cold tip of his nose nuzzled my neck while he left a blazing trail of kisses down it and breathed me in. I closed my eyes and rested my head against his, savoring every bit of contact I got from this man who seemed to want to devour me and keep me at an arm's length at the same time. "You're quite the goddess of the forest, you know that?" he asked me, pulling away to press another soft kiss to my lips before meeting my gaze. His sea-green stare held me captive, and I surrendered without argument. "All of the creatures on Earth and somehow I found you... how?"

I sighed, then laughed a little to humor him; he had no idea what a goddess of the forest I actually was. I wondered if he'd ever know. No other humans had been privy to my background or reality, not even Zara, but something about this man made me feel like he might stick around to find out. Maz squawked and flew off again, giving us space: *Get a room!* I was sure to get an earful about this once I met him back at home. "Now that you've found me, do you intend to keep me?"

"Only if you'll allow it, although… I get the feeling you can't be kept."

We made it back to the car without getting lost, much to my adventure partner's great relief. Before we returned to the city, though, I showed Earwyn that Deception Pass also had a beach, which seemed to make him feel more at ease. I watched the tension leave his body as we approached the water. I certainly understood having your "place," and we spent the remainder of the evening strolling along the beach, occasionally stopping to peek into tide pools while Maz pecked at barnacles on massive nearby rocks protruding from the shore. The water and the breeze coming off of it were frigid, and as a result, the beach was nearly empty. We wandered it until there was no more light to be found in the sky, and at some point, Earwyn's fingers interlaced themselves with mine again. The touch sent a jolt of electricity through my body, but when he stopped me in my tracks and dipped me into another soft kiss in the moonlight, I thought I might not mind being kept after all. Not only that, but I wasn't sure I had a choice.

CHAPTER NINE

*T*he next time we saw Earwyn as a group was on the eve of the winter solstice. When he'd invited us all to celebrate at his apartment, I hardly expected it to be for that reason. Most humans didn't celebrate the earth or nature or the seasons in that way, but any excuse for me to embrace my roots was beyond welcome. Worst case, we'd brush it off as me being "quirky" or a "hippie" – something I was all too used to. Earwyn was involved in ocean conservation, though, so how much room did he really have to talk? That man was a hippie, too, and his passion for the sea rivaled my own for the forest. Honestly, it made me swoon. As long as I didn't have to go *into* the ocean, I could probably find a way to appreciate it as much as he did.

I spent the morning putting together recipes I'd amassed over many decades; they were carefully filed away in my mind and had been passed down amongst generations of Yannavi folk. After placing everything in colorful glass containers to travel with, Zara and I took a rideshare over to the apartment building that Earwyn and Firth had been staying in during their time in town. Apparently, the Salt and Earth Alliance had an apartment that they kept solely for Earwyn and Firth's work visits. With my limited knowledge of human economy, I couldn't understand how anyone could afford to have an apartment on hand for infrequent use; the Alliance must have been a pretty lucrative employer with money to waste. Because I didn't think the clunker could stand any extra use, we decided against driving ourselves. There was also some suggestion that there'd be a lot of alcohol involved this evening, so we assumed driving wouldn't be the smartest idea. Of course, I found myself aching to stay with Earwyn for longer than just a dinner party, but knew that he had strong limitations that seemed to put stoppers in all of our passionate interactions.

The sun went down a little after four p.m., which was about when we found ourselves entering the rather large, swanky downtown Seattle apartment building. I'd never set foot in such a high-end complex and again, wondered how a conservation organization could afford to put their staff up here indefinitely. The exterior of the building looked classy and ancient, with stained glass windows and stone architecture, while the inside was modern and had every imaginable amenity.

Even the doorman was better dressed than we were, but he tipped his hat and let us in with a smile.

I wore a long, cotton, emerald gown with sleeves that had an intricate lace design; the delicate lacework pattern allowed my bare skin to show through its design. Over the dress, I wore a cream-colored hooded shawl that made me feel like I was back home gathering goodies for our celebrations in the winter.

As we rode the elevator up to Earwyn's floor, Zara stopped to look me up and down. "That outfit is over-the-top, Michelle." She reached out to touch my shawl, rubbing the fibers between her fingertips. "What is this? Wool? Geez, sprout, did you go and shear the sheep yourself?"

"Oh no. Is it bad?"

"I'm obsessed. Earwyn is gonna lose his mind."

"Since when do I care about some dude liking my clothes?" I asked, turning away from her and back toward the elevator door. When the elevator was silent for a moment, I sighed. "Shoot, I do care. I really care. Are you sure he'll like it?"

Zara smirked, then rolled her eyes a little. "Chill. He's gonna love it."

I smiled to myself and swiveled side to side a little, using the feel of the fabric swishing around my bare legs to relax me a little. I wasn't wearing much underneath and felt hopeful that Earwyn would soon learn that fact, too. Meanwhile, Zara was dressed in a velvety black skater dress and platform boots. Her faux hawk was styled perfectly, and I noticed that she'd recently shaved the sides of her head, which really made the colors of her floral tattoo pop. Somehow, we contrasted and complemented each other perfectly. I loved that about us.

After Firth let us in, I set my bag with all of the containers down on the kitchen counter of their place, which seemed to have all of the fixings that our apartment had, only about one hundred times nicer. He must have really liked spending time with Zara because most folks would've much rather spent time in a swanky, all-inclusive apartment complex–resort hybrid than our rundown, restaurant-top apartment. How many microwave pizza pockets had he eaten when he could've been using this gourmet kitchen the entire time? I was certain this apartment even had heated toilets while our apartment had creaky floors and clanging pipes. Yikes. Bugs? None here. I didn't mind them, but Zara had made it clear that they were not supposed to be a staple in human households.

"You didn't have to bring anything!" Firth boomed, looking at the spread as he let us in. The larger brother looked comfortable and casual in a flannel button-up shirt and jeans, though the latter hugged his massive legs so tightly I thought they might rip if he moved too quickly. I hoped for his sake that it was an illusion and they were unnaturally stretchy. He wrapped Zara in a big hug as she entered and even lifted her off the floor as he did so. It was cute and my cheeks warmed at the sight; I loved their comfort with each other. Meanwhile, I was antsy beyond belief and yearning for something like what my roommate had. That longing was entirely new to me, but ever since I'd met Earwyn, not one of my other connections held any appeal to me. Yes, I wanted comfort, wanted closeness, and warmth, but only from him. The exclusivity of those desires was foreign to me and admittedly, a bit scary. Still, the thrill of the unknown was a bit stronger than my fear.

"It's my pleasure," I signed to Firth, still slowly, as I took the covers off each of the dishes. I'd made a spiced Anjou pear bread, cardamom orange cookies, and a parsnip soup; Earwyn and Firth had assured us all of the main food items would be taken care of, so I went with sides. I also crafted a sparkling beverage (similar to Sprite) from pine needles I'd gathered the last time I'd spent a day in the woods, as well as an animal feeder for the men to hang from their apartment balcony. It was made of a small hoop structure I'd woven from fallen twigs, coated in suet, and rolled in seeds, nuts, and dried fruit. Something told me this particular building wouldn't be pleased with them welcoming wild birds and squirrels onto their landing, but I left it anyway.

Once everything was unwrapped, I pulled two small gifts out of my bag and set them on the counter as well. Firth's gift was a candle, the scent of which reminded me of home, and for Earwyn, I'd managed to knit a scarf over the last few nights. With that said, I hadn't known how to knit until three nights before our gathering and as good of a teacher as online videos were, the scarf was nowhere near perfect. It had some misplaced holes, and one end was wider than the other. Even so, I'd made sure to wear it around my neck to sleep the night before so I could tell Earwyn he now had something that smelled just like me. My heart raced at the thought; would he wear it? Or would it end up in a drawer somewhere? Surely this was way too much for a man I'd only been around a few times prior, and yet, our bond felt like one decades in the making.

Before I had the lids packed away in my bag, Firth and Zara wandered off to the living room where they'd laid out an array of board games for the evening. The couple chatted away, Zara's legs flung over Firth's massive quads, while I removed my shawl and looked for a place to drape it. I barely had it off my shoulders before I felt Earwyn behind me; he was a presence I'd learned I couldn't deny, whether it was his body or his scent or just the way he occupied space in his confident quietness. "Allow me," he said softly, almost as if he were right up against my ear. A slight gasp left my lips as his fingertips graced my shoulders and he removed the shawl the rest of the way.

I turned to face him with a smile, though I knew my cheeks were flushed and any hint of nonchalance had left me. "Thank you."

"No, thank you," Earwyn insisted, hanging the shawl on a coat rack nearby. "I told you you didn't need to bring anything; we've got everything handled... though, something there smells incredible. I only hope what we ordered can live up to your homemade creations."

"It's not often that someone invites me to a winter solstice celebration," I confessed, then looked him up and down. "You look nice," I added, reaching up to place a hand on his chest. The cotton, horizontally striped black and gray shirt he wore must've been the softest thing I'd ever felt, and it was perfectly complemented by his olive green corduroy slacks. His heart hammered against my flesh, and I couldn't help what I blurted out next. He placed his hand over mine, pinning it in place: a gesture I'd grown accustomed to even though I wasn't sure of the reasoning behind it. "Can I kiss you?"

Zara hollered from the couch, "Just do it, girl!" Of course, she didn't know the extent of his hesitation from the other times we'd gotten close, nor did she know much about our conversations… how soft, sweet, complex, and mysterious this man was. Something about him suggested that he needed more communication and forethought than perhaps was typical of most humans. When Earwyn placed a soft hand on my cheek and leaned forward to sweetly initiate the gesture, I smiled against his lips and laughed a little. He felt familiar, even with our limited interactions, and I'd been craving that closeness since the first night we'd pulled apart from each other. Even if this was all I got from him ever again, it was nice. It was perfect. I would treasure it for the rest of my days.

I helped serve up dinner, including the additions I'd brought. When I went to the kitchen to slice up the pear bread and serve it in a small wicker basket, I inadvertently ran the blade of the bread knife over my finger instead of the loaf. Unable to help the hiss of pain that escaped my lips, I wrapped my finger in the opposite hand in frustration. Blood seeped between my fingers, and the flash of crimson mesmerized me.

"You alright over there? Cut yourself?" Earwyn asked from his spot on the couch.

"That's weird, Michelle never gets hurt," Zara mused aloud, already a little tipsy from the libations the brothers had provided. "She sure is clumsy, though!"

"Huh, yeah, that's me…" I forced laughter as I stared at the blood dripping from my finger onto the granite countertop. I didn't really bleed, not usually at least. It wasn't that I wasn't able to, I just never hurt myself enough for an injury to make me bleed… These little bumps and cuts typically healed before they had a chance to weep. Because of my lack of familiarity with injury in general, I wasn't sure what to do next, but soon Firth appeared at my side with a previously unopened first aid kit and helped me apply a bandage with his massive hands. "Thanks…"

I caught Earwyn looking at me, concerned, from across the room. People cut themselves, this was fine… except I wasn't "people," I didn't cut myself, and this wasn't fine. This was concerning. I tried to push the thought of its implications to the back of my mind; I was supposed to be enjoying myself, enjoying my friends, not panicking over a cut.

After a night of board games, music, good food, and good conversation, I found myself melting into the couch I'd been sitting on with Earwyn. The cushions had undoubtedly molded to the shape of my body over the course of a few hours. I was tired and full and also more comfortable than I'd ever been, leaning my tired head on Earwyn's shoulder as he took the last turn in our game of Monopoly when he quietly asked, "Will you stay?" My eyes must have widened a little, shocked at my wholesome man's implied intimacy, because he then added, "It's far too late for you to be heading home." It seemed Zara and Firth were already heading to the brother's room for the evening, so it didn't look like I had a choice in the matter either way; I didn't like the idea of leaving without Zara, even if I'd somehow wanted to. It had always been our promise to look out for each other.

When I looked up at Earwyn with a smile, I joked, "This is a nice couch. I wouldn't mind testing it out. I'm about to fall asleep anyway." I also wouldn't have minded peeling Earwyn's clothing off with my teeth, but I wouldn't dare ruin just how perfect everything had been that evening.

"No, no, I can take the couch."

I snorted and brushed him off. "I think I'm glued here." He

kissed my head and tucked me in before leaving. What I didn't expect, however, was that once I'd dozed off comfortably on the couch, having shed some of my outer layers of clothing and donned one of Earwyn's blankets, I'd be woken by his warm presence above me. I was so shocked by this new development that I was certain I was dreaming. "Mm, this is nice," I mumbled against dream-Earwyn's soft lips. "Too bad it's not real life," I sighed, eyes still closed when he pulled away. "But I'll take what I can get."

Earwyn, ever patient and understanding, laughed warmly at my confusion and sighed. "It is real life, but I'm sorry I can't give you more, faster." The next thing I knew, I'd opened my eyes to find that he had hoisted me off the couch and was carrying me back into his room. When I remembered that moment later, I'd be shocked at his strength; lifting someone as tall as me was not an easy feat, even for big strong men. I sighed happily, nuzzling into his neck, and breathed him in. How was he so warm, even in the cold of winter? He locked the door behind us and set me down gracefully, cradling my face and locking eyes with me in the dim light of his bedside lamp. I glanced around briefly to find that Earwyn's bedroom was just as swanky as the rest of the apartment. It boasted floor-to-ceiling windows that looked over the glittering city; the Space Needle shone boldly in the distance. Against one wall was a massive California king size bed, layered with fine sheets and blankets of silver and blue, the headboard of which had geometric patterns fashioned into its wood. An electric fireplace with a driftwood and stone insert crackled across from the bed. A line of suits and the rest of Earwyn's fine clothing filled the slightly open closet, and nearby was the door to the master bathroom, which was likely just as over-the-top. The room was luxurious, clean, and masculine. Much to my pleasure, it smelled like him.

"I'll give you all of me if you can be patient, though I'm not sure how much of a prize that really is," he told me seriously, as if I wasn't as desperately head-over-heels as he was for me. It almost felt like an insult for him to be so self-deprecating. "But for now, can we take baby steps?"

He could've talked me into anything in that moment as his jade gaze burned into mine, spreading heat rapidly through my entire body. Unable to produce coherent words, I nodded as if in a daze. His smile in response suggested that he hadn't expected such willingness, and it pleased me even more to see him so genuinely happy. What was that? Walk off a cliff, Michelle? Sure! Anything to put that smile on his face again. God, it was beautiful, like seeing the sun for the first time. "Good, then let me worship you," he directed as if he were finalizing a business deal. "Let's face it, that's all I've dreamt about since we first met."

I gasped as he sank to his knees before me in an ultimate show of submission. Before I could choke out some commentary about how worship didn't seem like much of a baby step, nor did I feel worthy of such behavior, he was lovingly running his hands up my thighs, his fingers exploring the flesh beneath my dress. My head fell back involuntarily, and I whimpered at the contact. "Wyn," I said with a sigh.

"Wyn?" he asked aloud, pressing kisses to each new inch of bare skin he revealed as he pushed the gown up over my calves and thighs. He sounded amused at the nickname.

"That's what I call you..." I panted, fumbling to explain myself and feeling lightheaded because I was in a position I'd only ever dreamt of happening.

"When do you call me that, Michelle?" Earwyn purred as the gown crept up smoothly to my waist, exposing my legs fully as well as my panties. They matched the gown, of course: green lace. I typically didn't put that much effort into clothing coordination but found myself very, very glad I'd planned it out that night.

"When I think of you," I breathed, finally, willing the words to flow as easily as they did for him. Then, I confessed, "When I touch myself."

He kissed between my legs, spreading warmth through the fabric of my underwear and to my flesh, and smiled against my skin. "I like Wyn." Seconds later I found my precious gown on the floor and me standing in front of Earwyn in nothing but my panties and bra while he admired me. There was something strangely erotic about the way he looked at me in his fully dressed state. Supposedly, he worshipping me, but I would have been content to be at his mercy instead. I licked my lips at the sight of the straining bulge in his slacks and reveled internally in my triumphant femininity, but told myself to focus on what I was allowed to have that evening. Baby steps, I reminded myself.

"You're a goddess," my golden-maned man said finally, smiling as his gaze traveled up my body to my face, where I was undoubtedly blushing. I couldn't help but wonder how this Earwyn was so much more sure of what he wanted than the one I'd kissed in my hallway and on the beach and in the forest; perhaps he needed to be in charge, even though he seemed to be physically submitting to me. There was no doubt that this man was topping from the bottom. "Have I scandalized you?"

"No," I said honestly. "This just isn't a juxtaposition I'm used to."

"I can imagine." He sighed, running a hand through his hair. "I think I can distract you from the strangeness, though, if you'll let me. Can I touch you?"

"You don't have to ask. I trust you." Admittedly, though, the genuine earnestness and tenderness in the way he asked for permission turned me on even more. Maybe he was modeling what he needed from me. "Touch me."

His lips found mine while one of his hands tangled itself in my hair and the other grazed my side, settling on my hip for a

moment while his tongue explored mine. I'd missed this. I'd
thought about it nonstop since his first night visiting our apartment, and while the memory was nice, the real thing did not disap-
point. Heat bloomed in my belly, and I clenched my thighs shut
against the dampness that was spreading there. I wanted to devour
this man alive, to consume him like the depths of the ocean and
hide him away from the harshness of the world. I wanted him bare
and open. Apparently, he had similar thoughts; he trailed blazing
kisses down my throat, shoulders, and onto my chest, where he
took one of my nipples into his mouth. "God," I panted.

"Are you religious?" Earwyn asked, lifting me up off the floor
so that I could wrap myself around him as he carried me to the
bed. He laid me down with a grace and elegance I'd never seen a
man exhibit – and only very few women – and I looked up at him
through a hooded gaze, suddenly aware of just how exposed I
was. I trembled slightly in excitement.

"After this, I might be."

The sandy-haired, green-eyed Adonis of a man leaned over me
to press a sweet kiss to my lips. I could taste the faintest whisper of
myself on him. "Let's hope I have that grand of an effect on you."
When he ran his hands down my legs, pulling my panties down as
he did so, I saw stars again. How could such gentle, simple
gestures leave me gasping for breath? I still felt confused by his
selfless approach, but eventually was too lost in sensation to dwell
on it. I told myself to be present. I owed him that. "Beautiful," he
murmured, then leaned down to press his lips to my bare cleft. "So
soft and sweet, like the rest of you." My eyes fluttered shut, and
my back arched helplessly into the mattress, where he reached up
to lace our fingers together and pin one of my hands into the
sheets. Once again, I was being gently restrained, guided, led from
beneath. I was panting, breathless in an instant. I was desperate for
more, and he delivered, laying his tongue against my lips before

using it to spread them and lap at my folds. When he found the sensitive bundle of nerves between my thighs, he sucked on it expertly, then ate me soft and deep until I was gripping his hand and his expensive sheets for dear life.

"Come back to me," he whispered against my inner thigh, breaking our union just as I was teetering on the edge, looking into the crashing waves of the ocean threatening to pull me in. I gasped as he left me writhing. "I love you like this." I could feel his gaze on me as he raked it up my body. "You're divine, stunning… so soft and warm and open for me," he told me, running a hand up my belly so that he could knead one of my breasts. "You're as hungry for me as I am you. I could touch you like this for days." Then, he pressed another kiss to the union of my thigh and pelvis, groaning against my flesh as if that act alone had him undone.

"Is this worship or teasing?" I whimpered, devastated at the loss of contact but amazed at his ability to read my body so well already. For someone so reserved and, according to my assumptions only, inexperienced, I felt laid bare. Earwyn read me so easily, it was as if he knew every inch of me and had for his entire lifetime.

"Both," he confirmed, waiting until my breathing had slowed a bit before licking me again. His sandy locks brushed against my legs as he worked me. When he plunged one, then two rough, slender fingers into me, I found myself grinding against his hand and nearly begging for more. "I love how you squeeze me," he mused, and I wondered how hard and hungry he was beneath those finely pressed clothes and his reserved exterior. Was he imagining me squeezing his cock just as desperately? I was, too, but even the thought of his face between my firm thighs had a storm brewing within me.

"I wish— you'd let me— squeeze you elsewhere—ah!"

"Me too, goddess," Earwyn agreed almost sadly, but loud

enough that I could hear him over my own frantic breaths. He leaned over me, still working me with his dexterous touch, to kiss me hard and deep. His tongue swept into my mouth, which was dry from breathlessness, and I wondered if this was some sort of power play for him. I was completely at his mercy, but he was merciful... so merciful... I wrapped my arms around his neck, grinding my naked body against his clothed leg as he pumped his fingers in and out of me, his thumb caressing my clit in perfect time. "Stunning," he labeled me, moving to press kisses down my throat. "Let go now. Let me hear what it's like when you touch yourself and think of me. I need to know..."

"Yes!" I gasped, throwing my head back into the bed and grasping one of my breasts with my free hand. I found myself overwhelmed by Earwyn's ethereal beauty, the feminine satisfaction of being enough to move past barriers with him, the sensation of his tongue, his fingers, his husky but loving voice... "Oh, oh God," I whimpered, unable to stop the crest of an explosive wave of orgasm from crashing over me. I cried out, gripping his fingers tightly and near sobbing with pleasure, "Wyn, it's so good, oh, God..."

I was tender and weak when Earwyn finally kissed my damp throat after riding out my climax, sliding his fingers from my sensitive tissue before crawling up to join me on the bed. He lovingly repositioned me so that I was fully on the bed, then pulled a blanket up over my bare body in a way that suggested he wasn't hiding me, just keeping me safe and warm. The bedding smelled like him; this would be a fine place to die, I thought. I breathed it in and let my head swim. Whatever happened there was perfect, right, even if it was disorienting. I would ride that wave without question.

"Mmm," I murmured, and nuzzled myself into his chest, beyond content. I wasn't sure how much time had passed before my eyes finally fluttered open, but when I looked up at him, his smile immediately lit another fire within me. More. I needed more. I tried to calm myself, though, and appreciate the selfless creature holding me. "What about you?" I asked, unsure of my phrasing; normally I would've initiated something, but he'd made it clear that he had boundaries. "Can we get creative? With... baby steps?"

His resounding chuckle warmed me even more, but he seemed unsure. I cringed internally as I felt walls going up between us once again; this dance with him was so delicate that each step needed to be perfectly choreographed or I could lose him entirely. I didn't want to risk that, but I couldn't let fear stop me from loving him. "What did you have in mind?"

I reached down to move the blanket off us, then tugged Earwyn's sweater up slightly, exposing a few inches of his midsection. Unsurprisingly, he had what I'd heard referred to as an Adonis belt – v-shaped grooves in the muscles of his lower abdomen. It only seemed fitting considering how godlike he was. Then, slowly, so that he could stop me if needed, I unbuttoned his pants. It was challenging with one hand because of how hard he was straining against them. He was panting. He seemed shocked, though, when I grabbed his hand and slid it into his boxers. "Touch yourself for me," I suggested, knowing that anything more would be too much. When he complied, I marveled at the sight of him fisting his cock beneath the fabric of his clothing, then climbed on top of him to straddle his legs. He looked embarrassed, nervous, but unable to deny the pleasure of what he was doing to himself while I watched. I kissed him hard and deep, desperate for as much of him as he'd give me. I grabbed his free hand and pressed it to my breast, kissed his throat, whimpered in his ear at the fact that I was drenched again because of him. As his body tensed with his impending release, I crushed my lips to his and pleaded, "I want it all." It seemed so much more intimate that way, him sharing this personal familiarity while mostly clothed and with me barely touching his flesh, and I was desperate to soak it all in.

He came with rough, shuddering jerks, spilling himself fully onto his tensed abdomen. Before he could protest, I lowered myself farther down the bed and lapped up every last drop. I wanted to worship him, too.

WINTER

CHAPTER TEN

$\mathcal{E}$veryone and their mom has seen the Nutcracker ballet. I, apparently, didn't fall into either of those categories because I was ecstatic at the idea of attending a performance of it at the Pacific Northwest Ballet. While I'd mastered incorporating seasonal coffee drinks into my routine – peppermint mocha this time of year – I was pleased with myself for acquiring yet another human-life badge. Zara had apparently seen this performance a million times, but she humored me because "Male ballerinas have big packages that you can see through their tights! I dig it."

Firth echoed the sentiment with the sign for "same." Well, there was no arguing with that logic. Earwyn was less enthused about the prospect of seeing big dicks in spandex. Regardless, we all used it as an excuse to dress up and go out together. Doing things as a group of four had quickly become one of my favorite pastimes, especially because I found that being around these friends didn't drain my energy tank like most human interaction did. As a result, I didn't wake feeling hungover or need recovery time the next day; I just wanted more. It had even begun to replace some of my time in the forest, which I could not have anticipated ever happening but didn't mind. It was nice to think that I could have that powerful of a connection elsewhere. Was Earwyn becoming as crucial to my existence as the forest always had been?

The lobby of the venue was decorated for winter holidays, including bunches of mistletoe in every doorframe leading into the theater. I had a love/hate relationship with this time of year in the human world. I loved feeling surrounded by nature. I felt at home, between the Christmas trees, wreaths, and now the little red ribbon–wrapped greenery bundles hanging everywhere. It smelled divine – a woodsy person's dream. On the other hand, all of that nature was dead, empty of the magick I could normally awaken within it. I cocked my head at the hanging plant, immediately drawn to the sprig of foliage miraculously appearing indoors, and was about to ask Zara about them when I saw a young man pull his boyfriend into a kiss underneath one of them. Ah, another strange human custom to add to my mental encyclopedia. Mistletoe is a parasitic plant, so it seemed a bit odd to me that it was apparently a symbol of love and affection to the humans, but who was I to judge the customs of another race? If they wanted to kiss under the leech plant, I wouldn't be the one to stop them, even if it was a sign that they were embracing sycophantic relationships.

When the coast appeared clear, I reached my fingers up toward a bare doorframe entry to the theater and willed my own tiny sprigs of green littered with white berries. The only thing that was missing was the red ribbon the other bunches had, but my magick didn't really extend to man-made materials like polyester ribbon. As I brought my hand back down to my side, itching to pull Earwyn into a kiss based on this human tradition, my head began to spin. The room spun. I felt depleted: a new sensation following such a minor creation or summoning. Sometimes magick made me feel alive and spry, other times it left me a little drained, but to feel this sucked dry I typically would've needed to summon an entire forest from scratch or bring someone back from the brink of death. I leaned on the wall for support and closed my eyes, willing myself to feel grounded again. Thankfully, Firth and Zara had wandered off to get drinks before the show started, so my only audience was my date and other ballet attendees filtering through the open door to the theater. The latter noticed nothing; for all they knew, I was simply having a hard time holding my liquor.

Without a word from me, Earwyn slung an arm around my waist and pulled me off the wall so that I'd lean my weight against him. He looked concerned, but in his true stoic and discreet fashion, didn't want to draw attention to me unless I wanted him to. He escorted me to our seats before asking, "What's happening? You're flushed."

"I'm always flushed around you," I whispered, lying through my teeth even though I desperately wanted to spill my guts to him. This was all wrong. I tried my best to neutralize my panic outwardly and encouraged my friends to enjoy the show. I wanted to enjoy it, too, to enjoy Earwyn and our newfound adventure together. I tried desperately to focus on his fingers interlaced with mine and the way his thumb stroked the back of my hand while he watched the ballerinas glide across the stage. When the vertigo didn't subside, however, I waited for a break in the performance and excused myself without saying much to the group. The air in the building was stifling, so I found myself stumbling out into the winter Seattle air, where I was relieved to find my familiar. I looked up at him in a panic. "What's happening to me, Maz?"

When I heard nothing in return and the small bird cocked his head at me in confusion, my panic increased tenfold. This was my bird, my familiar, right? I noted the chip in the side of his beak and the way his feathers lay against his small body, glistening blue-black in the streetlights' reflection. Yes, this was my Mazus. I would've recognized him anywhere. After all, we had been together since he was hatched from a tiny speckled egg, hundreds of years ago. "Can't you understand me?"

He cocked his head the other direction, then let out a small, irritated chirp. Much to my dismay, we drew the attention of some passersby. "Damn, is that girl talking to a bird? Downtown Seattle, y'all... shit never ceases to amaze me. Let's get outta here."

My head swam and my heart threatened to crawl up through my throat. I couldn't go back in and watch people leap across a stage as if nothing was wrong! Big dicks in spandex would not be enough of a distraction from this crisis. I definitely couldn't talk to Earwyn about this... or Zara, for that matter. A loneliness I hadn't felt in my time in the human world crept in, cold and hopeless; I couldn't even talk to Maz. I put my hand up toward the tree, and the corvid jumped into it without hesitation, his beady black eyes boring into me as he glanced at my face before rubbing his own against my fingertips. At least he still knew who I was, even if we couldn't talk to each other...

My phone buzzed in my pocket, and I realized how long I'd been missing from the venue. Without looking, I knew it was Earwyn, but I couldn't bring myself to answer. Instead, I did the least productive and most impulsive thing I could think of – I shoved Maz into the pocket of my coat, making sure that his little head was poking out before I sprinted toward my apartment. I was running through the city with a bird in my pocket. For once, I fit right in without additional effort.

When I finally got into my apartment, I slumped against the door to my bedroom. Maz jumped out of my pocket and hopped around my room as I fished my phone out and dared to look at it. I had missed calls from Earwyn. Then Zara. Hell, Firth even tried to video chat me, too. Guilt overtook me.

TEXT FROM EARWYN

Michelle?

Michelle, where did you go?

Hey, I'm really worried. Are you okay?

Please just tell me you're okay. I'm worried something happened to you. Did I do something?

At least let me know you're safe. Please!

I shook too much to type out a coherent message in response, so, fearful and confused, I called him.

When Earwyn answered, I heard panic in his voice that I'd never witnessed from him before. My heart sank. "Oh, thank God, Michelle. *I've got her on the phone, she answered.*" Firth and Zara's voices were muffled in the background; I'd pulled them all away from the show, and they were all worrying about me. Part of me felt awful, while the other couldn't help but bask in the fact that I had so many people who loved me. My gratefulness was fleeting as I remembered once again why I'd abandoned them that evening. "Are you okay? What happened? Where are you?" I could picture him pacing back and forth, running his hands through his hair. I'd worried him.

"I'm sorry…"

"You don't have to be sorry. Whatever happened, it's okay… it'll be okay. Are you safe? What do you need?" Earwyn had seen so many horrors, been subject to so many horrors, that he was assuming the worst. I could only guess what his imagination had put him through in the time he didn't know where I was; I had no doubt that place was dark and full of terror. I couldn't be the cause of his going there ever again, not if I could help it.

"I… um, I'm okay," I managed to reply eventually, picking at my fingers as I watched Maz explore my windowsill from inside. He glanced back at me a few times while I spoke on the phone, almost as if he was checking to see if our connection had been restored. If only it were as simple as needing to reset a router. I, too, had hoped that it was a fluke thing, something I'd imagined, and that I was just having a momentary freak-out, but that wasn't the case. When he looked back at the window, he tapped on the sill with his beak as he discovered a crumb of food I'd left there for him earlier in the day. "I think... um, I think I'm sick. I'm sorry. I started feeling really sick, and I just had to get home."

Earwyn let out a sigh of relief on the phone. I could almost hear a stifled laugh in his voice, as if he were chastising himself for being so stressed. "You're sick... okay, it's alright. It's okay. *She's sick, she's okay. She went back to the apartment.*" He sounded like he was trying to convince himself. "What do you need? Can I come take care of you?"

"No! I mean, no, I wouldn't want you to get sick, too, you know? I'll be fine, I'm sorry I scared you." Tears welled in my eyes; he was being so sweet, so generous, just like he always was, and I wanted nothing more than to invite him over and tell him every-thing. It broke my heart that I couldn't.

"What if I have medicine delivered? What's hurting? I could order soup..." He was silent for a moment, and when I didn't fill the space, it seemed he had realized that I wasn't going to take him up on any of his offers. "There's this really good place near your building, and I bet they would deliver if I—"

"It's okay, Earwyn, I'll head home soon and make sure she's okay," Zara told him in the background. "Don't freak out. I'm sure she's fine. Maybe she just needed to be alone for a bit."

"You don't need to apologize, Michelle," Earwyn finally told me. "I'm just glad you're safe... I'll come check on you tomorrow."

"No, Wyn, you don't—"

"Tomorrow. I'll see you tomorrow." I couldn't argue with him. When he spoke again, the voices of Zara and Firth were even more muffled, as if he'd stepped away from them. A car whizzed by in the background. "Michelle…"

"Wyn?"

"I love… loved seeing you this evening. I'm sorry it got cut short and that you're feeling unwell. Please get some rest, and if you need me, you know how to reach me… sweet dreams."

It seemed cruel that I should be so wrapped up in whatever was happening to me that I couldn't give Earwyn's almost-confession-of-love the attention it deserved. He'd given me the perfect opportunity to jump in and save him from his own awkwardness by beating him to the punch. Oh God, had I just admitted to myself that I loved him? This was *not* the time for huge revelations! If only I hadn't bothered with that stupid parasite plant at the ballet, then none of this would've happened.

I choked back a sob and shoved the tangled remnants of my fancy hairdo out of my face.

Mazus trilled from the windowsill and cocked his head at me in confusion. I wished I could explain to him what was happening.

I spent the rest of the night in the bathroom, where I tried to convince Zara that I had a stomach bug through my creative use of vocal sound effects. "You know, it's probably better if you and Firth go back to his place. I'm going to be holed up in here all night, monopolizing our only bathroom…" More fake puking noises. When I thought they had left, I turned to the plant stand by the small bathroom window, its glass frosted with the ancient age of our apartment building. My plants were still fine, it seemed, but that could've just been because I was taking care of them and could've had nothing to do with magick. I stroked the leaves of a neon-green pothos, and nothing happened. It didn't perk up at my touch, didn't lean in to my fingertips like a small animal being petted. I found one leaf that looked a bit dingy and yellow, and when I held it between my fingers, instead of recovering, it snapped off and fell to the tiled bathroom floor to die. I choked back a sob.

I had heard the front door of our apartment open and close, which caused me to assume that the couple had left as I'd suggested, but sometime later, there was a knock at the bathroom door.

"Sprout?" That was Zara's nickname for me that no one else ever heard; it was an inside joke about my green thumb and also how big I was in comparison to her. We thought it humorous for her to call me something so tiny. I found it charming and sweet; it made me think of a name a mother might call her child and it warmed a part of my heart that longed for protection and connection. Despite my confidence in myself, I also found it endearing to be related to something small and fragile: two things I was not normally, but I was feeling more fragile by the moment.

"Zara." I sighed, unable to muster any more convincing words to encourage her to save herself from my mystery illness. She could see right through me, so perhaps it was time to drop the facade.

"Come on out, I haven't heard you barf in a while."

I stared at the crumbled brown leaf on the floor for a moment before kicking it under the vanity. When I opened the door, Zara said nothing. She simply took me by the hand and led me back to my bedroom, where she instructed me to get into bed. She tucked me in, then returned with water, crackers, and a small trash can; she was playing along, just in case. When she climbed onto the mattress next to me, she pulled my head into her lap. We must've been a sight to behold, with her small body shielding and coddling mine, which felt twice her size. She stroked my hair, which was splayed across the top of her lap like a blanket of tawny vines.

"What's going on?"

"I wish I could tell you."

Zara was silent, stroking my locks in the same repetitive pattern as if it were helping her think. It helped me calm my frantic breathing, at least. "Earwyn is really worried about you, sprout."

Guilt crashed over me. "I know."

"Listen," she murmured, tucking a stray wisp of hair behind my ear, which made it easier for me to see her out of the corner of my eyes. I crushed my eyes shut in an attempt to fight back tears; she could see right through me, even if she didn't know exactly what was going on. That was friendship: this unique type of soulmate that knew the depths of my being like no one else ever would. "What's really going on? This isn't like you, but neither is spending all of your time with the same person."

"I feel like I'm losing myself," I confessed.

"In Earwyn?"

"Maybe, but that's not the problem. I *want* to lose myself in him. Something else is wrong and I… I can't figure it out, Zara."

"Does it need to be figured out tonight?"

"I don't know…" I chewed my lip, then forced my eyes open and looked up at my friend.

"I mean, what if I wasn't me anymore?"

"You're you. You'll always be you. You're you without trying, sprout. Now get some rest… maybe text lover-boy again so he doesn't have a heart attack." Zara smiled at me, her honeyed eyes soft and warm, none of their usual spice to be found.

"You think he might?"

"He's got it bad for you, girl." She handed me my phone, then stifled a yawn. It was late.

"He almost said…"

"I heard."

"What am I supposed to do if he says that, Zara?"

"Oh, come on, it wouldn't be the first time someone's gone all ga-ga over you."

"This is different." I sighed, fiddling with the case on my phone as I lay there. I couldn't put it into words how it was different, but it was; I was being consumed by this man. Whatever he was feeling, I felt it, too. That was different for me. Before typing out a text to him, I set the phone down on the bed next to me and met her gaze again. I realized then that we'd had very little time to connect like this in months. "And Firth? How are things with him?"

Zara chuckled, a silly, spritelike noise that spread warmth through my chest, even with my impending mortality. She leaned back on my headboard and looked up at the ceiling, no doubt hiding a blush from my question. "This is supposed to be about you!" she insisted. "But they're good. I like him a lot, sprout... it's easy being around him, and we get each other, we have fun together, the sex is amazing, but..."

I waited silently, holding space for her thoughts. So far, I hadn't heard an issue.

"I feel like there's so much I don't know about him even though he's always with us. Do you feel that way about Earwyn? Like, are they just reserved or what? Hell, I still don't know what they actually do for work. It's like they operate in a different universe than us. The hotel, the cars, the money. He feels like such a freakin' mystery to me. Like, don't get me wrong, it's a mystery I like having to solve, but still... who is he?" When she finally stopped rambling, she looked down at me, flustered.

It was true; we knew so little about these two men who seemed to have filled every free space in our lives. Their charm had somehow blinded us to their mysteriousness, but it was becoming abundantly clear that we were being kept in the dark. It was only slightly reassuring that I wasn't the only one who felt that way.

I wanted to tell Zara all my thoughts, but I settled for "I know what you mean." If only Zara knew everything about me, I could confess to her about my magick disappearing, about terrafolk, about the little things I'd noticed about Earwyn, my suspicions about him maybe not being human either.

"Well, at least I'm not totally crazy." Zara laughed, ruffling my hair a little. "But that's a problem for another day. Listen, I don't know what's up with you, but let's do something to at least take your mind off it."

I surrendered. I wanted to figure out the answer to everything right then, but I knew there was no way; it was late, I was drained in more ways than one, and I honestly just missed my best friend. Sometime later found us on the couch under a pile of blankets, eating Chinese food from our favorite place, and watching movies. We left the subtitles on because we'd gotten used to putting them on for Firth. I texted Earwyn that I was feeling better and I'd see him tomorrow. Before then, though, I needed to figure out what was happening to me.

CHAPTER ELEVEN

*E*arly the next morning I managed to get an appointment with Dr. Jansen, and when she explained to me that all of her clients had taken advantage of a same-day appointment with her during a time of crisis, I felt uniquely human. Given the circumstances, however, being human did not feel like an accomplishment. Why couldn't we bond over something less severe than our mortality?

"I'm losing my magick, Dr. Jansen," I blurted out, pacing her office despite her encouragement to take a seat and drink some water from the cooler next to her couch. "I'm getting weaker by the day, I can feel it, and I don't know what to do. What happens when it's all gone?"

"Michelle, I've never seen you this escalated before."

"That's because I've never lost my magick before!" I froze in my tracks, realizing that I'd exploded at her even though she wasn't to blame. "I'm—"

"You don't need to apologize. It's okay."

I chewed my lip, then took a deep breath and forced myself to take a seat on the couch I sat on every week with Dr. Jansen. It took me a moment, but eventually I got myself a paper cup of water and sipped it quietly.

"I want to remind you that I still don't understand how your magick works, Michelle, so I'm just going on what I've gleaned from our conversations over the past few months, okay? And truthfully, I still haven't quite determined how 'your magick' and your background plays into the challenges you're facing here in the, um, human world."

I nodded, agreeing that this was probably the closest to "on the same page" we were going to get. I didn't have time to explain the inner workings of an entire society to her, nor did I think she had the ability to follow along with such an involved backstory.

"This may be a stretch given how you've reacted to me bringing it up in the past, but is it possible that you're losing your magick because you've been away from home for so long? Away from Yannava?"

A chill coursed through my veins, and I had to set my cup down because my fingers started trembling. "Why would you say that?"

"Well, sometimes when we start to lose ourselves a little bit, we need to return to our roots, to ground ourselves. For you, it sounds like that may be more literal than it is for most," Eline noted, offering a small smile with her last statement.

I set my jaw and sternly replied, "I can't go back."

"Mmm, I'd gathered that this might be a barrier for you, Michelle. Why is that? Why can't you go back? I would imagine that your family would welcome you home easily since you left on good terms and had simply left to explore the human world for a bit. We've all gone on these adventures away from our homes before. Needing to return eventually is normal. In fact, sometimes those adventures remind us of all the things we were missing from back home."

"I can't return to Yannava, Dr. Jansen." I picked my cup back up and swished the water in it, letting myself be momentarily distracted by the way it circled the inside of its wax-coated vessel. When I took a sip, I met her gaze again, acutely aware of how her dull gray eyes were focused on me. I supposed this was how therapists looked when they were on the verge of a breakthrough with a client; I did not want to be part of this breakthrough. I wasn't ready. But even as I sat there, I felt my energy waning.

"You know what I'm going to ask next."

"I can't go back," I started again, dropping my gaze before my confession poured from me, "because I had too many responsibilities in Yannava, Doctor. Too many people relied on me and wrongly so. I'm not meant to lead an entire civilization. I'm not strong enough. I wasn't strong enough then, and I am certainly not strong enough now. It would be an injustice for me to return to my people… and fail them yet again. I promise you, they don't even want to see my face right now."

CHAPTER TWELVE

"*K*ind of chilly out here for a forest baby, isn't it? Want me to keep you warm?"

The hair on the back of my neck rose at the oddly familiar voice, feeling uneasy because it wasn't familiar in this setting: in the middle of the woods, where I was supposed to be finding answers and reprieve. It didn't belong here. In fact, no one but me belonged there at that moment. I pulled my fingers from the dirt and wiped the tears from my face with the back of my smudged hands, effectively smearing my face before I stood. "Anala." What was she doing here? Had she been following me? The fact that we'd found each other in the human world had always seemed like a happy coincidence to me, a way for me to keep in touch with my roots, but her presence now seemed the opposite. It almost felt sinister. I searched her face, desperate for answers and unwilling to make a total fool of myself by asking for them when she seemed so perfectly comfortable; she must've known something I didn't. She was dressed in high-waisted jeans and a mustard-yellow knit top, her outfit complemented by dark red lipstick, heavy eye makeup, and of course, manicured fingers. Her feet, which seemed out of place in their bareness, were also done up with matching red polish. Sunglasses, which were absolutely not needed in that day's climate, hung from the collar of her shirt. "Isn't it cold for *you*?"

Stupid question, she was obviously fine. Not a clever comeback.

The Indian woman cocked her head to the side, her onyx locks tumbling gracefully over her shoulder as she did so, and offered me what felt like an empty smile. "No."

"Well, what are you doing here?"

Anala clucked her tongue at me in chastisement. "Surely you can't think you're the only one who needs to recharge every once in a while. Besides…" She smirked, casting a glance at the looming shadow of Mt. Baker behind her. "You're nearing *my* territory."

Volcanoes. Of course I knew that Anala was fire-folk. In fact, it explained a lot about Anala: her volatile and explosive nature, the heat of her touch. It didn't explain some other details that now nagged at me, like how we had come across each other in the first place. She had told me she was visiting from another community of volcano-dwellers, yet none of it felt right. "And what do you want from me?" I suddenly felt very uneasy around her. It was an odd feeling to have toward someone I'd shared so much intimate time with. As she approached me, I made sure not to take my eyes off her for even a second. She was different; this was not the person I'd spent countless nights with, flirted with, slept with, cooked breakfast with. Her energy had changed, and though I couldn't tap into it, I could sense it. I knew enough about her kind to have a healthy fear of them, too. Fire is dangerous, especially in a forest. Hot, yes, but also explosive, destructive, and harmful. She could burn me in more ways than one.

"Don't be silly, Michelle," she chastised me, gracefully walking over to a large nearby tree. I fought the urge to run or shield myself. Fire was dangerous; everyone knows that, but especially people who dwell in trees. She wrapped a slender hand around one of the tree's protruding and now leafless branches as she spoke, the evidence of its fall shedding crunching under her bare feet on the forest floor. "I don't want anything from you. I simply came to tell you to be careful around that man you've been spending time with." She clucked her tongue at me again, the sound grating and obnoxious. "He could be bad news, you know."

I raised an eyebrow. This didn't feel like jealous ex-girlfriend business. It couldn't be. Two magickal beings just wouldn't bicker about some man. It was clear that all of the strange signs that I'd been forcing myself to ignore meant something. Whether it was good or bad remained to be seen. On its own, him being one of our kind didn't mean a whole lot. Regardless, I didn't like being spoken to like a child, nor did I like her selective information sharing.

"I mean, you're losing your magick, right babe?"

I gritted my teeth in anger. Why did she know that? How long had she been watching me struggle? And how was my magick related to Earwyn? Nausea gripped me as I considered the possibilities, one of which involved me falling for a man who had been sent to destroy me, to punish me.

"All I'm saying is, some combinations can be deadly…" Anala added, gripping the tree branch tightly. Ember crawled out from her sleeve and propped herself up on the tree, where she watched Anala closely. She slid a perfectly manicured thumb nail into a crack in the timber, and I watched as an electric bolt of red slid through the tree's core, causing it to heat up and burst with flame from the inside. The newt marveled at the flames, clearly unaffected by the extreme heat, then returned to Anala's hand. When she removed her fingers from the tree, she dusted them off on her pants and turned to leave. "Watch your back, girlfriend! He'll bleed you dry; you know how *men* are!"

Grasping at my fleeting control over the situation, I shouted after her, "Anala, stop!"

She halted in her tracks, but didn't turn to face me. In an instant, the energy of our interaction switched from teasing to serious intensity. I swallowed hard, willing myself not to turn and run.

"Tell me what's going on," I said through gritted teeth with as much confidence as I could muster. It turned out to be next to none, and my words squeaked out pitifully, like air escaping from a balloon. "Tell me what's going on," I attempted again, digging my feet into the dirt, praying to whatever gods were out there for a whisper of strength or resilience. "Or I'll—"

"Or you'll… what?" When the other woman turned around, I swore I could see actual flames in her molten stare; it was clear that she was not playing around any longer. I wondered if my frequent, recent rejection of her advances had only fueled this rage toward me. How long had she been harboring such incendiary hatred toward me? And how much did she know? "As far as I'm concerned," she continued, no trace of her teasing smile present any longer, "you couldn't make a fucking blade of grass grow right now… so what is it you're threatening me with, Michelle?"

I wanted to cry. She was right. I had nothing, and she could've probably knocked me over with a strong enough thought. Before I could talk back, she continued. "You know, you piss me off," she confessed, stepping closer to me as she spoke. At first, I thought the trembling beneath me was simply a side effect of my weakness and overwhelm, but then I heard rumbling from the rupture in the ground behind her, and fear coursed through my entire body. "You think you can do whatever you want, go wherever you want, have whoever you want… well, not anymore, sister," she hissed. The volcano hissed, too, and steam rose in the air above it. "I don't know who died and made you queen, but your time is *over*."

Without a second thought, I turned on my heel and sprinted back toward my car. By the time I had buckled myself into my seat, my phone was vibrating repeatedly with warnings that Mt. Baker was showing sudden, unexpected signs of an impending eruption.

CHAPTER THIRTEEN

To say that my return home left me feeling vulnerable and confused would have been a colossal understatement. I felt utterly alone in my discomfort, too, because there was no one I could trust to speak to; Zara couldn't know about this dilemma, Earwyn potentially had ulterior motives, Firth was with him, and now Anala had me on guard around even her. I missed the days when she'd simply been an overly eager hookup. Perhaps I'd pissed off the wrong fire princess; that bitch was ready to knock me out on sight. I couldn't even vent to Maz!

Then, as if on cue, there was a knock at the door that caused me to nearly crawl out of my skin in panic. I'd forgotten that I'd agreed to let Earwyn come over and "take care of" me the night before. A burning sensation clawed its way up my throat as if to add insult to injury. Was this fucking heartburn? Holy hell on earth.

"I'm coming," I croaked out, hesitantly approaching the front door. My mouth was dry, and my fingers trembled. I twisted the sleeve of my shirt in one hand and the wad of fabric quickly became damp from the sweat of my palms. I felt unhinged.

I opened the door nervously after looking through the peephole and, once I'd confirmed that no one else was in the hallway, pulled Earwyn in by his collar. He looked alarmed, but I didn't care. I shut and locked the door behind him before shoving him into the living room. As he stood there, clearly startled, I couldn't help but drink him in. Aside from the disheveled collar of his shirt, the rest of him looked pristine; he wore a black t-shirt, tapered khakis, and a jean jacket. His blond hair draped smoothly over his broad shoulders, and I swallowed hard as I took him in from head to toe. The sharp peaks of his upper lip made me lick mine before I urged myself to remember why I'd been on edge just seconds ago. How I'd like to scale those mountains, but they threatened to lead me to my death.

"Are we doing some sort of roleplay thing?" Earwyn stammered as he reached up to straighten his collar. "Because I can be all for it, I just need a heads-up… and I don't really feel comfortable with—"

"Who are you? Who are you, really?" I hissed finally, hand outstretched to fend him off and hopefully muster what last little bit of magick I had left in my body. I flexed my fingers as if that would ignite a spark. It didn't. I could feel my energy draining as I stood there on the verge of tears. It couldn't be coincidence that Earwyn had come into my life only to be followed by the loss of my magick. Was he responsible for this? I feared then that charming me had all been part of a plan that I'd fallen for, and I felt set on edge by Anala's suggestions from earlier. I swallowed hard at the thought of how I was falling; even as we stood there at odds, I couldn't help but admire the curve of his jaw. I wondered briefly if he thought I was having a bout of short-term memory loss or spiraling into early dementia.

"This isn't really the welcome I'd been hoping for," Earwyn responded, swallowing hard and running a hand through his hair. The action stirred up some of his signature scent and I had to stop myself from inhaling deeply. "You said I could come over. I've been looking forward to it all day." He dropped one of his hands, which had been holding a bouquet of wildflowers. They were bright and beautiful despite the cold weather; violas, winter jasmine, and sprigs of pine. A couple of petals fell to the floor unceremoniously, and my heart wept for the disarray we were in. Everything really was falling apart.

"Just tell me," I insisted, holding back tears.

"Earwyn. You know that. You know me, Michelle."

"Where are you from, Earwyn? Why are you here?" I was nearly shouting at that point, but I couldn't care less about my volume or the attention it might draw from our neighbors. If this was the end of me, I had the right to go out screaming. It was likely, though, that they didn't care how much noise we made. People in the PNW tended to keep to themselves, I'd learned, and not bother with others if they could avoid it. I hated that.

"Right now? I was coming to talk to you and bring you these flowers. I wanted to make sure you were alright after what happened at the ballet. I mean, what happened at the ballet, Michelle? I still don't know… are you sick? Did you need time away from me? …And did you get those alerts about Mt. Baker? Do we need to leave?" Earwyn's tone changed to frazzled excitement and then back to confusion, a mix of emotions I hadn't seen from him before. "But I'm guessing that's not what you were asking. I'm in Seattle for business," he told me calmly, as if that would answer all of my complex questions. This just made me angrier; how daft did he think I was? That answer hadn't been enough before and it certainly would not be enough now. I immediately felt suspicious and wondered what he had come to talk about.

I scoffed. "What *kind* of business, Wyn? Earwyn. What kind of business, Earwyn?" I scolded myself mentally for using the nickname I had for him; it had almost become a replacement for his full name in my mind. I'd said it so many times over the previous months, probably said it in my dreams even. I forced myself to push through instead of getting caught up in the details. "Look, I *know* you're terrafolk, too, and that suspicion didn't bother me until my magick started fading… Now I can't even keep a damn plant alive! So you better have a good explanation because right now it's hard to believe this is just a coincidence."

"Your magick is fading…" Earwyn repeated as if testing out the words. I hated that he seemed oblivious to what I was saying; if he was strong enough to steal from me, he was likely stronger than me in general… and if he was here to steal, he had to have known what he was stealing! I tried to make sense of it all in my mind, but the more I considered it, the more frustrated and depleted I felt. This wasn't like me. "It's… complicated, Michelle, much more complicated than we have space for in this heated conversation. Don't you think something as serious as that accusation deserves a sit-down conversation? There's a lot to unpack here."

His continued reticence angered me. I channeled that anger and flicked my wrist in the direction of one of my many plants, which immediately shot out vines and wrapped them around Earwyn's ankles, bringing him to the ground. Dizziness immediately overtook me, and it was clear that had been the very last crumb of my magickal ability. He hit the floor with a loud thud as I sprinted for the kitchen drawers to find a knife. Seconds later found me straddling him to keep his arms in place as I pointed the knife at his throat. I was out of breath. Exhausted. I also had no clue if that was truly my last bit of magick or if it would eventually regenerate… It certainly hadn't felt like it was regenerating so far. Ah well, at least I would die having defended myself a bit. If his magick was as strong as mine had ever been, strong enough to steal mine right from me, a knife would do very little to protect me unless I was very handy with it. "Why sit when you can just lie down? Start. Explaining," I growled through gritted teeth.

"I'm Earwyn... of Ulmos."

"Ulmos," I noted, stifling a sigh of relief at the confirmation of his race. Still, I was uncomfortable with the thought of him being so secretive. It felt like the tactful omission of my own race had been the right move to keep myself and the humans safe whereas Earwyn's lie struck me as malicious. Not only that, but the realization that he was a member of one of the most feared and ruthless kingdoms of terrafolk set me on edge. I used the tip of my blade to brush his hair off one side of his neck, which quickly exposed a set of shimmering, golden gills. They were mesmerizing, but didn't move as he breathed in through his nose. As far as I knew, I'd never encountered an Ulmosi on land, let alone in the city with humans, so I'd never expected to see gills on someone in the human world. I still felt unsure of how I'd missed them, though. I reflected on the way Earwyn spoke and dressed, his resources, his affiliation with human organizations... it all pointed to one thing. "And you're probably a prince, am I right?"

"Was a prince, I think." His eyes remained locked on mine, but his gaze was impassive. Was he really so unthreatened by me? It couldn't have been so; I felt his heart racing under my thighs and his pulse against the blade of the knife.

"And Firth. Who is he? Who is the man that's been spending a lot of time in my house while you're out doing 'business'?"

"For all intents and purposes, he's my bodyguard, but I'd say he's more of a friend at this point. A brother, like I told you. Ulmosi would probably call him other things, though, because he's now associated with a traitor prince."

"I knew he was too charming to actually be related to you," I growled, still furious and panting. Did I really think an insult was going to work in my favor? "Why didn't I notice his gills? It doesn't matter. You have to leave."

"Why?"

"Your explanation..." It took me a moment to formulate my thoughts, and upon my reflection, I was able to calm myself a little. It wasn't fair that I had made him out to be a criminal when I, too, had withheld information about my identity. However, my fear that the loss of my magick had something to do with him amplified my insecurity. "Look, I know I'm not exactly innocent when it comes to withholding the truth, but... my magick is..." I paused, swallowing hard. "It might as well be gone now. I can't hear my familiar anymore. That's terrifying," I confessed, suddenly ashamed at my previous reliance on my magick. I felt naked. Laid bare before this man I barely knew and, much to my dismay, wanted nothing more than to know fully. But the many unknown details of our situation kept me at arm's length from him. I realized then that so much of my confidence came from a power that no one else around me had and that without it, I wasn't sure how to operate. It seemed a wonder to me that anyone felt comfortable in this world without that sort of protection; the potential for an untimely death had certainly cast a cloudy haze over my outlook.

"Please." Earwyn softened, his words barely above a breath. He looked suddenly very unsure of his ability to explain himself out of this situation, but desperate to convince me otherwise. "Don't make me leave."

I could've surrendered right then and done whatever he said without a second thought, but I tried to fight back. "Why shouldn't I?"

"I couldn't bear it," he told me, the honesty in his gaze almost painful. "I was sent here for business with the humans, but the longer I stayed, the more I realized I was actually looking for you. I just didn't realize it until that first night I saw you at your work. Then, every moment we've spent together since has just solidified it. I'll try to explain it, I promise you, but I'm not here to take anything from you... and I only came tonight because I couldn't stand to stay away. I just wanted to make sure you were safe."

"But you thought you should stay away," I reframed, wondering what it meant that he was supposed to be doing business with the humans and somewhere, that plan had gone so wrong that he was now viewed as a traitor to his people. From what I knew, the Ulmosi were not a group to mess with; they had limitless resources at their disposal, and they were ruthless. Suddenly, I worried about what might happen if they came after us. Would Zara be in danger just because she was associated with me? It seemed foolish, careless to drag a human into the affairs of non-human creatures when the result could be deadly or dangerous at best.

"Your life seems great, Michelle," he told me honestly. "You've got pretty much all I could ever hope to have. It didn't seem right for me to come and mess that up, but I'm selfish."

"How would you mess it up?" I gritted my teeth, hating any negative comments against himself because they felt like an insult to my taste. We sat in silence for a moment, the pounding of my heart all I could hear. My thighs strained against the fabric of my jeans as I remained poised on top of the other creature. I wondered for a moment what I could do to save face if Zara wandered in, but the thought quickly left my mind as I recognized the look on the prince's face. I'd seen it before. "Why are you looking at me like that?"

"You're beautiful."

"I'm holding a knife to your throat," I reminded him, weary with exhaustion and fighting a surge of other sensation that was rushing over me. I wondered if it was my position of perceived power that had me feeling heated or just being this close to Earwyn again. Regardless, my body was certainly rebelling against my brain. Surrender seemed like the easier option.

"It's a butter knife."

Before I could convince myself to stop and think, my lips were on his. I shifted to free his arms, though my fingers remained wrapped tightly around my useless weapon. It took next to no effort for him to knock it from my grip and intertwine his fingers with mine. For how perfectly they laced together, the action may as well have been accompanied by the click of a lock. He could've easily rolled me underneath him, but I was grateful when he didn't, and instead traced his free hand down my side. It felt like an act of submission and good faith; I was desperate then for any sign that he wasn't about to overpower me in a way that I didn't want. "Earwyn," I breathed against his lips, shuddering from his soft touch.

"Let me stay," he stated, a nearly silent plea to me, so soft that it was more of a question than a command.

"My magick," I gasped, unsure of how to get my brain back on track as my body rebelled against it. "I can't just—"

"I know," Earwyn began, then corrected himself. "I mean... I don't know, but I can only imagine how terrifying it is to feel your magick slipping away. I do know that we'll figure out what happened. We'll get it back. There has to be a way. Until then, we'll keep Firth close for your safety." At that moment, I wanted nothing more than to curl up in his arms and sob. How could he be so sure that we'd figure it out? And why did he want to figure it out with me? That type of commitment and devotion seemed better suited for people who'd known each other for centuries, not days. "Why would you do that for me? You barely know me, Earwyn."

"It's the right thing to do," he said, seemingly without a second thought. "That and—" This time he paused, clearly mulling over his next words before releasing them into the world. "I think I'm in love with you."

"You don't even know me, Earwyn," I told him calmly. I'd heard those words before, sure, from overly eager lovers who didn't actually know much about me aside from my ability to make them feel good. Something about Earwyn's tone was so genuine, so certain, though... I considered for a moment and added, "Without my magick, I'm nothing. Hell, even with it, I—"

"That's not true. I know it's a big part of you, your identity, and I'm sure it is part of what drew to me to you... but you're more than your magick."

"I don't know if I believe that," I confessed. "I don't feel connected to the earth like I used to. I feel like I'm..." I trailed off, searching for a way to describe the sheer hopelessness that accompanied my new mortality. "Untethered. I'm not grounded anymore."

We sat in silence. I knew there was no way for Earwyn to understand what I was feeling. Prior to losing my own magick, I would not have been able to imagine how bleak things looked without it; it was all I'd known up until that point. The fact that he was still there, was trying to understand, was priceless, however. When he finally spoke again, he met my gaze with a fierce intensity. "We'll get your magick back. Until then, I have resources... Let's use them."

"And right now?"

"Right now... let me keep you grounded as well as I can. Let me love you."

I nodded thoughtlessly as his lips found my throat and let him kiss my flesh until my head spun. "Love me," I breathed, my words a desperate plea.

We tumbled toward my bedroom with reckless abandon, bumping into walls and leaving boots, socks, and retreating vines in the hallway without a care. I couldn't recall where the butter knife went. Zara would likely find that I'd just adapted to her organizational style. "You'll tell me what you like?" I asked when we finally stumbled breathlessly into my bedroom. In that moment, despite my fear and uncertainty, I wanted nothing more than to please him and to forget the chaos we were surrounded by. Being close to him, intimate with him, had always made me feel more present and in the moment; this time I hoped it would be an escape.

The corner of Earwyn's mouth quirked up and he laughed a little. "Your guess is as good as mine."

"You haven't..." Despite my being a highly sexual person, the idea of someone choosing not to have sex wasn't that strange to me. It was more like the fact that Earwyn was so stunning, so soft, and probably older than my hundreds of years... To think that he'd spend that time without the physical affections of another, though he clearly desired it on some level, confounded me. I felt oddly selfish and entitled for being in this position with him. That didn't stop me from imagining a million other positions I wanted him to put me in.

"Not consensually," Earwyn replied matter-of-factly. For such a dark truth, the softness in his gaze only hardened briefly. When he came back to me, it was with the same enamored stare from moments before.

My breath caught in my throat at his admission, but eventually I managed to keep the conversation moving, "And it doesn't bother you that I have?" Humans had a way of keeping track of these things and using them against each other; it wasn't my style, but it had become something I was used to.

"I should hope you've had plenty of wonderful experiences in that domain, and I wouldn't mind contributing to them if you'd allow me." The look on his face was so painfully genuine that I didn't know how to react. "I may not be experienced, but I'm eager." My heart shattered, but Earwyn, ever giving as I was learning, tried not to let me dwell on the news he'd just broken. I supposed this was us getting to truly know each other, as fast as it seemed.

I swallowed hard and looked him in the eyes, searching them for something as heavy and dark as his admission. There I found only lightness, longing, and appreciation, though. "Is that why you think you love me?" I blurted out against my will, pretty sure I had effectively ruined the moment. I had to tell him, though. "Because there will be others, Earwyn. In fact, most people will treat you the way you should be treated... and you shouldn't settle for the first person to appreciate you just because you aren't used to it." The words felt like a dense weight on my tongue, difficult to maneuver, but necessary; I couldn't let this man love me like an abused animal loves its savior. That wouldn't be fair to either of us; it would deprive him of the possibility of finding the "right" person for him and me of being loved for who I truly was, not just a healing space for someone hurt and broken. "There are so many people who will worship you like you deserve. I'm not a rarity." I refused to let the abuse of his past make him think otherwise.

Earwyn laughed a warm, deep laugh, dropping the tension in the room immediately. "Goddess," he said, taking my face in his hands. I closed my eyes and breathed him in. "Try not to mistake my inexperience and excitement for ignorance. I'm certain I've encountered enough humans and our kind to know what I want, *who* I want, and what's right for me. To know who I love. I appreciate your desire to protect me, but... the only person who could hurt me now is you."

"I won—" My eyes fluttered open to face him, but he pressed a finger gently to my lips.

"You won't." My look must've said "How do you know? How can you be so sure?" because he smiled and replied, "Because you love me, too."

"Yes," I breathed, unable to deny his statement. My head spun. I felt ravenous and protective and confused and enamored and...

He gasped when I slid one of his hands into the front of my blouse and onto my breast, where my desire for him bloomed almost painfully in my chest. I was burning for him. "Michelle," he breathed, pressing himself to me so he could kiss my neck again while he gently kneaded my breast. When he delicately rolled my nipple between his nimble fingers, my head fell back.

"Mycel," I corrected him with a breathless whisper, telling someone in the human world my real name for the first time. "It's Mycel."

He chuckled as I helped him remove my shirt and glanced around the bedroom we were in, which was neat, but adorned with plants on every surface. "Of course it is." He smiled, then crouched in front of me to take my chest in his mouth. I desperately wanted to touch him, but felt bound by the information he'd shared with me earlier. What if I scared him off, crossed boundaries that I wasn't even aware of yet? Heat bloomed in my belly as his sweet, soft lips danced across my scorching flesh. How I yearned to feel them over every inch of my body.

Eventually, I pulled him off me gently by his hair and looked him in the eyes; a wave crashed through their stormy turquoise. I was certain I'd get lost in that ocean one day, but I didn't really care. "What is it?" he asked, slightly breathless.

"Can I touch you?" I asked him, my fingers toying with the hem of his shirt. When he nodded happily, I wasted no time in yanking the fabric over his head and tossing it onto the floor. What his shirt had been covering seemed a crime to keep cloaked. I made quick work of his pants and had him lying back on my bed a moment later. I stood in front of him in appreciation, marveling over each dip and curve of the muscular slabs that made up his body. To no one's surprise, he had the physique of a competitive swimmer, but his chest was lightly furred with sandy stubble that disappeared into his waistband. His lion-like mane was sprawled out behind him on my pillow. Stunning.

"What are you doing, Mycel?"

"Admiring you. You're a wonder."

"Admire me closer," he said seriously, a hint of desperation and maybe insecurity in his normally composed voice.

I dove for him with a ferocity I didn't expect from myself in that moment and crushed my lips to his as if my life depended on it – at that point, it may have, I didn't really know. He ground his hips against mine and leaned into every touch and kiss I shared with him until I arrived at the edge of his briefs, which I pulled down with my teeth. He fell heavily into my palm, and I tried not to stare or linger too long, but the weight of his erection ignited a flame in my core that made me want to devour him whole. "I need to taste you," I confessed, reminding myself that I would fight that feeling if this behavior crossed a line for him. But when he didn't argue or move to protest, I held him and ran my tongue up the underside of his cock, which elicited the most beautiful groan from his lips. His back arched into my mattress and every fiber of his muscles strained in a way that fried my synapses immediately. I squeezed my thighs together in response to the ache brewing between them and slid onto the bed on my belly so I could continue working him. Moments later I had him panting desperately as I stroked and sucked him deeply, one of my hands massaging his heavy balls.

Earwyn gripped the sheets, his knuckles white. "Ah, Mycel, please," he breathed, shuddering as I raked my fingernails lightly over his muscular thighs. I'd been with many lovers, some loud, some quiet, but never appreciated each hitched breath and gasping plea like I did with Earwyn's timid unraveling. I felt him tremble against me as his fingers tangled in my hair and felt each muscle of his spectacular body brace for the unrelenting wave of an orgasm when he stopped me with a gentle hand. Despite the desperate need to close the gap between us, I complied, and sat back on my heels while brushing my hair from my face.

I swallowed thickly and wiped my mouth with the back of my hand, watching him for a reaction, but found him with an arm flung over his eyes as if he couldn't bear to be seen. His cock bobbed heavily, red and pulsing as if he'd been milliseconds away from release. Why deny himself that? I wanted – no, needed to watch him let loose, and with how stressed this man obviously was, he needed it as badly as I wanted to see it... "Wyn? What is it? Did I hurt you?"

"You could never," my lover assured me again, chest heaving, but I had difficulty registering the pain in his eyes when his gaze finally met mine. "I just need you closer." Maybe one day Earwyn would tell me more about the experiences that had made that moment so difficult, yet so tender, but I didn't want to pry. I wondered briefly who had it in them to hurt him with such violence. Instead, I joined him on the bed and lay in his arms, tracing shapes over his bare chest while his breathing calmed. His cock bobbed savagely and dripped precum onto his belly. I stopped myself from licking him clean. "Closer," he breathed. I nodded in understanding and slid out of my pants and underwear, kicking them onto the floor with his clothing. Cool air from the slightly cracked window sent a chill through my body and hardened my nipples into peaks as I climbed onto Earwyn, straddling his waist. The heat of his erection notched between the lips of my sex as I leaned over to kiss him softly. The air between us seemed devoid of oxygen, thick and heavy with longing but also a need for comfort. I could've stayed there forever, rocking myself against him, his chest hair teasing the hard points of my nipples, but we both needed more. I was ravenous for him, and he was admitting a need deep inside of him that demanded attention.

"I'm here," I told him, then wrapped my legs around his waist to pull him on top of me. It felt crucial to surrender control to him, given his past. What did I have to lose in trusting this man who'd only ever worshipped me? "As close as you want." The weight of his body on mine was exquisite, and I couldn't help but nip and kiss his shoulders as he positioned himself and slid gracefully into me in one fluid movement. He pressed his forehead into my neck hard as we adjusted to each other, and the soft, tortured moan that left him caused goosebumps to scatter across my bare flesh. I couldn't resist reaching down to grab his muscular glutes and pull him even further into me; I wanted to follow his lead, but I needed him then like I needed oxygen. Soon we found our rhythm together, and I relished every sweet gasp and groan, catching them with my lips whenever I could so I could hold onto them inside of me forever. I ran my hands down his back and assured him throughout, loving how he somehow knew the right ways to angle himself despite his inexperience. "There, right there…" I panted, urging him onward and arching my back into the bed as I grasped desperately at his flesh. It felt as though his body was made for mine in a way I'd never experienced, and I wondered if he felt similarly despite having little to compare it to.

"Goddess," Earwyn groaned, his pace becoming more insistent, hammering into me with his only regard being for our race to the finish line and our shared pleasure. As my body approached the edge, I leaned forward to swipe a bead of sweat from his collarbone with my tongue, leaving a scorching trail. I knew he didn't want me to watch him unravel, so as I felt him approaching the cusp with me, I crushed my lips to his with a whimper and pulled him close with my ankles.

"Please," he murmured against the now kissed-raw flesh of my mouth, his facial hair tickling me as he did so, "I need this... need you."

"You have me." The words had just tumbled from my lips when he sunk himself further into me, groaning hopelessly as he emptied himself, a battering ram hellbent on claiming me. I followed suit, unable to help what his sounds and desperate clutching did to me. "Wyn, oh, yes!" Pleasure washed over me like a rushing tide, warming every part of my body and leaving me dizzy and breathless. I gasped against his sweat-slicked shoulder, trembling as we came down together. I felt tears pricking my eyes, a new sensation I'd never associated with sex before, and pressed them closed tightly as I held him.

"You have me," I told him again, tucked so close into his strong body that it almost felt like we'd become one person. He said nothing, but I didn't need him to. I felt his heart beating against my chest and knew that he'd meant what he'd said earlier; I was safe and he'd never dream of hurting me. We would try to figure this out.

CHAPTER FOURTEEN

"*I* can't fully understand why they are set on destroying everything we have with the humans, but it's clear it's been in the works for a long time... longer than I've been alive... I think it's my relationship with them that has the Ulmosi set on their plan, though." Earwyn lay in my bed still, a thickly muscled arm behind his head as he watched me pace around the room.

"You really don't feel like you're one of them," I murmured, noting how he referred to his people as a group that didn't seem to include him.

His gaze followed me, but he seemed elsewhere mentally, at least for that moment. "No... I mean, I suppose I understand it all to an extent; the humans have abused the ocean since the beginning of time. They're destroying it. Little *conservation* efforts aren't enough to make a difference. The only real way to heal the ocean is to—"

"Get rid of humans altogether," I interjected, not shocked by that conclusion but not pleased with it either. I crawled back into the bed next to him, feeling cold and empty at the thought of destroying an entire race of beings.

"Precisely... and this partnership is the perfect way to lull the humans into thinking they're *in* with the Ulmosi before using their position to leverage the situation. I can't fathom what that will actually look like when the time comes, but it won't be pretty."

"But you don't want to follow through with their plan," I tested out, trying to make sense of the situation. It was curious to me how much Earwyn separated himself from both humans and the Ulmosi in his speech; clearly, he didn't feel like he belonged to either group, and I wondered if he had a true home. As the oceanic man lay next to me in my bed, draped in a sheet and sprawled out next to my naked body, I listened to him explain how he'd come to do "business" with the humans and why. The story shed an undeniably bad light on him due to his willingness to lure the humans into an alliance that was truly one-sided and wrought with betrayal, but I felt like I knew better than to assume, given the trust I'd forked over so far. There had to be more to the story. "Why help them?"

"I didn't think I could leave. You don't leave the Ulmosi; they brainwash us from birth to believe that you'd rather die. Besides, where would I go and what would I be without my status? And would I continue to live and be like the Ulmosi if I separated from them?" he asked honestly, closing his eyes as I traced a finger down his chest. I didn't want to answer that in a way that would derail him. "Then I realized that my family was just using me for this plan... and that my only value to them was as a bridge between these two worlds and as a royal who could produce an heir that would further those malicious goals. Firth is the one who encouraged me not to return after he saw what it was doing to me and what it would do to our home... and to the humans, who have been nothing but decent to us despite their shortcomings."

"An heir?" I raised an eyebrow at the thought of Earwyn having children with some Ulmosi princess; if the rest of their people looked anything like he and Firth, she was likely stunning. Is that what jealousy felt like? I cringed internally and told myself I would rather avoid that feeling in the future as it certainly wasn't serving me then. Why obsess over someone else when I was in bed next to the most beautiful creature on the planet?

"Yes." Earwyn swallowed hard, then turned to me with that stormy gaze. Just as before, he seemed perfectly calm, as if he knew so much more than he could possibly fill me in through words. "I'm engaged."

I leapt from the bed as if it were on fire, not caring about the fact that I was still fully nude. Crossing my arms against my chest, I turned away from him. I hadn't thought much about the concept of holy matrimony and how that played into my relationship with Earwyn since I initially assumed he was married, but something inside of me screamed that what we had done would now be labeled as wrong. "I want to believe there's a good explanation for you being engaged, given our current circumstances." I sighed, rubbing my face as I stood in front of him. Then, I gestured to the fact that my ass was out and we'd just had some of the most intimate sex I'd ever experienced. "But it's a bit challenging for me to understand how that could possibly be."

"It's a carefully structured arranged marriage, Mycel," Earwyn told me, propping himself up on one arm. He looked amused, almost as if I were a jealous girlfriend throwing a fit over a friendly coworker. I tried to follow his lead of being carefree about his engagement, but it was harder than I expected. "It's strictly a formality. It's political at best."

"You're still tied to her. You're engaged, Wyn."

"By the laws of the ocean, sure, maybe. Do you know who else follows the laws of the ocean? Lobsters. And they're really not very bright... Also, they eat garbage. Besides, she doesn't own my heart." He added the last part seriously, his tone pivoting. "Nor my body any longer."

I paused at his phrasing and immediately felt sick. "She's the one who hurt you," I stated, not needing him to reply. My stomach turned at the thought of this woman who'd made sex a violent encounter for Earwyn instead of a loving or, at the very least, adventurous and enjoyable one. How had she looked him in the eyes and taken that from him? And who would want that, when an eager and interested Earwyn was one of the most beautiful sights in the world? I clenched my thighs at the thought of his passionate, engaged self from moments prior. I was torn. I felt guilty for even letting the topic linger as long as it had.

"If that brought me here, to you, then I'm glad to have endured it."

"Don't say that," I pleaded. I was torn by my concern for him and my disgust at the thought of him enduring some sort of sadistic gauntlet to reach me. No one could be worth that sacrifice. "How could your parents allow such an arrangement? Do you... get along with them?"

Earwyn's gaze hardened again, and I knew immediately that I had poked yet another tender spot. "How can I?"

I chewed my fingernail as I stood there watching him. As much as I always wanted to learn more about him, I could tell I may have gone too far; there was only so much deep diving we could do into our emotions at once before we felt completely burned out. And if Earwyn had been honest about wanting to learn everything about me and spend forever together, we had plenty of time for these conversations. "I'm sorry, I—"

"Parents are supposed to protect their children, Mycel," he told me flatly, staring up at the ceiling. "They're not supposed to use them as pawns for political warfare, especially when it results in them being abused and violated."

I swallowed hard, my heart crumbling for him. I didn't want to change the topic in a way that seemed dismissive, but I couldn't let him sink any deeper. There was too much at stake. "Then pray that I never run into any of them, magick or no. Speaking of…"

"I don't know what's happening with your magick," Earwyn confessed, running his fingers through his hair as he lay in bed and watched me begin to pace again. Once we dropped the topic of parents and fiancées, he relaxed again. "No one knows about our interactions besides myself and Firth, who is my greatest ally. Besides," he pondered aloud, "my magick hasn't been affected, and I'd imagine they would target me first, if anything. Punishment for leaving the kingdom beyond their set parameters would likely be extreme."

"But earlier you said you weren't sure if you'd keep your magick or your lifespan if you left," I mused. Our kind weren't exactly immortal, but we didn't meet harm very easily, and our lifespan was exponentially longer than that of the humans. If our longevity was linked to our magick, I realized then, I wasn't ready to die. I looked out the window, still standing next to the bed, and noticed rain beginning to fall. Before I could comment on what his magick must be like, Earwyn directed a finger at the window latch, which popped open and sent a mist of raindrops into the room. I laughed a little as they swirled around me even though they made my already naked self much, much colder. Water and I seemed to be getting along a little better the more I got to know Earwyn.

"It's still here for now," he told me honestly, smiling a little at the way the water droplets landed on my previously warm flesh and dripped down my body. "Are you cold?"

I nodded, then leapt onto the bed again. "Warm me up!"

"Then you'll tell me more about you," Earwyn instructed,

pulling me up with strong hands so that I was straddling his chest. I stared down at him with admiration I hadn't felt for anyone up until that point. He'd made me feel safe and seen. He'd bared his soul to me as much as someone could this early on in a relationship. All he'd asked for in return was a bit of vulnerability, and that, it turns out, I was happy to provide. "And we'll start figuring this out."

The "yes" that hissed out from between my lips was both in agreement with his game plan and a response to the feeling of his handsome face diving between my thighs. He spent the next thirty minutes licking me, fucking me deep with his fingers while gripping my thighs with his free hand, bringing me to orgasm after rolling orgasm until I was boneless and ready to spill my story.

As we fell asleep, I rolled to look at him and noticed smile lines at the sides of his mouth. They hadn't been there earlier that day. He was aging.

CHAPTER FIFTEEN

*L*iving in a human world while facing the perils of magickal kingdom drama was challenging. It was not exactly easy to call off work because your magick is fading or because you're gaga for the prince of an underwater realm and can't focus on bartending; I had to do some sleuthing to figure out what excuses most people give their boss for missing work. In fact, my internet search history probably made it clear that I was an alien, but I tried my best to maintain the human charade while spending the rest of my waking moments piecing together what was happening to myself – and, unbeknownst to him, Earwyn. I had yet to tell him about the signs of his aging I had noticed – I didn't want to worry him, and maybe we'd find a way to reverse it before it became an issue. My own impending mortality had shaken me, and I didn't want the same for him.

We never had a formal discussion, but moving forward Firth seemed to know me a bit better. We all knew to keep the situation under wraps from Zara, though, who needed to be protected from our world at all costs. With any luck, we'd resolve all of this without her knowing and live happily ever after under the guise of a mediocre human life, looking forward to seasonal coffee beverages, gardening, and frequent, passionate sex with very little responsibility... bliss.

The weather was frigid with the first snow of the season falling when Earwyn and I made the trek back to my homeland looking for answers. We needed to move quickly and reliably, so we took one of Earwyn's work cars: a white Maserati Levante. It was shiny and fast, and when I stepped on the gas, my entire body felt like it was being sucked into the driver's seat. It gave me a thrill, but I was a bit too preoccupied in my thoughts to enjoy it as much as anyone else might have.

When we arrived as close to the edge of the forest as we could navigate the car, I slid my boots and socks off and chucked them in the backseat, blissfully unaware of just how much that machine cost. I sank my toes into the frozen ground with a hiss, then a sigh, desperate to maintain contact with the earth even if my body was losing its tolerance for extremes. I'd stand in the woods long enough to grow roots if that was what it took for me to reconvene with Mother Earth. Earwyn, meanwhile, looked frozen. He wore what most would consider an outfit appropriate for a Seattle winter – thick jeans, a gray turtleneck, black peacoat, and black leather boots – but it did little to shelter him from the cold of the actual wilderness. I shot him an empathetic smile, then wrapped my scarf around his neck and kissed him softly, hoping I could provide a temporary bit of warmth. Then, I led him into the woods.

Maz flew overhead, a constant lookout for both of us now that he'd been introduced, albeit wordlessly, to Earwyn.

How I wished it was under different circumstances and that I could take all the time in the world to teach my man about each native plant and animal. I smiled inwardly at the thought of

Earwyn feeding critters in my woods one day; he was such a soft, sweet soul, and I knew they'd welcome him with open arms.

As we approached the kingdom of Yannava, deeper into the woods than any human could ever stumble, those daydreams were rapidly extinguished.

A young Yannavi guard stopped us abruptly, landing on the frozen ground in front of us with a thud; it was clear that we'd been tracked as we got farther into the woods. I looked at the warrior, then up at the trees where there were no doubt many other of Yannava's protectors, and back to the young man again. "Turn back," he said firmly, barely meeting my gaze, but instead staring straight ahead, jaw hard. I couldn't see his eyes from the shadow of his heavy helmet; it looked to be of brushed bronze and was decorated with an intricate leaf design that helped the soldier blend into the forest scenery. Just seeing this armor sent memories of home flooding back to me in a rush. "You cannot pass this way."

"Don't you know who I am? I'm one of you! I was born in this forest." I challenged him, shocked and annoyed by my own pompous tone. Living in the realms of terrafolk was not like living in the human world. There were no tabloids or photo albums and our art was not like that of the common people; portraits were not commonplace. It shouldn't have surprised me that the guards of my realm didn't recognize me when I should have been a staple in everyone's knowledge. And yet, I felt rage bubbling inside of me. "My name is Mycel."

The young Yannavi's expression changed, and he tilted his head slightly. In respect?

A burst of hope shot through my chest – he knew me! My people remembered me! I hurried to speak before I lost the nerve to. "I've been gone a while, but I need to speak with my aunts, I mean my..." I paused, swallowing hard because I knew the title would feel foreign in my mouth. "Let me pass. I am your queen."

Unsurprisingly, the party of soldiers did not drop to a knee or bow. "You *were* our queen," the guard stated, confirming my fears. "And we've been instructed not to allow you entry into Yannava as well as to distance ourselves from the traitor prince and anyone fraternizing with him," the young soldier stated, jerking his chin in Earwyn's direction, "lest we risk banishment. We have no interest in being on the wrong side of the Ulmosi. You need to leave." I'd been reduced to an accomplice of the traitor Ulmosi prince. How they knew what he looked like, I couldn't even begin to speculate. Maz unleashed a loud caw in the distance, a warning for me to abide by the rules of the Yannavi guards and pick my battles. He was right; I had very little energy left to use. Was it their agreement with the accusations against Earwyn that had caused them to side with Ulmos or just their fear of their power? Since when did my people, of all magickal people, have a vendetta against humans?

The silence that followed hung heavily in the air, and I struggled to process what felt like such a vast difference from the last time I'd visited my home. I was no longer welcome here. I clenched my fists, willing the forest to feel my rage, but nothing happened. The ground didn't rumble with my fierceness, the plants didn't band together to push me through the wall of guards. There was only silence and what I soon realized was the sound of my shallow, frantic breathing. When I looked at the guard again, he held a sharpened blade toward me. "Now. By order of the Stewardesses Hyssop and Clove."

I gritted my teeth at the names of my aunts and what they'd allowed to occur during my time away from Yannava. Our kingdom had always been ruled over by women and, in the past half century, my aunts had been appointed temporary rulers of the kingdom due to the absence of a ruling queen or heir to the throne.

Hyssop and Clove weren't inherently poor rulers, though this news of their decision-making was clearly beyond disappointing. I couldn't help but wonder what threats they'd faced to put them in a position where their guards would turn me, of all people, away. I gritted my teeth, partly unsurprised that Clove would have allowed such a thing to happen but convinced that Hyssop would have resisted such a decree; she was Clove's wife and not related to me by blood, but a just and ferocious leader as far as I could recall. I saw her long, stern face in my mind as I stood there, replaying the guard's words over and over.

I had been exiled.

"Let's go," Earwyn said finally, grabbing one of my balled-up hands to guide me away. The intensity of his hold on me suggested that he truly feared for our lives, but I couldn't bring myself to get there with him. Perhaps I simply had a death wish.

"Why should I?" I snarled suddenly, shaking his hand from mine. "This is my home!" I bet I knew this child's parents. And grandparents. And great-grandparents.

The blade inched closer... so close, in fact, that I could see the matching leaf decor on its handle. I knew the blacksmith who had made this sword.

An arrow was pulled from its quiver somewhere in the trees.

"Not anymore," Earwyn reminded me, voice as even as it could be. He reached another frozen-fingered hand for mine and gripped it tightly. "Not right now." I knew he was trying to keep me calm, but grounded in reality, and to get us both out of what was becoming a dangerous situation. Without my magick, this young forest-dweller could easily kill me, and if Earwyn retaliated, he'd be dead, too. He just didn't know it. Perhaps that fueled my anger more; the image of harm coming to Earwyn was something I simply couldn't process.

"And hopefully never again, traitors."

"Traitors!" the trees shouted in a chorus of shame and rejection. "Go back to your humans!"

Maz's screech into the distance signaled that it was time to leave or face our fate in the forest of Yannava. I wondered briefly if they'd allow my familiar to return or if they wouldn't recognize him either.

As we hurried back through the forest, I found I was barely holding myself upright; none of my usual grace remained. Maz flew over us, leading us back toward the car because my sense of direction also seemed to have failed me. I was grateful for his intuition and the way he seemed to "get" me even when our communication had been stifled. It's no wonder humans make so many different gadgets to tell you where to go; it feels nearly impossible when it's not second nature to you. The car had just crept into view when a crunch sounded from behind me, followed by Earwyn crying out, "Ah! Shit!" I'd never heard him swear before. Something in me caused me to turn rather slowly, and when I found him lying on the ground with his hands around his ankle, I gasped. More than pain, the look on Earwyn's face was shock; this was a novel experience for the prince of Ulmos. I hurried back to him and got to the ground next to him, looking from his face to his ankle. It was already swelling.

"Shh, it's okay," I assured him, helping him to his feet. We still needed to go before the Yannavi realized we were nearby. There was, no doubt, a bounty out for the capture of the prince, though I wasn't sure why we had initially been allowed to leave. This injury would expose our weaknesses to them if they ever caught up to us. I flung one of Earwyn's arms over my shoulder and wrapped an arm around his waist. "It's not broken, just try not to put your weight on it. Let's get you back home to rest." After years around humans, it was easy to slip into caretaker mode; I'd gotten used to their fragile nature, but I'd never expected to have this intimate of an experience with it. "It's okay," I said, lying to myself. This didn't feel okay; my world felt as though it had gotten much, much smaller.

Earwyn was silent as he hobbled down the mountain with my help, until finally he commented, "You don't seem surprised that I'm hurt." He was panting as we walked. I could feel him staring at me out of the corner of my eye.

"I'm not."

"I've never," he managed between labored breaths, another novel experience for him, as he navigated the steep, rocky hillside with my support, "been hurt like this, Mycel."

"I know, baby," I choked out as my foot hit the black of the parking lot. Tears welled in my eyes. I'd heard tales of terrafolk royalty taking away the magick of their people as punishment, but I never imagined that my own people would do such a thing to me. And yet it appeared there was no other explanation for what was happening; Ulmos was clearly very powerful, and my association with their traitor prince had labeled me a traitor as well. This felt almost as serious as if he were dying because, in a way, he was. I wasn't ready to explain that he was fading just like I was. This was how it started, this was how it felt: disorienting, painful, and scary. The worst part was not knowing how much longer this left us with. First, it was our magick, but with that came our prolonged lifespan. Were we destined to be truly mortal after every bit of magick was gone? What did that mean? Did we get a normal human lifespan and if so, when did it start? Both of us had already lived hundreds of years, well beyond the life of any known human... It seemed ironic that we'd be labeled traitors and turned mortal as punishment for being compassionate toward the humans. It felt like our people were saying "If you love them so much, they're your people now! If you want to live with them, you'll die with them, too!"

CHAPTER SIXTEEN

"*P*lease talk to me," Earwyn begged after a stint of painful silence during the ride home. I was driving as if we were being followed even though I knew that a clan of magickal forest dwellers wouldn't likely run out into civilization and chase us down a highway, nor would they load up into an automobile to do so. "I know it hurts to be turned away so plainly from the place where you grew up and spent most of your life, but don't let that be the end of it for you."

"There's nothing for me to say, Wyn," I told him seriously. I gripped the steering wheel so hard my knuckles were white, and my still-bare toes pushed into the gas pedal as we veered down an icy mountain road. I could hardly feel my feet aside from the pins and needles that indicated that they were finally thawing out a bit. "No answers, nothing. They act like they don't even know I'm one of them... besides, we have other things to focus on. Your ankle..." I sighed and glanced down at his footwell before looking at the road again. He ignored my concern.

"*You* know, Mycel. You know where you're from and where

you belong. Nothing can change that, least of all some youngling who is just carrying out misguided orders from their rulers. Soon you'll go back, and they'll see the mistake they made. It's all a big misunderstanding; they're not going to exile one of their people. We both know Yannava is nothing like Ulmos – it's not as brutal, not as vicious."

"Where do I belong? Where is home?" I scowled, my tone venomous. I felt defensive, angry. I hated that my walls were building themselves up around me and between myself and Earwyn, but they were. My anger was taking over everything and wrongfully so; if I didn't get it in check soon, I'd alienate my only ally and the only person who truly knew me. "Where do I belong, Wyn?" Up until recently, I'd always known who I was, for better or worse. I'd known where I was from, what I was, who I was, what I liked… I knew that even if I felt out of place in the human world, I had a home to return to that would always understand me, no matter what, no judgment.

"Yannava," Earwyn told me confidently, watching me as I drove. I could see him from the corner of my eye with his soft gaze and warm presence. He looked pleased with his answer. Didn't he ever get angry? Doubtful? Did he have an ounce of rage in his ever-patient brain? The scenery passed us in a snow-covered white blur. "Don't let anyone else take that away from you. You know where your home is, Mycel, and your people need you."

I wasn't sure what came over me at first, but I pulled to the side of the road with a jerk, the car slipping a bit from my control on the ice before it finally stopped. I cut the engine and found myself breathing so hard that the windows of the car began fogging up even before I turned to look at Earwyn. The air in the vehicle was thick and stifling, not only from our breath but also the tension from our encounter in the woods.

"What is it?" he asked, obviously startled by the change in our plans, but as always trying to be calm for my sake. I felt a twinge of guilt for how much of a rollercoaster this man had been put on by the women in his life; I made a promise to myself that one day soon our lives would calm down again.

I raked Earwyn over with my gaze, his bronzed flesh looking out of place in the contrast of the frozen forest outside our windows. His nose was slightly pink from the cold, and he had his hands stuffed into the pockets of his coat despite the heat blasting in the car. He was beautiful, soft, and safe. Understanding. Judgment-free. I swallowed hard as I noticed the signs of his aging from his own magick fading and wondered if he had noticed yet, too: a streak of gray hair in his sandy mane, a slight crease between his brows. Neither of those things made him any less beautiful, of course. "I know where my home is," I breathed finally, my body relaxing as if the weight of the world had suddenly left it.

"Good." A triumphant smile had just crossed his lips when I flung a leg over the center console of the car and made my way onto his lap. It wasn't the easiest feat given our respective sizes, but soon our faces were only inches apart, and I had his sculpted jaw in my hands as I locked eyes with him. I tried to be mindful of his hurt leg, but found that I desperately needed to be closer to him than the driver's seat allowed. "Goddess, are you sure this is —"

"It's you," I breathed, tilting my head so I could press a kiss to his cold lips. The frozen tip of his nose brushed against mine and I smiled against his skin, pleased with my realization. I felt relieved in a way I'd never experienced before. If home was here, right in front of me, then that was all I really needed and more than I could ask for. All I needed to do now was keep it near me and keep it safe. "It's always been you. Not the forest, not the sea, not the earth or the moon. Just you. With magick or without, for however long we have; it doesn't matter. You are my home."

"Me?"

"Marry me."

The prince of Ulmos didn't reply, but instead kissed me tenderly at first, nibbling on my lower lip. He pulled away after a few seconds and met my gaze, his expression pensive and a little pained. "Mycel, you know marriage is…"

"I know," I assured him, wanting more than anything for him to know that I understood why he was hesitant, understood why the idea of marriage didn't seem as romantic and carefree to him as it may have to other people; I could never dismiss what he'd been through or assume that I could erase it all from his history. "I know, it doesn't feel safe or sacred to you." I wanted him to know that I really did understand and that my question – or demand, rather – came from a place of love, not of selfishness. "I would never want to discount that, Wyn. I just want to show you what it can be, with us. I just want to love you for however long we have. I want you to know that marriage doesn't have to be a prison… it can be a promise."

Earwyn's gaze was pained as he, no doubt, recalled the events that had led him to resent and fear the idea of marriage. Who wouldn't when it came to mean entrapment, force, and pain? I prayed that his eagerness to please me wouldn't allow him to agree with something he truly disagreed with. Within seconds, though, he was peeling my blouse from my shoulders and laying blazing kisses across my flesh. How had his lips warmed so quickly? I didn't care. I wanted to devour him whole so that he would be with me always and the feeling of home would never leave me again; my tender heart wouldn't survive any further abandonment, especially not from him. "Wyn," I breathed, tangling my fingers in his hair as he kissed down my chest. His gaze was half-lidded and hungry. Meanwhile, his fingers found the buttons of my jeans, and then he met my gaze again with a questioning look. "Yours," I told him honestly, smiling a little as he leaned me back onto the dashboard of the car, where he unbuttoned them so that he could slip just one pant leg off me. Neither of us had the patience to do much more undressing.

"What would you promise me?" he asked, breathless and frantic as he unzipped his own slacks, freeing himself with a stifled groan. His cock bobbed heavily and I had to stop myself from marveling at its size and power. The way he was painfully hard and ready to go – with me, for me – at a moment's notice flattered me endlessly. His peacoat hung off his shoulders, awkwardly restraining him in a way that made his chest and arms bulge under the fabric of his shirt, but he wasted no time in pulling my panties aside as he welcomed me forward onto his lap.

"To love you, always and forever… with everything I have, Wyn," I said again, this time almost pleading with him.

"I love the way you love me," Earwyn told me, "so eagerly, so genuinely." He bit his lip hard as he slid me down onto him, and I couldn't help but tip my head back in response, almost as if that would make more room for him inside of me. "So openly."

I gasped as the broad head of his cock hit a tender spot inside of me. I put a hand on his shoulder to steady myself, then slid off of him and back down again, thrilled at the way our bodies together set fireworks off inside of me. I needed him. I needed him for longer than a mortal life would allow, but I would take whatever the universe would allow me. I reached down and tugged the buttons of his shirt open, sliding my fingers beneath the fabric so that I could connect more of my body with his. It was an honor to know him so intimately and to love him like this. "It's what I was made to do," I breathed, stealing another kiss before rocking myself against him again. I slid myself down onto him fully and swore I could feel him deep in my chest as I ground my hips into his.

"Yeah?"

"Mmhm." I nodded, riding him at a consistent pace now. Earwyn thrusted up to meet me, and we moved together like waves crashing ashore, each one bringing us closer and closer together.

"You were made for me," he panted.

"Yes."

"Made to love me... made to take me like this, Mycel, all of me."

"Gods, yes, Wyn..." I crushed my lips to his in desperation, loving the taste of sweat on his upper lip where he'd been frozen and trembling before. "Every inch," I murmured between smaller, softer kisses, then took his lower lip between my teeth as he hammered into me. The car bounced in our parked spot on the side of the highway; much more of this and we'd soon be rolling down the road.

"And what happens when you get sick of me?" he asked suddenly, our faces hardly a breath apart. "Marriage... it's... it's supposed to be forever."

"It's not a cage, Earwyn. I won't keep you unless you want to be kept."

Earwyn swallowed hard. "Keep me."

"Marry me."

"Yes."

SPRING

CHAPTER SEVENTEEN

*W*e married in the forest because it was the only true home Earwyn and I had come to know. Despite being unwelcome in the kingdom of Yannava, the forest wasn't like the ocean, where just stepping foot into it seemed dangerous and likely put us on the Ulmosi's radar. Here, we could explore and be present as long as we steered clear of Yannava. I picked wildflowers and put them in my hair in a makeshift crown and found my lover barefoot, in a clearing. Light streamed through the canopy and glistened on the surface of a nearby pool of water. The rushing of a waterfall could be heard intermingled with the chirping of birds and the rustling of leaves. I could handle a water-fall, I thought, especially if it was with Earwyn.

The scars on Earwyn's neck shimmered a pale gold; it had been months since he had last used his gills to breathe, but I still found them oddly beautiful. They were a symbol for where he'd come from, what he'd endured, and a place he'd ultimately outgrown for the better. In fact, his time earthside seemed to have done him well overall. He seemed brighter, happier; not as stormy as he'd used to be, but still as passionate and complex... all of the things I loved about him without as much of the suffering. I was certain I never wanted him to change, until I saw him smiling more and more at peace each day.

"How will I know where to meet you?" he'd asked me that morning, clearly nervous despite both of our peaceful excitement. We'd spent the night before chattering about how we would wed and what we would do to celebrate. When we drove ourselves to the forest, he intertwined his fingers in mine as we rode in silent comfort. We exited the car with our respective outfits – Earwyn's laid carefully over his forearm and mine tossed over my shoulder in our contrasting styles – and I blew him a kiss as we ventured into the woods to prepare for our most sacred ceremony.

I chuckled and told him that I trusted he would find his way back to me, to our place, just fine. The forest had a way of leading people and creatures to the paths they were meant to find; his path would always lead to me, I knew that. The same stifled giggle came over me when I spotted him barefoot, in a clearing surrounded by small fly agaric mushrooms and clover. The feel of the greenery between my toes was heavenly and almost as blissful as the sight of my wonder across from me. I was certain I saw a squirrel pester him about his hair before scurrying away with a disgruntled shake of its head. It appeared as though the critter had been trying to hide an acorn in his wild locks. Huh, he really was fitting right in.

"That's enough, little creature..." he muttered, waving the beast off as he turned toward me. Either I'd lost my usual stealthy woodland gait, or he'd learned to sense me no matter where we were; the latter was more comforting and romantic. "Mycel," he breathed finally, as if he'd just recalled how to speak. The name sent a burst of heat through my heart. How long had I hidden my real name? And how like-home it felt for those brief syllables to tumble from his soft lips... goodness, when had I become such a sap? I cracked a smile at his greeting.

I closed my eyes and leaned into the touch of his rough, slender fingers as they fiddled with my hair, tucking an extra flower behind my ear. Things move slowly in the forest, like seasons and creeping moss and mighty, ancient trees, so we moved slowly, too. I wore a sheer, floor-length white dress with a plunging back and neck. It swept the ground as I walked, gathering little twigs and leaves as I went. The surface of the dress was embellished with glistening pearls: a small reminder of Earwyn's homeland, which I knew he loved if he could separate it from the harm of its current rulers like I had with the woods. The fabric felt lovely against my flesh, which was mostly bare beneath aside from undergarments of matching white lace.

Meanwhile, Earwyn was dashing in a coffee-colored suit, cream vest, and white shirt. I'd brought him a bundle of wildflowers and tucked them neatly into his jacket pocket. "Wonder," I addressed him, pressing a kiss to his palm as he caressed my cheek. I ran my hands down the front of his shirt, savoring the hard slab of muscle beneath the fabric. The top few buttons were undone, and a few inches of his bronzed flesh showed through. His hair was neat, tied at the nape of his neck with a bit of twine, and he looked heavenly as ever.

"Goddess."

Human weddings need officiants, witnesses. In the forest, there's a witness every square inch of earth. Everyone watches, but no one judges; bugs don't care if you're rebelling against your nature, just that you don't step on them. The wind will wrap you in its arms regardless of your affiliations. I sighed quietly in relief at this realization. I loved the woods despite the turmoil we were both facing and felt glad to share these moments in a place that brought my heart and body peace.

"Mycel," Earwyn began again, taking my hands softly in his. He squeezed them a bit, a gesture of extreme assurance, and gazed deeply into my eyes. It always impressed me that he seemed to bare his soul so authentically and without fear. "From this day forward, I promise to cherish you infinitely. To climb the highest mountaintops or dive to the deepest depths of the ocean by your side. I'll love you now until forever; even when we return to the dirt of the earth, my soul will embrace yours forevermore. I'm yours always."

It took me a moment to remember to breathe and respond to his vows with my own. "Earwyn... Wonder," I addressed him, fiddling with one of his fingers as I searched his gaze. It was so easy to get lost with him. "Though it took me some time to realize, you're my home. I'd always felt a little out of place, even in spaces that I'm supposed to belong, until I met you. I see now that I belong wherever you are and that anything is possible for us when we are beside each other. Nothing makes me feel stronger and safer than your embrace or more understood than your listening ear. I have more love for you than there are leaves in the forest or grains of sand in the sea. I vow to love you forever and always."

"You're my first love."

"You'll be my last," I told him honestly, smiling a little to myself at what that realization meant. There was nothing more beautiful to me than the comfort I felt in realizing he was my last true love, forever.

We soaked in the beauty of each other's words in silence for a few moments before I remembered to pull my ring for Earwyn from where I'd tied it into my hair; there hadn't really been anywhere in my outfit to tuck it away, so it hung on the end of a small braid behind my ear. The ring was made of charred maple, a band of copper, and a strip of shed deer antler, and Earwyn admired it lovingly as I slipped it onto one of his strong fingers.

"You made this?" he asked quietly, holding his hand up to admire my craftsmanship in the filtered light of the forest. The textures of each material contrasted the others in a way that symbolized how our differences could work in great harmony and strength.

I chuckled and held up a splintered finger as a trophy of my work. "Yep!" It would've been easier with magick, but I had poured every bit of myself into that physical manifestation of my love and commitment for him. He snatched my hand into his and kissed my tender, bruised fingers, then slipped his own ring lovingly onto one. The metal was warm from being in the inside of his jacket. It appeared to be white gold, which glistened sharply and was fashioned into decorative, red-gem encrusted leaves that held up a lavender conch pearl. It was breathtaking: complex and intricate, like our love for each other had to be to withstand the challenges we'd faced and would face. From the moment it touched my flesh, I felt infinitely bound to him… so much so, even, that I immediately tangled my ring-clad fingers into his hair and pulled him to me for a soft, but thrilled kiss. He tasted warm and sweet, and the way he melted into me was something I'd not soon forget.

A giggle burst from my lips against my will as sheer bliss overtook me. Seconds later found us lying on the forest floor, the soft moss of the ground acting as a blanket for our warm embrace. I kissed him again and again. "My husband."

The sun was beginning to set when the sound of water interrupted us. When I turned, I was assaulted by the sight of a man standing at the edge of the pool nearby. He looked slightly familiar; buzzed hair and a stern expression, but was missing the warmth I'd come to expect from Earwyn and Firth. There was no doubt this man was one of his kind, though. His clothing suggested he might be a soldier; he wore a metal helmet with a sharp, ribbed fin across the top and a suit of armor that looked waterproof and flexible. The armor consisted of shoulder plates, gauntlets, and greaves, all in a shimmering blue-green, which were layered with what looked like a medieval wetsuit. When Earwyn noticed my pause, he did not follow my gaze. It was almost as if he could sense the other man. Perhaps he simply saw his reflection in my eyes. As we stood, my stare locked onto the intruder and Earwyn's piercing mine, the woods fell silent. I recognized the change from when the birds watched a predator take down its prey. Part of nature, yes, and an event that required respect and mourning; we all return to the earth, after all. I panicked internally at what this meant for us. Were we the prey here?

After several attempts to clear his throat (I'd later realized from the unfamiliarity of the forest's fresh water versus the salt of his homeland) the man spoke. He never left the pool of water, his boots immersed in the rocky sand of the water's edge, and appeared perfectly comfortable as the material of his outfit dripped heavily. Spikes of limpet-tooth armor lined the outside of his wetsuit. "Prince Earwyn of Ulmos." The man bowed his head so deeply that his helmet tipped forward, threatening to slide off of his head. "I've been instructed to escort you home by order of the king and queen. Your betrothed expects your prompt return as well."

Earwyn stiffened. "I no longer answer to that title nor am I *of* Ulmos." He refused to turn toward the other man, and I could see the pain in his eyes at the mention of "home." A creature of the earth should feel in their element regardless of location, and yet the concept of belonging had become such a delicate matter to the both of us. Still, the woods were silent, and the reality of the pair of us being exiled set in. No one was coming to help us, no matter the outcome of this conversation. I gripped my husband's hand tightly, spinning the ring around his finger without thinking. When he finally turned toward the soldier, his fingers remained intertwined with mine. "Please," he stated through gritted teeth, forcing what little politeness he could muster, "deliver that message to the king and queen."

The soldier remained stoic, continuing to avert his gaze in a show of respect. "Unfortunately, Your Highness, I've been ordered not to return without you and to collect you at any cost."

There was no time for Earwyn to respond with words. As soon as the soldier raised his hand, flexing his fingers toward us, Earwyn's hold left mine and gripped his own throat. I watched in horror as he gasped for air and blood trickled from under his fingers. His gills were reopening themselves against his will and the air of the forest was quickly suffocating him. Like the guard, he was being made unfit for land.

A horrified "stop!" escaped me as I sank to the ground with him, unsure of what to do. He needed to be in the water, but bringing him into the pool would only close the gap between himself and his captor. "What do you want? Please, please stop," I begged, looking from the guard to my quickly paling man. "He belongs here! Why is he being summoned?" As I dug my toes into the earth, I begged silently for someone to come to our aid. Where were my people? This wasn't necessarily our forest, but I usually felt them everywhere, and yet, now, nothing, not even in my time of need. Where was Firth? We'd wanted this ceremony to be inti-mate, private, but now we were in desperate need of back-up.

I frantically placed my hands over Earwyn's and hoped for a moment that I could muster enough energy to keep him earthside for a little bit longer. I thought it was working when he took a deep breath, but I soon found myself depleted and panting. I couldn't wrap my head around this dark magick that had allowed the guard to not only reopen Earwyn's healed gills, but stop him from being able to breathe regular air as well.

"That's no business of yours, *fairie*. Bring him here," the soldier ordered harshly, his magick working as intended. "Or you'll watch him die."

I looked back into the sea-green eyes of the only person I'd ever truly loved and knew that I would be the one to carry him back to his torment. I had to. Selfishly I realized that a world without him would not be worth existing in, so watching him die just to save him from returning to Ulmos was not an option. When I flung his arm over my shoulder and dragged him to the pool, he begged me, "My... Mycel... find Firth." I felt sick with myself, but I wouldn't let him bleed to death or suffocate here in the woods. I wondered for a moment if this guard would bring back his body simply as a trophy if I let him die. I imagined what they'd do with it in Ulmos and how they'd parade him around as a traitor either way.

I gripped his fingers as I lowered him into the water and watched him heave a breath of relief. "I'm coming to get you," I promised him, not knowing how that would be possible or when I would be with him again. But before he could respond, the guard had grabbed and pulled him into the water. His fingers slipped from mine, leaving his wedding ring in my hand. When they vanished, the token of our love slipped through my fingertips and into the water. I gasped, trying desperately to chase it through the pool, my eyes blinded by tears.

It was gone.

He was gone.

The forest exploded with bird chatter.

I sat in the water and screamed.

CHAPTER EIGHTEEN

*I*t didn't take me long to find Firth; Zara's panicked yells hit me as soon as I entered our apartment building. I slipped into our unit and locked the door behind me, hoping that no one else had heard her and called the cops. There I found Zara crouched on the floor over Firth's massive figure, which had obviously been left for us as a warning. I wondered briefly how someone had gotten into our apartment if it was seemingly impossible for the guards to leave the water, but told myself to focus. If we ever got through whatever this hell was, we'd have plenty of time to muse over logistics.

"Zara, move," I told her sternly, pulling her off Firth. "You have to be quiet." My blood rushed in my ears, and my vision swam. It was a wonder I'd gotten there safely in the car.

"What do you mean 'be quiet'? There's a dead dude in our living room!" she hissed, angry at the suggestion but complying with my physical redirection anyway. "And I happen to really like that dead dude!" She scrambled backward on her hands and feet, watching the scene before her unfold in horror.

I didn't have the energy to reply, so I began scanning the large Ulmosi's body for any signs of injury. I saw his chest rise and fall, though his breathing was shallow, and wondered if they'd done some ungodly thing to him that the likes of my waning magick couldn't undo. Once I noticed the rapidly growing red stain on his shirt, I was able to tear the fabric and identify the wound on his abdomen that had clearly been made by a non-human being, but it wasn't totally foreign to me. It wasn't necessarily made by a Yannavi, but it was something I could fix, something land-based in its harmful magick. I sat back on my heels and sighed. There wasn't time for me to process the implications of the fact someone close to us, to me, had likely committed this atrocity against our group, against our family.

"Let's get him to the couch. I can fix this."

Again, Zara complied, but the look she gave me said "You have a lot of explaining to do." Sometime later I found us loaded in the car and me pouring my heart out to my roommate.

"You're some sort of fairie?"

"Kind of, but don't use that word... it's, uh, kind of a slur. Also, Earwyn and I got married," I blurted out, gripping the steering wheel with trembling hands. I had only realized I'd left out that important detail when the flash of white fabric on my thighs caught my gaze: my wedding gown. Had I really been wed in this cloth only hours before? Now it was stained with my husband's blood, a painful reminder of how our wedding had ended. I couldn't bring myself to look at Zara as I drove, knowing that she was likely staring at me with her mouth agape. A sense that I had betrayed her washed over me. "I didn't think it was important for you to know all of this. Now I see it would've been downright dangerous, but... I shouldn't have lied. That wasn't very friendly of me. I just, I didn't even know how to—"

"I wouldn't have believed you anyway," Zara confessed with a sigh.

"I don't think that's true. You've never doubted me before," I told her honestly, realizing that I'd never thanked her for how gracious, how loving she'd been to me when she really had no reason to. She just was. I owed her the truth, but it was also my duty to keep her out of harm's way, especially because I hadn't been able to do that for either Earwyn or Firth. My chest burned as I thought of Firth, still, barely breathing on our couch because of me... I couldn't even let my mind wander to what Earwyn might be experiencing.

Silence hung over the car for what felt like forever until a trembling sob erupted from me against my will. My roommate said nothing. After all, what was there to say? But she reached over and put a soft hand on my shoulder, squeezing it a bit as I drove.

The Olympic National Park crept into view.

Once the car was in park, I practically sprinted in the forest. It was hard to ignore the silence there. Normally I would've felt the presence of our people, my powers, and my home, but there was nothing. My chest ached as I searched for each native plant I'd need to fix Firth... without magick, it was tedious. Nothing spoke to me. It felt like every moment away from Earwyn put him more and more at risk of being harmed. He'd been gurgling blood when I last left him, which wasn't promising for his survival. Hopeless, I crawled on the forest floor, examining each plant that came into sight. There were many plants native to the Pacific Northwest, and unbeknownst to most humans, many of them had properties that made them ideal for healing. Because humans were so oblivious to the properties of these plants, the misuse of them often had negative consequences, and because I now had very little separating me from humanness, I was at risk for meeting the same fate if I misjudged. Asking Zara to help brought me comfort, but I couldn't risk letting her identify anything fully on her own either; I'd never forgive myself if she met harm like the rest of my loved ones had.

"I have to fix this," I muttered to myself as my knees sank into the freshly wet dirt of the forest. "Have to fix this. Come on. Come on!"

In my frustration, I'd forgotten one of my greatest allies and best resources: "Maz!" I gasped, sitting back on my heels as I pulled my fingers from the dirt. He would know. Where was he? He hadn't vanished like everything else had, but I also didn't hear him like I usually did in the back of my mind. Hesitant, but hopeful, I wiped a dirty hand on my dress and then used it to belt out a piercing whistle. "Mazus! I need you!"

I didn't hear him coming like I normally did, but soon he was there, in the dirt before me, his blue-black feathers glistening in the filtered light of the forest. I looked at him closely. "Maz... I can't hear you anymore, but I need your help." I looked at him with pleading eyes, and he met my gaze with his onyx marbles, unflinching, unblinking, and focused. He tilted his head; he was listening. I could have kissed that little crow, but instead I tried to focus.

Meanwhile, Zara was staring at me as if she couldn't believe the extent of the ridiculousness she was being forced to endure. Fairies. Magic. Elopement. Now talking to birds in my bloody wedding dress. How she hadn't turned me over to my therapist, I wasn't sure.

"Yarrow," I told Maz, holding his gaze with mine. I prayed to whatever gods might be listening that my familiar could still understand me in some capacity; whether it was my words or just my energy, I didn't know. "Like this." I used my fingers to make the shape of a plant with multiple shooting stems, then used my other hand to gesture at the top of the stems as I described the plant, "little flowers here, white, maybe yellow?"

Maz cocked his head and for a moment, I feared I had just been speaking at a creature who wouldn't be able to comprehend my words, but then he hopped off toward a clearing. A clearing, yes! I should have remembered where yarrow was generally found, but in the past I would have just thought of it and been led to it effortlessly. When Maz cawed from the clearing, I followed his noises and found him pecking at a just-bloomed yarrow plant of vibrant gold. I pocketed a few handfuls, filled my water bottle in a nearby stream, and booked it back to the car with Zara and Maz in tow.

* * *

Because Firth was so large and difficult for Zara and myself to move as dead weight – and without the help of my magick – I ended up cutting his shirt open to treat his wound. Beneath the fabric of his shirt was a vest made of limpet-tooth armor. I sighed as I disassembled a portion of it to access the growing gash in his side; the fact that his Yannavi attacker had known how to get through this nearly impenetrable armor meant that the Ulmosi had been so eager to punish Firth that they'd shared one of their greatest secrets. If Earwyn had a similar vest, I hadn't known about it, but with Firth as his bodyguard there was likely no use for him to wear one, too. I couldn't imagine how long they took to construct either and how precious a resource they were for the Ulmosi.

Day 1

On the first day without Earwyn, without Firth's voice or big body moving around our tiny apartment, silence overtook the two of us who were mentally present. Without speaking, we took shifts watching Firth on the couch, where his chest continued to rise and fall consistently enough for me to be unconcerned about whether he would live, but desperate for him to wake up. Zara, on the other hand, seemed to listen for nothing but his breaths. When she was "off" her shift watching him, she dragged herself into the kitchen and attempted to feed us both. At first, she tried to act like everything was normal; she put the same amount of effort into preparing meals for us and even dished up a bowl of food for Firth as if there was a chance he'd sit up soon, well and hungry.

I couldn't bring myself to eat. I took each snack and meal out onto the balcony where Mazus waited patiently and tossed the black bird each scrap, which he gobbled up. At the end of the day, however, he looked stuffed as if he were only consuming my leftovers as a favor to me. Exhausted, but unwilling to hurt Zara's feelings and her attempt to keep me alive, I was grateful for my familiar's efforts.

In the evening, I begged him to fly over the ocean as far as he was willing. When he returned, shaking his small head, I at least knew that Earwyn's body wasn't floating somewhere in the Pacific. That would have to be enough to get me through one day. As I sat on the balcony with Maz, waiting for Zara to tag me in for my shift with Firth, I twisted my wedding ring around my finger absently. It had been less than twenty-four hours without Earwyn, and I felt empty aside from the scene replaying in my mind; I could see his pained expression as I lowered him into the water only for him to be dragged away against his will, back to the place where he'd endured torture and manipulation throughout most of his life. How could I have done that? How could I have subjected him to such horror when I'd promised him a safe haven, a place of healing? If I got him back, would he ever trust me again? I swallowed hard and looked at my ring, the one I didn't deserve, and decided that I had to make sure he was safe again if nothing else.

Even if he decided that my betrayal was too much to ever forgive, I had to make sure he was alive to make that decision.

DAY 2

I was ravenous, but unable to keep even a single bite of food inside of me. I became fast friends with our bathroom, where I vomited every time I attempted to eat and fought back nausea that plagued me the entire day. It felt cruel that the universe should cause my grief to also manifest physically. What else did I have left if I was just a sobbing, puking mess?

DAY 3

On day three, Zara had to go back to work. I'd requested a longer weekend because I was supposed to be on my honeymoon. That fact in itself made me feel sick and sorrowful. Instead of spending the day in laughter and love and – no doubt – endless passionate sex, I spent it obsessively cleaning the apartment, which had grown even messier in the chaos of Zara's daily cooking. It was easy to see how each of us was coping – or attempting to cope, rather. Zara cooked. I cleaned. Neither of us really ate. I puked. We both cried. Rinse and repeat.

DAY 4

When Zara stacked yet another dirty dish on the counter, I could have screamed. I angrily put it into the dishwasher while staring at her. She didn't notice.

DAY 5

My once lush and bountiful balcony of plants had quickly turned shriveled and yellow. Whether from my lack of magick or just neglect, I wasn't sure, but I pulled our trash can onto the landing and began sweeping armfuls of plants into it without a care. It felt pointless to pour my energy into these shrubs when I couldn't even take care of myself. I was just about to chuck one last plant – a small pot of rosary vine – into the trash when Zara caught my wrist.

"Don't toss this one."

"Why shouldn't I?" I queried, exhaling deeply in frustration.

She plucked the small vase from my fingers and held it up in front of my face. "It's not a total loss. See? It's mostly green. Don't let a single yellow leaf take away from that." Zara wasn't even a "plant person," and yet she grabbed my pruning shears, trimmed the dying leaf, and replaced the single plant on the balcony where it had previously been.

Maz rubbed his face on the plant's leaves as if he was glad to see an old friend.

Day 6

I realized on day six that it was the longest I'd gone without speaking to my husband since the day I'd met him. I stared at my phone, which I kept charged solely in hopes of hearing from him, and read every text he'd ever sent me. I looked at our call logs. I listened to his voicemails. I figured out how to "lock" each and every single one so that they wouldn't vanish off this strange human electronic device; surely that would've completely sent me over the edge.

"Michelle, hi, Earwyn here. Just saying hi. Hope to see you soon. Take care."

"Michelle, hey, pick up please. Where did you go? Are you

okay? I'm still at the theater, Zara and Firth are inside but I'm starting to panic. Did something happen? Please just… call me back. Let me know you're okay."

"Mycel, hey, it's Wyn. …Wyn, I love that nickname. You know I've never had a nickname until now? Three hundred years and no one thought of a creative way to shorten Earwyn. Oops, I think someone heard me. Did I say three hundred? I meant, um, thirty. In any case, I'm thinking of Indian food for dinner. Let me know what you'd like, and I'll bring it back to the apartment. Umm, okay, bye."

"Hey Mycel. Can't sleep. You're at work. Wish you were here instead." He yawned. "I miss you."

This one was a whisper. "Hey. You're lying in bed next to me asleep, but I needed a way to immortalize this feeling. You asked me to marry you today. That's the coolest thing that's ever happened to me. My ankle is the size of a baseball, but still. Coolest thing ever. I love you. Gotta go, you're talking in your sleep." Laughter. "Did you know you snore? Okay, bye."

Maz watched me from my bedroom windowsill, where he trilled and chirped at me to get my attention with no luck; even though we had stopped being able to truly understand each other, he had never stopped trying to connect with me. Nothing could pull me from my thoughts. What cruel punishment it was to meet the one person who made me feel whole and accepted and held only to have him ripped from my arms. I had failed him. I had sent him straight back to that which he had desperately tried to heal from.

Day 7

I couldn't sleep.

. . .

DAY 8

I slept the whole day.

DAY 9

Finally remembered to shower.

DAY 10

On day ten, it became too much for both of us.

"This is your fault!" Zara screamed, throwing another plate on the floor, where it shattered immediately. The linoleum of our kitchen was decorated with silverware and dishes that she'd swiped off the counter in her rage. I tried not to flinch every time a new item joined them. Maybe the screaming and clattering would wake Firth if we kept at it for long enough. "If you'd just told the truth or, I don't know, maybe gotten a little more concerned when things started getting weird… but no, you don't seem to notice when things are weird… then maybe Firth wouldn't be in a fucking coma on our couch and Earwyn wouldn't be—"

"Don't," I responded, furious, but not completely disagreeing with her accusation. I gritted my teeth as I stood there in the carnage of our argument, Firth's still body lying in the midst of it all, unaware and unassuming. The guilt I'd already laid upon myself was agonizing, but to have someone actualize my fears by speaking them out loud – I couldn't handle it. I wouldn't let her put that into the universe. "Don't say it. You know there's no coming back from that."

"He's—" Zara started, sliding another plate off the counter and onto the floor. She punctuated each word with another shatter: "— probably—dead!" The look on her face, though still fierce as ever, betrayed her distaste with her choice in insult. That was low.

Lower than low. We'd worked so hard to ensure that her beloved would pull through, and yet I had no clue where mine was, what torment he was suffering, or whether he still drew breath. To remind me that he might be stiller than Firth was now seemed the ultimate betrayal.

The only thing that stopped me from charging her right there and then was the alarm buzzing in my pocket, indicating that it was time to go to work. I had to go, had to maintain some semblance of normalcy, and if I was lucky, catch Anala. She was the only suspect I had earthside. I swallowed hard, then walked over the shattered remains of our dishware still barefoot and glared at Zara. "Probably," I forced out, my mouth dry and painful. "But if I let myself believe that, then what?" I wiped my face with the back of my hand, grabbed my boots, and left. "Then nothing!" I added before I swung the door shut. The door slamming behind me must have rattled one last bowl off the counter because another crash echoed through the hall as the door closed. I knew what happened if I let myself believe that; that was it for me. There would be no returning to Yannava, no hanging out with Zara and Firth, no exploring the forest or the sea. There would be nothing. How could there be anything left for me when my everything no longer walked this plane? I bit my lip hard as I pulled my boots on in the hallway of our apartment building, completely oblivious to the side-eye a passing neighbor gave me; it was probably in their best interest to leave me alone unless they wanted their kitchen redecorated as well. I didn't realize then that I hadn't put on socks. That would come back to bite me in the ass later, probably, when I had to fight through my shift with sweating feet that would make me want to crawl out of my skin.

Mazus landed on every nearby branch as I walked down the street to our restaurant. Before I opened the door, he let out a piercing "caw" as if he were demanding that I meet his gaze.

Normally I met his demands to check in in a much more amicable and appreciative way, but nothing was normal anymore, and I wasn't sure what I was becoming under the stress of our current situation. "I'm fine, Maz!" I hissed, waving him off. I'd likely feel guilty for that later, too.

I wasn't fine.

I was spiraling.

Day 11

I was mixing a drink at the bar at work when I spotted a head of onyx locks bobbing through the restaurant accompanied by a physique I'd become intimately familiar with prior to meeting Earwyn. Rational thought left me, and I dropped the glass on the counter, oblivious to the patron asking me where I was going mid-order. He'd looked wary when he'd first approached me – in fact, all of the regulars had; I hadn't been able to keep up my carefree, playful facade all week.

"Anala, you bitch!" I growled, grabbing the shoulder of the woman I'd spotted in the bar. I didn't register that it wasn't her before spinning her to face me and roughly holding her by the arms.

So, on day eleven I lost my job for harassing a customer. I didn't argue. What use was there? What value did money have when the world had practically stopped turning? I had barely been holding it together through my shifts anyway. I wasn't sure how I'd explain my lack of rent money to my roommate.

I came home from my last shift to see that Zara had meticulously cleaned the entire apartment in what I assumed was an apology. I didn't have the energy to care.

. . .

Day 13

Springtime used to be my favorite time of year in both Yannava and Seattle. In Seattle, it's a welcome break from bleakness, big coats, and the often-blinding decor of the holiday season, though I do understand the humans' incessant need to put twinkling lights on everything when the days get shorter. In spring, people plant flowers and go running. They wear sunglasses. They say odd things like that it's "way too hot for my PNW blood out here." In Yannava, animals come out from hibernation, and all sorts of plants begin to bloom. But this spring felt bleaker than ever. Any hint of sun felt blinding, and the warmer temperature threatened to suffocate me any time I stepped out of the apartment… hell, any time I stepped out of my bedroom. I had to, though, to continue trading shifts with Zara in keeping an eye on Firth as he healed. Here and there, he'd groan or shift slightly in his unconscious state. I tried to listen closely for any sleep-talking that might hint at who had harmed him, but no luck. Despite Zara's harsh, hopeless words about Earwyn, I held on to faith that Firth would make a full recovery. I wouldn't wish the crushing agony of not knowing on my worst enemy, let alone my best friend… and she was still my best friend, cruel words or not.

I kept my head down as we traded shifts that day, but we were passing each other in the hallway at one point, and I accidentally bumped Zara. I was so much bigger than her that I sent her into the wall of the hallway by accident. Even if I didn't have my magick, I still had my unusual size and lack of grace to keep people away from me.

"I'm so—"

"It's fine," she told me with a sigh, seeming hesitant as she looked up toward me. The hallway of our apartment was small, putting us much closer to each other than two feuding roommates would've naturally been. "I wasn't looking where I was going."

I couldn't bring myself to meet her gaze. Instead, I was counting down the seconds until I was back in my room, watching Maz preen himself on my windowsill, and saying a silent prayer for Earwyn. I wondered briefly what Dr. Elina Jansen would say about my behavior.

"Thanks for taking care of Firth."

"It's my fault he's hurt." I shrugged, not dismissing the seriousness of that misfortune, but insisting that thanks were not necessary; perhaps I should've taken every single care shift to show just how remorseful I actually was.

Zara didn't acknowledge my comment. "We'll get Earwyn home, sprout. When Firth wakes up, he'll tell us what to do, and we'll get him back... and we'll take care of him, just like we are with Firth, until everyone is healed and happy again. We can do that. We will do that." Zara looked up at me tiredly, and I saw a silent apology in her gaze. Everything was so raw and tender, she wouldn't be the one to repeat what she'd said to me, even if it was to make amends.

"... if he's alive."

"He's alive, sprout. He has to be. Your story doesn't end here."

Day 14

Zara left a plate of snacks outside of my bedroom door. This time, I shared them with Maz instead of trying to offload all of them on him. He looked thankful... and fat, with his blue-black feathers jutting out of his now-round body at awkward angles.

Day 15

On day fifteen I stood on the beach that Earwyn and I had waded into after the charity gala. The water wasn't nearly as frigid as it had been then. I saw no beauty in the ocean anymore; it had taken the one thing I loved most and committed itself to his torture. As I walked out into the water, the sand squishing between my toes and my clothing growing heavier as it took on moisture, I sighed. It was pulling me in just like it did him. It was claiming me, just like it had him… at least I could be connected to him in that way, but it was all wrong. I was supposed to consume him, to claim him, to devour him, not the relentless ocean. I walked until I couldn't walk any farther, then let a small current knock me onto my back in the water. I floated. I floated for longer than I could keep track, the overcast sky of Seattle shielding my eyes from the sun in what felt like one last display of mercy from the universe.

Maz was nowhere to be found… even he had left me.

When my mouth felt dry and parched, I glanced around me and realized that I couldn't see the shore anymore. My hair spread around me on the surface of the water in a matted, tangled web. Despite my lack of movement, fatigue soon overtook me, and I couldn't stand to keep my body afloat any longer. I let myself float with just my face above the water, my body's natural instinct to stay alive overpowering my desire to be washed away forever and become a blip in the lives of the people I knew. Soon I began dipping beneath the surface. I had nothing left. I pulled in one last deep breath as my head dunked under again, this time not bobbing to the surface again.

I was sinking.

I watched the filtered daylight shimmer through the water's surface as I sank deeper and deeper, fish fleeing from me as my body cut through the water. I'd have to breathe it in soon. I'd have to submit if I really wanted to let go. I put my hand on my chest and held my wedding band close to my heart in one last act of everlasting love, then closed my eyes.

I'd see Earwyn soon.

Better yet, maybe the ocean would see this as a trade, a sacrifice. If my death caused it to release Earwyn back to the surface, back to the human world where he was safe from the abuse of his kingdom, it would be worth it.

But the universe had other plans, and they were not so merciful. Before I could inhale the brine of the sea and submit to the ocean's depths, something was pushing me aggressively to the surface of the water. Soon, I was at the top again, gasping for air against my will and being shoved through the water toward the shore. It pushed me with a speed that could only come from an ocean dwelling animal until I was at a depth that I could stand in, then vanished. I turned back only in time to see the fin of a shark dip back into the water. My back ached from where its snout had shoved me what felt like a mile back to shore.

I wasn't allowed to die, to give up, yet.

Day 16

On day sixteen, Firth gasped awake. Zara screamed from the living room, where he'd remained under our care for nearly three weeks now, being rotated and changed and dabbed with a cool towel by whichever one of us was "on duty." When his eyes opened, Zara was crouched over him, staring down at him lovingly. She was practically vibrating with joy when I re-entered the living room, and it looked like it was taking everything in her not to tackle the giant man. I was impressed at her restraint. We sat him upright, and after holding a glass of water with a straw to his lips for a drink, Zara pressed her lips to his in a reunion kiss that made my heart ache.

We fed Firth and helped him shower and change before I relayed the events of the day we'd all lost our normal lives. He nodded in understanding as he ate, and then I dropped my request on him. "I need you to help me get into Ulmos." Zara signed in translation next to me, not expecting an exhausted Firth to have the strength or focus for lip-reading.

He shook his head immediately. "It's not safe."

"I don't care," I told him seriously. "I have to get Earwyn."

"I'll go, it was my job to protect him."

"No," I argued, shoving his fork back up toward his mouth. "Listen, don't talk."

He rolled his eyes at my phrasing, but didn't stop me. Instead, he dutifully took another bite of room temperature pasta salad while staring directly at me. "I need to get him back. You need to rest and heal. I need you here with Zara in case anyone comes back to finish what they started. So you will help me get into Ulmos, no matter what it takes. They'll kill him and harm all of the humans if we don't. I'd imagine any family you have there is in danger as well." I realized then just how little I knew about Firth – did he have family in Ulmos, aside from his would-be brother, Earwyn?

Firth was silent, swallowing hard. A moment later, he set his jaw and added, "Earwyn would hate me for letting you go after him. He wants you safe more than anything. Just as it was supposed to be my job to protect him, it's my job to protect you and Zara." He glanced at his lover for a moment, his gaze softening, before he looked back at me, where he recomposed himself.

"I'm the reason he's gone, Firth... if I don't get him back, I'll never forgive myself. I can't live like that. Besides, he won't be around to hate you if he's dead."

He gave me a curious look, as if he doubted I had that ability to rescue our friend. I promised to explain more later, but it made no sense nor would it keep him safe in the moment to provide him with further information now. I begged Zara to help me convince him and then stay behind as well to take care of him for however long I was gone. What a huge sacrifice I was asking them both to make for someone that, in the grand scheme of things, they barely knew. After all, perhaps it had been my people that had harmed Firth. I prayed that he would understand when I explained it was under the orders of his leadership, who were now most likely puppeteering his best friend.

"I can't give you magick," Firth stated finally, with a sigh, as he resigned to help me. "I don't even have any of my own... it started fading around the same time Earwyn's did, you know."

"I know. I just need to get into the kingdom. Then I'll take it from there."

"You need to breathe underwater."

CHAPTER NINETEEN

"I t's going to hurt," Zara told me, interpreting for Firth and me as I lowered my fully clothed self into our apartment's clawfoot tub. The large man sat on our closed toilet, steadying himself with his arm on the counter; he was still weak, and even this task was asking a lot from him. I thought for a moment that this experiment might be better in Firth and Earwyn's apartment due to the size of its tub and materials we'd have access to, but realized that it wasn't safe to go somewhere we'd be so easily found; their names were, no doubt, on the registry at the security desk, and Firth showing up would mean that he wasn't dead as they'd planned. Zara was interpreting for Firth and me because he wasn't strong enough to stand over the tub and speak to me. The tub was filled to the brim with cold water, and sprigs and splotches of different sea plants floated at the top: seagrass, red algae, and kelp. Zara had also dumped what seemed like an entire container of store-bought sea salt into the tub. The smell had even filled the hallway, and though it was unpleasant, I was appreciative of her willingness to wander around the grocery store and

beg nearby scuba divers to help her find supplies for what might
be a suicide mission.

"I can handle it," I told her, though a chill had already started
coursing through my veins. I had to handle it. What else could we
do? Stand by the ocean and pray for his return even though all
magick and community had left us to die alone? By Firth's calcula-
tions, this was the only way to get me to breathe underwater.
Apparently, he'd read about it somewhere in Ulmos, though
whether it was a historical book or just a myth, he couldn't recall.
Not very promising, but who knew Firth was the researching type?
It would likely only work because I was terrafolk, whereas trying it
with a human would undoubtedly lead to their death. That didn't
mean it would be easy for me, though, or that it was a sure thing
by any means. My clothing was drenched with the weight of the
water by the time Zara hoisted Firth to his feet above the tub; there
was no way someone of her stature had the strength to hold my
large body down.

The giant looked me in the eyes for a moment before placing
his hands on my shoulders. "You have to breathe it in as soon as
you can," Firth said seriously with what seemed like genuine
concern in his eyes. Perhaps he didn't completely hate me, or
maybe my willingness to die trying to get his friend back was
enough to get me back in his good graces. "If there's any chance of
this working, you have to stay under and breathe it in." I think we
all knew that I was our only chance at getting Earwyn back and
keeping everyone from the Ulmosi's wrath. I tried to push the
thought of failure from my mind as the vision of my dead body
floating in the tub while Earwyn's floated in the sea cropped up in
my brain. As poetic as that ending might have been, it would be
too soon for us. We hadn't had enough time together. Like Zara
had said, it couldn't be the end of our story yet.

"Don't go easy on me."

Zara peered around Firth's massive frame to shoot me a worried glance, chewing on a hangnail as she looked down into the tub at me. "You can back out," she told me seriously. "We can find another way to get him back. This isn't our only option." But even as the words left her lips, we all knew she was lying. Sure, they'd let me back out, but it would be even more my fault if Earwyn never returned or the humans were slaughtered by the Ulmosi... I offered her a sad smile in return, then nodded at Firth to give him the go-ahead.

The next thing I knew, I was being pushed under the water, and the crushing coldness of the bath covered my face, filling my nostrils in a rush. Despite Firth's warnings, my first instinct was to hold my breath. I went under without a fight, and seconds ticked by where I couldn't quite convince myself to give in and attempt a breath. Eventually, my remaining oxygen withered away into nothingness, and when I realized that the next step was submitting, panic set in in full force. No amount of positive thinking or reminding myself of my purpose calmed my racing heart and the excessive cold spreading through my drenched body. I'd never teetered so boldly on the edge of dying before; that was one part of mortality that would take a long time for me to adjust to.

Then I started to thrash, sending water sloshing over the sides of the tub, almost as if my body thought it could displace enough to purchase me some more air. Firth held me steady under the surface, rearranging his hands so that he was pinning me down evenly across my shoulders and midsection, despite what I'm certain was Zara's panicked screaming. I wouldn't have been shocked if she was climbing the giant sea-man at that point, begging him to drop this plan altogether. He kept his word, though, and anchored me to the bottom of the tub without hesitation. I wondered if it was cathartic for him, sort of punishing me.

I squeezed my eyes shut against the burn of the saltwater and prepared to die. It hadn't worked. How foolish of us to think that simply trying to drown me would give me gills, would grant me entrance into Ulmos, which would just be the beginning of my negotiations to free Earwyn. I'd let everyone down, and as my body continued to struggle without me, I let my brain surrender to agonizing doubt and failure. I would never see Earwyn again. He would suffer because of me, and so would the humans, and Firth, and Zara... despite the darkness of my shut eyes, something drifted into view. Wispy, golden locks floated through the water in my clouded vision like rays of sunshine, caressing my cheeks in a tickle until Earwyn's godlike face appeared in my mind. My chest warmed from the inside at the sight of him, and I wanted to sigh in relief, but he leaned down to kiss me before my lips could part. I surrendered, like I always did with Earwyn, and pressed my mouth to his. Water flooded my parted lips, and despite my body's instinctual fight, I swallowed and breathed in. If this was the end, at least I got to see him one last time. "I'd never dream of hurting you," he whispered to me sweetly.

It was just us for some time, lost in each other as I suffered the burning pain of water inhalation; the softness of his lips was only enough to temper the agony and abuse I was putting my fragile mortal body through. Eventually, what snapped me from my subconscious was the metallic taste of blood. Fearful that I'd hurt Earwyn in some other superficial way, my eyes snapped open to see nothing but the murky tub water tinged pink with my own blood and Firth staring down at me while holding Zara in both of his arms. He looked calm, but Zara still verged on hysterics.

I breathed. It burned, but the pain wasn't in my lungs anymore. I moved my hands to my throat, where blood continued to seep into the water, and felt the torn flesh of my new gills. I winced as my fingers explored the now throbbing gashes in the sides of my neck, which pulsed with each new breath they took in. Fuck, it hurt. It burned. It had worked, though, and as the water stilled in the absence of my frantic thrashing, I saw my roommate and friend clearly, and gave them a weak thumbs-up in what was left of the water in the tub. I tried a few intentional breaths under the water and found that, aside from the pain of my new gills having been torn violently through my neck due to necessity alone, it was manageable.

Sometime later, they hauled me out of the tub, and I promptly flopped over toward the toilet, where I vomited immediately. The burning sensation of bile leaking from open wounds in my throat is one I wouldn't soon forget.

CHAPTER TWENTY

*U*nfortunately for everyone involved in our rescue mission, I wasn't the world's strongest swimmer. I could get by – I'd even been known to explore a bog here or there – but diving to the depths of the ocean with a brand-new breathing method was an entirely different story. This meant that every day was spent on the nearest beach, getting myself acclimated to the water, to going deeper, to visualizing my goal. I had all the time in the world, as did Firth. Well, not all the time… it was hard to forget that every day we spent on land was another day that Earwyn's life and the fate of all humanity hung in the balance. Zara remained employed thanks to our diligent efforts. She needed to maintain her employment in case I never returned; I couldn't be responsible for ruining her entire life by leaving her without a job on top of everything else I'd dragged her through.

As I practiced, Firth sat on the shore with Zara, carefully disassembling the limpet-tooth vest he'd worn under his clothing for so long and tailoring it to fit my frame, which was large in its own way, but had different curves than his. He also had to reconfigure other pieces of apparel he had with him; the Ulmosi wore a water-resistant fabric made of seaweed fiber during their time swimming and then changed into plain clothes when they were actually within the kingdom, which was basically a small ecosystem and society deep within the ocean. Existing within it would be easy enough; it was the getting there and getting inside without raising any red flags that would be challenging.

I surfaced after what felt like a particularly unproductive dive; I was slow, angry, and easily distracted by the plethora of predators that seemed to be more and more present the deeper I dove. If I'd been exploring the depths of the forest, I'd be fearless, and if Firth had been in my place in the ocean, he'd likely have nothing to worry about animal-wise. But these were the hands we were dealt; Earwyn was deep in the ocean, and Firth couldn't go get him because he still hadn't fully recovered. Any sign of him approaching Ulmos would likely sound the alarm as well.

As I walked onto shore, I frustratedly ran my hands through my sopping wet hair, wringing it out and grimacing at how frigidly cold the air was against my wet body. I'd donned a wetsuit to make my outings look less suspicious to humans, but I just wasn't acclimated to the ocean the way that everyone else seemed to be. I wasn't sure why I even bothered with the suit, knowing that I couldn't get into Ulmos with it on; it'd be a dead giveaway that I wasn't one of theirs. Even Zara seemed befuddled by my discomfort and resistance. I sat on the shore and looked at the water, feeling hopeless and empty.

As I sat, I replayed my most recent predator encounter that had rapidly driven my depressed self back to shore. Another shark, like the one that had pushed me back to shore on the day I'd been content to drown, had confronted me during this swim.

"Let's go."

"There's nowhere to go," I muttered, resting my chin on my crossed arms, which I'd perched on my tucked knees. I didn't bother turning to look at Zara, who was undoubtedly wearing a fiery, annoyed expression on her mousey face. "No amount of pep talks is going to make me better at this... and time is just ticking away." I shoved my fingers into the sand pitifully, ashamed at how much of a downer I'd become, but I was tired. Just tired.

"You just need inspiration," she told me sternly, grabbing me by the shoulder of my wetsuit. "Now get your wet ass in the car, and let's go." She got me upright, threw a towel at my face, and gestured for both Firth and me to follow her.

After we dropped Firth off at our apartment, I slumped into the passenger seat with the towel draped over my head and groaned. I didn't bother asking where we were going, but hoped it was somewhere that I'd be fine not wearing real clothes. If Zara was dragging me to an aquarium or something, I'd kill her myself. When I felt the car stop, I lifted the corner of the towel to see us parked in the back of Earwyn and Firth's apartment building: Odyssey. "You want me to be inspired by a near-death experience?" I asked, obviously annoyed. "Didn't we already try that once?"

Zara rolled her eyes and tore the towel away from me, then held a door key card out to me. "Shut up," she muttered, rubbing her face in irritation. "Firth still had this, and it's likely that the room is still being paid for by Salt and Earth. Go in through the back entrance and see if it opens. Maybe seeing Earwyn's stuff will give you the boost you need." She then unbuckled my seatbelt, waited for me to open the door, and shoved me out of it the moment she could. I didn't see how it would work; if anything, this could send me spiraling into some sort of comatose depression. But I went in.

I was quick and quiet, feeling strangely out of place as people's private conversations bled into the hall; the rest of the world had kept moving, continued, gone on, despite this one room being left completely alone. I felt lightheaded as I pulled the keycard out of the single pocket in my wetsuit and steadied myself before holding it up to the pad above the door handle.

I walked through the rooms as if I were in a museum of the world's most precious gems; each article of clothing folded on a surface, each piece of paperwork, shaving implement, toothbrush, they were all special in their own way and not to be disturbed. Perhaps if I left them as they were, someday Firth and Earwyn would return here to pack up and carry on with life with Zara and myself. Perhaps we'd have one last seasonal celebration here while helping them do so. Would I make pine soda again? Would we exchange soft and intimate gifts? My fingers trembled at the thought when I finally made it into the room Earwyn had been using for so long. Whatever he'd worn to bed the night before our wedding was strewn over the bed. The scarf I'd made him was on the nightstand of the side he'd taken to sleeping on when we were together. We'd gotten ready together that morning, but I hadn't noticed it.

It turns out I also hadn't noticed that he'd left a small envelope with my name on it on his nightstand. I surrendered and disrupted the museum exhibits, grabbing the envelope and flinging myself onto the bed, where I wrapped his pajama pants around me like they held me in an embrace. I opened the envelope and held the letter up above me to read, letting myself sink into the bed.

To my goddess, on our wedding day:
Wow, a wedding. What do I call you after today?
Wife? Partner? Your Highness?

No word seems to be enough to encompass all that you are and will continue to be for me. In life, there are many paths to choose from; I know now that any path with you by my side is the right one. Thank you for being my home, my reason, and my shelter from every storm.

Tonight, we celebrate.

Yours, forever and always,
Wyn

I tucked the card into my now-dry wetsuit, pressing the paper against the flesh of my chest where it could be closest to my heart. Eyes pressed shut, I envisioned Earwyn's face: hard and withdrawn until he'd opened up to me, then soft, tender, and beautiful. I thought of the stern lines of his jaw and the way the corners of his mouth quirked up into a sly smile when I'd said something funny… the way his thumb rubbed the back of my hand to reassure me. I knew Earwyn more intimately than most, and knowing him meant knowing his gracious and forgiving nature. I told myself that maybe he would forgive me and understand why I'd done what I'd done in letting the guard take him. Either way, I had to see him again to find out. I twisted my wedding band around my finger and felt a pang in my heart as I thought of the one I'd made for him in so many painstaking hours. He would always be worth that amount of pain and sacrifice and then some.

"I need forest time," I told Zara with an exhale as I flopped into the passenger seat of the car, where Zara had been waiting for me. On my lap was a bag full of items I'd taken from the room.

"Like… good forest time? Or… 'and that was the last time she saw her roommate again' forest time? Because I really can't deal with a missing persons situation right now, Michelle."

I chuckled for the first time in weeks, Earwyn's card filling me with a whisper of optimism and hope. "First of all, I technically don't exist as far as humans are concerned, so I don't think the cops would be much help. Secondly..." I smiled, pressing my fingers to the card in my shirt. "If I'm going to get my husband back, I should probably bring his wedding ring."

* * *

THE HARDEST MATERIAL TO FIND WAS THE SHED DEER ANTLER. IT WAS important to me that I stick to the original make-up of my wedding band for Earwyn because it had meant so much to me the first time; I knew it wouldn't be exact, but I hoped that this reforging would indicate the renewed strength our relationship would have once I rescued my husband.

I pulled a cord of copper from some of my old jewelry and peeled the strip of wood easily from a tree, but when it came to finding a deer antler shed, the universe felt to be working against me. I scoured the forest floor, desperate for something that would've normally been abundant during that time of year and yet, nothing. It was impossible to find even a scrap of antler left behind and that was all I needed, just a small sliver. Grateful for the growing length of daylight, I kept up my search because I knew I wouldn't be able to keep looking forever; there was no room for recreational forest time anymore, and the days between then and our rescue mission were ticking away. This was my last chance.

I had just sat down under a large tree with a sigh, considering my trip a failure, when rustling sounded from nearby. Maz cawed above, using a tone we'd both determined to mean "be on guard" and so I stood suddenly, feeling grateful that he could be my eyes when I had such limited vision in the forest anymore. When I turned toward the noise, I found myself face-to-face with an unnaturally massive white-tailed deer buck. Though this species was typically relatively small, this one seemed like something out of a fairy tale: an old God of the forest, no doubt. I stifled a gasp, knowing it would feel too loud for the presence of such an ethereal creature. There were only a few feet between us, and it met my gaze easily, seeming to bore into my soul with its dark gaze. Its nose was shiny and wet, black like an oil slick, and its white accents were as crisp as a bright cloud. Its antlers, which were oddly still attached to its head, reached toward the sky like flames, curving in an intricate and magnificent pattern. Moss hung off each bony tendril as if this creature had grown into the earth and only now left its post as a stationary being. I traced them up toward the trees with my eyes and marveled at their size, their thickness, and the deep green of each strand of mossy covering. Mortality had made me skittish, so when the beast stepped closer to me, I flinched and had to force myself to remain steady and in one spot. I met its gaze once more, then bowed my head in respect. The forest seemed to still and silence as we stood there.

The deer snorted, huffing into the cool spring air, and I felt the wetness from its breath hit my face in a sharp gust. I bowed my head lower, willing myself closer to the ground without toppling forward. This felt like I was face-to-face with a predator; deer weren't typically, but messing with the old creatures of the earth was an unpredictable and dangerous pursuit. They demanded respect. When he didn't budge, I dropped to my knees in a show of submission. I felt isolated here, in the place that was supposed to be my home, unable to connect with my very roots… and in my isolation, I couldn't tell if this manifestation of the forest was a welcoming sign or a foreboding one. Perhaps the forest was telling me to leave or be killed, to flee before causing any more damage. But I couldn't bring myself to turn and run, even if that meant I was keeping myself in harm's way. This was my home, and I refused to be exiled from it again. I couldn't, I wouldn't turn and leave. I placed my palms on the ground in front of me, keeping my head and my gaze low, and sunk my fingers into the earth in desperation, willing myself to grow roots and be reabsorbed into the earth. "Please…"

The deer snorted again as it regarded me and my act of submission, no doubt judging whether it was acceptable or not. I'd never encountered an old God like this, even when I'd spent every day in the woods as a citizen of Yannava, and yet here I was, head to head with one when I was the least connected to my people and home. I couldn't quite figure out what this meant for me, what it meant for us. The next sound, however, caused me to squeeze my eyes shut in fear and quickly accept that this interaction might result in one last show of mortality; it was the loud clanging of antlers knocking together before they hit the ground before me, tumbling over each other into the dirt. When I looked up, the beast was still shaking its mighty head, then turned to leave just as quickly as he'd appeared with a trot so powerful that it seemed to shake the ground. The antlers remained, stacked on top of each other where they'd fallen in front of me, with one speared into the ground as if the deer had planted its flag there.

It took me some time to shake myself from my stupor and reach out to wrap a hand around one of the antlers, even with Maz pecking at me to get my attention. He hopped around the antlers to inspect them, then bowed his own head at the offering that the deer God had given me, had given Earwyn and me. It felt like a sign of things to come. I took one antler, knowing that I would only have use for a small piece of it, and fashioned the remainder of it into a new blade with a leather wrapped handle that would fit in my boot; if I was heading into Ulmos with no magick, I'd at least need some form of protection. The universe knew I couldn't get by on my charms alone and that a piece of a forest God might act as a bit of a shield. I left the second antler for another creature to use.

CHAPTER TWENTY-ONE

"I wasn't sure I'd ever see you again, Michelle," Dr. Jansen told me. I didn't bother correcting her on my name even though I'd shared it with Earwyn, Firth, and Zara in the weeks prior. Therapy had been at the bottom of my list of priorities since I'd lost my husband. According to the doctor, however, most people sought out therapy more when tragedies befell them. Instead, I'd avoided my appointments altogether. It wasn't until my encounter with the deer that I'd considered seeing Eline again, and even then, it had taken immense self-argument to get me to make another appointment with her. The disappointment in her tone when I'd done so had been obvious.

"Neither was I," I admitted, spinning my wedding ring around my ring finger as I spoke. "I didn't think I could face you."

"Is that so?"

"It is." Hadn't I just said that? Human interactions continued to confuse me. "But it turns out I really needed to, just like I needed to face the reality of my leaving Yannava." I swallowed hard.

"Tell me about that reality."

"I left because I didn't want to lead my people," I confessed, finally forcing myself to meet the doctor's gaze. "I was in a position of power, but I failed. I felt powerless, unable to protect or guide them, so I left. I turned Yannava over to my stewardesses, and I left them... and now I really am powerless, Doctor. I have nothing. No magick, no connections, nothing."

"What happened? How did you fail your people, Michelle?"

I was shocked at her audacity to just come out and ask that question when we'd only barely grazed the topic, which was in and of itself very heavy. I looked at her incredulously, unsure of how she expected me to respond. A synopsis, perhaps? How could I recount such a situation in a calm, conversational manner?

When she noticed my hesitation, Dr. Jansen pulled her glasses off and rubbed the bridge of her nose. Then, she gestured at the couch that I was sitting on. "Why don't you lie down? Close your eyes." She must have realized that the suggestion seemed outlandish to me because she added, "I have some techniques that might make it easier for you to reflect on the situation."

The velvet of the couch felt soft and smooth against my bare arms thanks to the tank top I was wearing. I leaned into the sensation both literally and figuratively, then closed my eyes and attempted to home in on the doctor's voice. She lulled me into a state of quasi-relaxation I hadn't accessed in quite some time, but then quickly set me on edge again with her questioning. Nevertheless, I tried to remain in her imposed state of memory access, tried to allow my muscles, which were tense with fatigue, to finally relax a little.

"What do you see?"

"Home." I sighed, scanning my woodland kingdom in my mind. It was bright, full of greens and browns and the colors of various insects. Birds chirped in the trees. The sun shone on my cheeks. "It's bright, beautiful, and warm."

"You often speak of your home with such fondness, even when you describe the winters, which must have been harsh, living in the middle of the woods. In fact, I don't think I recall a memory you've relayed to me that has any negative connotation at all. So what went wrong? What changed this perfect image of home in your mind? What happens next?"

"What went wrong?" I repeated, struggling to keep my eyes closed and delve further into my memories. I'd resisted this for so long, and while I knew that Dr. Jansen was trying to lead me through a therapeutic exercise, it had done me well to avoid these deep dives as much as possible. Now, though, my avoidance was no longer serving me, so it was time for a change, as painful as it might end up being. "What went wrong was... my people allowing me any power at all," I mused aloud, trying to let my filter go. "But you know, it's all part of the bigger plan and you don't really have any say in it and it's a family thing..."

"You didn't like being in charge."

"I didn't mind it at first. In fact, I thought I was doing a decent job. Everyone seemed happy." I could smell wildflowers, could hear children giggling as they climbed trees in our woods. In my mind, I saw a tiny tot, no bigger than a human toddler, learn to grow her first flower with just the power of her magick; she was glowing in excitement at the little green sprout as it bloomed tiny white petals. "Then it started to rain."

"It rains a lot here in Seattle."

"Yes," I agreed. "I used to love the rain."

"How do you feel about it now?"

I bit my lip. I hadn't let myself think this far back. When I first arrived in the city, the rain would set me on edge. I remember the sensation of raindrops on my flesh making me feel like I needed to crawl out of my skin and escape. I had considered leaving Seattle, going somewhere warmer, drier, but my resources within the human world were so limited; I had no money, no car, no connections. Eventually, I exposed myself to the rain, against my will, enough to realize that rain in the city was likely safe. It happened all the time and no one panicked. I avoided it until I gradually reacclimated to it, tolerated it enough to appreciate it like I had in the forest before everything had gone awry. But thinking about what had caused water to be so traumatic for me to begin with…

"Afraid."

"You've told me about your fear of the ocean, of deep water. I would think rain is a lot different than that. What makes you scared of the rain, Michelle?"

"It didn't stop. It went on and on…" I told her, exhaling shakily as I remembered the heaviness in the air. "The ground turned to mud. After three days of playing in it, everyone started to worry. It wasn't letting up. The floors of our homes started to fill with water."

"Oh…"

"They came to me for help, for decision-making. They needed someone to guide them to safety."

"Who?"

"My people. It was my job to tell them what to do, my responsibility to protect them." The endless storm echoed in my mind, along with the rain drops, the squish of mud beneath my feet, the panic in the voices of my people when they came to me in the midst of the storm looking for help. The water was rising rapidly.

"What did you decide? What did you tell them to do?" Now Eline sounded genuinely curious for her own investment in the story, not just because she was guiding me through my own self-discovery. I couldn't see her, but I was certain she was leaning over her notebook, staring at me, hanging on my every word.

"I was scared, but they needed me to be confident. I told them we were staying. We couldn't... we wouldn't abandon our homes. I told them that Mother Nature and our connection to the earth would keep us safe."

"You had no reason to think otherwise. I'm assuming that had been true so far."

"I believed that it was the right choice."

We sat in silence for a few minutes, with Dr. Jansen seeming afraid to ask the one question that really, truly mattered: what happened next?

"So many of them... died," I choked out finally, squeezing my eyes shut as hot tears slid down my cheeks. "Children, Dr. Jansen... little children who were just learning about their magick and the world. Elders, too, who we were supposed to be protecting and showing our respects to as they lived out their lives. Homes collapsed in a mudslide, rooms flooded, boulders crushed people and their belongings. Many of them didn't know how to swim because why would they?" I was angry. Why would nature do that to us? "And even those that knew how to swim couldn't carry everyone to safety... there wasn't anywhere to go. The survivors sat in the trees for days, waiting for the rain to finally stop and the water to retreat." Silence again. "I buried as many of them as I could and helped repair what I could before I left." My eyes snapped open and the room slowly faded into view again, made blurry by the tears I couldn't stop. I had forced these thoughts from my mind for as long as I could remember, told myself that my time away from home was for pleasure only. I'd been lying to myself to protect my brain, but now everything was out in the open again. "I failed them and now I have nothing. No power, no home. All I have left is the need to find my husband and make sure he's okay."

"Isn't that worth something to you?"

"It's the bare minimum. It's my fault he's gone, so it only makes sense that I should ensure his safety."

"Hardly," Eline commented, her gaze impassive and hard to read as usual. "What happens after you get him back, Michelle? Will you return home?"

"If I get him back..." I pondered aloud, "and I return alive, I'll have to. I've left too much unfinished." And then I told Dr. Jansen something I only realized as I was saying it. "I don't know the extent of it, but my visit back home made clear that Yannava is in danger. They're being controlled by threats... making decisions that are very unlike them, unlike us, as a people."

"And yet you feel powerless..."

"I am powerless. If I go back, all I'll have to work with are my words. Hell, the last time I tried to return, they made it clear I'm no longer welcome."

"I don't think you're looking at this clearly, Michelle," Dr. Jansen commented, narrowing her eyes as she leaned forward to look at me closely. I must have looked confused because she continued speaking. "You may feel powerless... you may not have the magick that you think defines you, but prior to you being powerless, you would have never considered going back to help your people. You know that it's going to be a fight for them to let you in and yet... you're willing to return, now, with fewer resources than ever, to help them. I don't think that could ever be called powerless. I think it's stepping into your power. It sounds like you're fulfilling your destiny."

Somehow, I didn't think we were still talking in metaphors. Dr. Jansen continued, looking at me seriously as she did so. "When you return," she said with such certainty that I knew my return was inevitable, "tell them I sent you."

I usually didn't think of Dr. Jansen by her first name, Eline, nor did I know of any Yannavi with that name. I did, however, remember a story of one of our people who left the kingdom of Yannava to live among humans. It was said that she used her skills to help them, but that she still kept in touch with some of our people. "You're Elan."

CHAPTER TWENTY-TWO

*W*e waited until sundown for me to surrender myself to the ocean, and as I waded into the clear water, I was reminded of the first night Earwyn had slipped into my dreams. The thought of his body pressed against mine in sand much warmer than that between my toes brought some heat back into my body. I trudged forward until I was waist deep before turning back to look at Zara and Firth. I'd have no way to communicate with them, we'd realized, no way to update them if I was caught or if I found Earwyn dead. They'd just have to wait. "Go home," I told them with as much confidence as I could muster. "We'll be back soon." I said it several more times in my mind as if to convince myself it was the truth, then turned away from them and plunged into the dark, cold depths of the ocean. Home. Home. Home. Back soon. Back soon.

The crushing weight of the deepening ocean bore down on me, and eventually it felt like a chore to dive deeper. Like any other land creature, it was effortful to fight away from my normal source of oxygen, and breathing through my new gills still took some getting used to. Not only that, but my brain and body both continued to fight against my history with the water. The only time the ocean and I had seemed to be on the same page was when I had tried to let it eat me alive. Since deciding that I should stay alive, we had returned to our previous relationship of enemies.

I felt my inner dialogue debating whether or not to turn back just as the glimmering dome of the Ulmosian territory came into my bleary view. Gills or not, the saltwater still stung my eyes. Firth had described Ulmos to me as if it was something I could miss, like a turn while driving to a party, but it was truly impressive. I wondered for a moment if humans ever stumbled upon this glittering palace before remembering just how deep I was; they didn't need to hide like my people did because they were so far out of the way. The city was a colossal kingdom of blue and silver and green, all enclosed in what looked like a giant protective bubble. Inside, it seemed, life carried on much like it did on the surface; the Ulmosi walked, talked, and operated upright, with gravity and oxygen to aid them.

I gasped – or gasped as much as I could underwater – as a huge shadow with colossal tentacles moved past me, and I knew that if the depth didn't scare humans away, the existence of colossal squid likely would. If it was possible, a chill coursed through my body at the thought of being the beast's next meal and being torn bit by bit by that enormous beak. The ocean was terrifying.

Guards were stationed around the perimeter of the bubble, where one needed clearance to be permitted entry. The guard at the entrance nearest to me – who reminded me of both our beloved Firth and the guard who had ruined the most beautiful day of my life – began moving his hands through the water as I approached. I was grateful that I'd put some extra effort into learning Ulmosi Sign Language before this voyage, and I mentally thanked Firth and Zara for their oceanside lessons between my dives as I communicated with the Ulmosi guard.

"State your name and business," he signed. His communication was so fluid that it was clear he'd been using this language his entire life. Perhaps it was standard for all Ulmosi to be fluent. I tried hard to focus while still maintaining a neutral expression; after all, I had to convince this man that USL was one of my native languages. My brain felt fuzzy and tired, but I was so close...

Shoot. My name. "Mycel" was certain to sound the alarm in the sea kingdom; it didn't get much more forest-like than being named after part of a mushroom. I searched my memories for names Firth and Earwyn had mentioned while discussing home. "N-e-r-i-s-s-a."

The guard nodded.

"Returning home," I lied, "summoned by the king and queen." I held my breath while the guard looked me up and down. A school of fish swam rapidly past me, and I flinched despite my efforts to appear at home.

Though he raised an eyebrow at my less-than-comfortable behavior, the guard stuck a gloved hand through the wall of the dome. When I put my hand in his, he pulled me through immediately, and I was left standing on the platform next to him, gasping to adjust to the air within the dome. It was startling, going from using my gills to my lungs so rapidly, and I tried to stifle my rising cough so as not to draw any further alarm from the guard. The air inside of the dome was humid.

It didn't work. No sooner had I cleared my throat than the guard had pulled my wrists around my back and secured them with bonds. "I know you're not returning home. Another guard has told us to keep an eye out for you, so I suppose it's good you were already headed to see the king and queen..."

CHAPTER TWENTY-THREE

When I finally found my Earwyn, my husband, my missing piece, he sat upon his throne next to the woman he'd been promised to. "Yes, yes, that'll be just perfect for the royal wedding! And your coronation, of course, darling," she purred, talking at Earwyn while he looked disinterested. "I can't believe it's almost here!" The scene felt like something out of a nightmare.

The Ulmosi throne room was as overdone as the rest of their kingdom. Not only did it shine, it glimmered, and its excessive decor and wealth made me feel even more out of place and unsteady. It may as well have been the inside of a treasure chest. The walls sported floor-to-ceiling windows which peered into the depths of the ocean, and schools of shimmering fish, sharks, and the occasional octopus made their way leisurely by them. Glowing sconces lit the walls and sent glittering beams of light fluttering down the walls. The floor shimmered like mother-of-pearl, and in the center was a smaller dome, probably as wide as I was tall, that looked to be the inverse of how the city was structured. Instead of a dome of air inside of the ocean, this was a bubble that allowed the throne room's inhabitants to look at and possibly enter the ocean via a suspended bubble of water. It appeared to work much like the entrance to kingdom had, where it could be penetrated if necessary to cross into the other zone.

At the far end of the room were the thrones. Even in a crowd, it would've been easy to pick out the king and queen of Ulmos by their resemblance to the man I loved. His father sat upon a throne that looked to be made of driftwood and encrusted with jewels and white gold. The man was older, but not old by any means; in human years, he would have likely passed as in his midforties. He had the same blue-green eyes as Earwyn, but they lacked the tender depth that I loved so much. The older man had a perfectly kept beard and long blond hair that seemed to sparkle with the reflection of the sea when he moved his head.

His wife, whose gaze held a harshness that reminded me of the depths of the ocean... dark, empty, unforgiving... sat unamused next to him. Her dark hair was piled on her head in an intricate updo, and she was looking down at one of her perfectly manicured hands, seemingly inspecting her jewelry, when I was escorted in. She truly looked like a mermaid, the kind that lured sailors to their deaths, though somehow even less pleasant. It was hard to believe that these people had produced someone as gentle as Earwyn, and when I thought of the way he'd regarded them during our conversations, I felt anger rise within me.

Next to the royals were advisers. For being at the service of the royal family, the advisers were almost indistinguishable in their own luxurious apparel and appearances. The attire of the Yannavi royals couldn't compare to even the lowest tier here in Ulmos. Each wore rings, necklaces, jewels upon jewels. It was clear that any funding raised for ocean conservation under the guise of the Salt and Earth Alliance went primarily to fulfilling the Ulmosi royals' extravagant lifestyle. It made me wonder how their commoners lived. Did they, too, have access to riches? Or, in true Ulmosi fashion, did they live in poverty, begging for scraps from their rulers? It seemed like the latter was more likely, and for a moment, I imagined the people of Ulmos lining up outside of the castle to receive their weekly rations. My stomach turned. I had only seen the kingdom from afar before being escorted directly into the hall, but it would not have surprised me to see streets lined with trash in the neighborhoods, simply masked by the glimmering facade of the city from afar. They were, after all, very focused on appearances.

CHAPTER TWENTY-FOUR

"And what right do you have to be here, in the High Court of Ulmos? I don't recognize you, nor do I care to. Speak quickly and limit our wasted time," instructed one of the royal family's advisers. The man stared down his nose at me from his seat.

"I've come to collect my husband," I said firmly, though every muscle in my body was screaming with pain. Yes, I'd come to rebel against their move to betray the humans and rule the other domains of terrafolk, and also to rearrange some faces if needed, but I'd likely need the help of my partner first.

I looked directly at Earwyn, who was sitting on his throne in misery next to his betrothed. Outwardly, he looked fit as ever, wearing a shimmering ensemble of black and gray with greenish-blue accents; his vest, trousers, and cloak all matched expertly. He wore black leather boots that were shined to perfection. His hair, which I'd desperately missed running my fingers through, however, was in stark contrast to his previous self; his flowing locks were absent, and instead his mane was cut into short waves. As handsome as he looked, I knew better than to think this was just a styling choice. Everyone in the hall had long, shimmering, and well-loved hair; this was an act of damnation. My heart ached. Despite his neat appearance, however, his eyes were dark and heavy with sleepless circles, and his throat still bore healing bruises from where his gills had been brutally reopened by his arresting guard. They looked like a warning. His posture was impassive, as if he couldn't be bothered to add to the conversation by confirming or denying what I'd said, but when I finally met his gaze, it was clear that something was amiss. His eyes looked exasperated, desperate, concerned, and filled with longing. That was when I noticed his hands, which were "resting" on the arms of his chair, but looked as though they were straining against some invisible bonds. His nail beds looked dark, too, as if he'd been scratching at something, and I noticed some grooves in the wood of his would-be throne. While his ensemble had sheaths for what might have been a sword and dagger, no such weapons filled them. There were more important matters to consider, but I found myself briefly thanking the stars that his ring finger remained bare, and no one had filled my space there. How long had he been trapped there? How many public appearances had he made while confined to his throne, looking pristine but feeling like a prisoner of his own people? I didn't waste a glance on his queen-to-be, knowing that I'd need to be strong for both of us once I got Earwyn away from her. I didn't want to think of what had happened while I was away; what abuse had he endured?

The only reassuring part of Earwyn's appearance was the sea otter lying on a small pillow on the floor next to his throne. I recognized her as Genny, Earwyn's familiar that I'd never had the pleasure of meeting, but had heard about. He told me he spent some evenings on the shore with her, watching the waves come in.

Genny looked up at her person periodically and I sensed concern from her I hadn't seen in another animal's expression.

The court burst into laughter at my statement. I found it boring that they were so pompous, but knew that I had to entertain their conversation as a means to an end. My head spun, and my stomach cramped, but I managed to keep myself upright. I straightened my spine and lifted my chin. Even Earwyn's fiancée laughed, gesturing at me as if to say "Who is this woman?" I hated her. I wondered for a moment what they'd promised her for her part in this facade. If I had a chance to slap the smirk off her face before I left for either prison or home, I'd take it in a heartbeat.

"This seems like quite the desperate plea for attention when the prince's coronation is only days away," another older man noted with a scoff. It was a wonder this community had produced someone as soft and humble as Earwyn. "You're not the only Ulmosi with a crush on Lord Earwyn, but I hardly think that's grounds to cause such a scene. In fact, I'm uncertain of how you even managed to gather an audience with the entire court."

I rolled my eyes at the mention of a crush and honestly, at the mention of a scene; I believed I had it in my power to make a much greater one if needed, especially with the arsenal of information that Firth had equipped me with. "We've wed, so I'm certain it's a bit more than a crush at this point," I stated firmly, searching the court for the guard who'd taken Earwyn from me those weeks prior; surely despite his alliance he'd vouch for the fact that he'd found us in the midst of our wedding. "And you'd do right to honor that union above whatever this arranged nonsense is," I added, gesturing at the couple before me. I wasn't sure if it was the pain, the exhaustion and sacrifice to get myself there, or just my annoyance with the fact that I was having to explain myself to a court of snobs, but something about the scenario left me with very little tact. I despised royal business; there wasn't a group of creatures anywhere else in the hierarchy of our societies that I'd found to be more up their own asses, though somehow Earwyn seemed to have escaped that stereotype.

"And why should we listen to you?" an elder Ulmosi asked curiously, eyeing me up and down. I wondered briefly how often their plans were foiled, let alone by someone not even of their kind. They didn't know I wasn't one of their kind, though. I braced for additional questioning: *How did you get here? Where is the guard that helped you, so we can punish him accordingly?*

I pulled out the weapon I'd only realized I'd had moments before. Why had my body been rebelling against me? Why hadn't I bled in months? The chaos of my time with Earwyn had been so distracting that I didn't realize I'd believed us to be biologically incompatible until that moment, when I felt the flutter of life in my womb. "Because I'm carrying the heir to your throne."

The court gasped.

I looked to Earwyn again, part of me fearing what his reaction might be. I knew that providing Ulmos with an heir had been a dreadful thought for him, and I knew that breaking the news to him in a court full of creatures he hated was not ideal. When my eyes met his, however, I felt fresh air fill my lungs for the first time in forever. The relief I felt in his gaze was a reminder that I had made the right choices in my life recently and that this was where I was meant to be. His stormy gaze was deep and soft, only for me, but he kept the rest of his expression passive as if he were being held captive. He was, after all, and I knew that even when he held the highest throne in his kingdom, he would still be a puppet to the Ulmosi's ulterior motives. He wouldn't be Earwyn; he'd be a shell, and even if I wasn't his wife, I had to try to free him from that hellish fate. Anyone I knew enough to respect the way I did Earwyn deserved someone to fight for them, and since Firth was incapacitated, I owed this to him. I grounded myself in my stand as I awaited their judgment.

"Delusional," the man scoffed, sneering at me. "This isn't the first desperate attempt at gaining attention we've heard... nor would this be the first royal bastard if it's true. Get this peasant out of here and deal with her accordingly." He snapped his fingers at a guard who'd been standing near the door to the room. I steadied myself to be hauled off again, but was determined not to look frightened. I wondered how they would've dealt with an actual pregnant peasant; perhaps the automatic next step for me was to throw me in a prison cell where I'd starve to death along with my unborn child. Such an inhumane travesty would never have happened in Yannava, but it was clear that the Ulmosi were brutal, violent, and power-hungry. "We don't need a commoner child running around claiming to be heir to the throne."

"I wouldn't recommend that," I said clearly, glaring at the guard as he approached me. I wasn't sure what in my posture or words had actually made him listen, but he paused briefly, looking at his leadership for instruction. "I'm sure the entirety of Yannava would be disappointed to hear that the rightful claimant to their throne has been harmed or mistreated in any way, let alone while pregnant with the heir to their and another kingdom's throne."

"The rightful claimant to their throne has been missing for quite some time. Said to be fraternizing with the humans, no less," the queen-to-be finally piped up curiously, eyeing me as if she didn't trust what I was saying. "Besides, you're in Ulmos. What would a Yannavi be doing here, and how?"

"Yes." I nodded and stifled another eyeroll at their inability to put one and one together. I forced myself to hold my head up high despite my irritation with her involvement. "That's me. And the son or daughter I'm carrying will have the right to your throne and Yannava's. You know full well that harming a royal from another domain, let alone the highest royal who also happens to be carrying a child, will undoubtedly lead to a war you couldn't dream of winning." The ocean was deep and scary, I knew that, but I told myself that the forest had allies that the Ulmosi couldn't even begin to imagine. "You may have bullied my stewardesses into agreeing with you, but that was only because they didn't have me there to lead. That mistake will not happen again."

The court was silent as I stood there, willing my legs not to shake. "Now unhand my husband," I said firmly, savoring the way the title felt on my tongue. "And allow us to leave."

The crushing weight of my unanswered demand filled the room, and self-doubt began to creep in rapidly. I forced myself to stand up tall and face them head-on, but couldn't bring myself to look at Earwyn because I knew he would soften my already questionable resolve. When a mocking laugh burst from the woman on the throne next to him, the hair on every inch of my body stood on end immediately: Maren. I looked up at her to catch her glaring at her fiancé and felt my blood boil. "You were able to... knock up that fairie, but you can't even begin to satisfy me in bed?" she spat, glowering and clearly unbothered by the attention she was drawing to herself and the future king of their domain. Even though I knew the truth about their predicament, I couldn't help but feel embarrassed for both of them. When Maren stood from her throne to face me, however, I was taken aback. Her hair, so blond it was almost white, was done up in intricate braids that lined the sides of her head and trailed down her back, and her eyes were the palest blue I'd ever seen. There was no doubt that she was stunning, with perfect, petite features and skin like porcelain, but she looked hollow.

Earwyn, meanwhile, was straining so hard against his invisible bonds that I could see the veins in his neck threatening to burst. They'd really subdued him.

"Perhaps an alliance—" an older man spoke up briefly. When I surveyed him, I realized he must've been Earwyn's grandfather.

"That's enough, old man! Royalty or not," Maren spat, descending the stairs in front of her throne to approach me, "you're nothing but a dirty, greedy, little fairie." The rest of the court looked on in horror, though it wasn't clear if they were also feeling embarrassed or if they were just fearful of this wildcard of a woman. She stepped toward me threateningly, punctuating her words with the sharp clicks of her shoes against the marble of the hall. "You might be the perfect fit for our pitiful prince here, but I won't let you march in and take him just because you spread your le—"

I couldn't help myself. Having been stripped of almost all of my weaponry upon entry, I resorted to using all I had left and smiled inwardly when my fist collided with Maren's jaw. The resounding crack was one of the most satisfying sensations I'd ever felt, even though it resulted in a terrible ache in my hand and what was likely to be only short-term discomfort for Maren, who undoubtedly still had access to full magick. With any luck, I'd at least bruised her pride even though I'd probably broken a couple of my fingers. Her cheek shone red for a few seconds, and I reveled in the enjoyment I got from her shocked expression. Priceless. After all she'd done to my husband, it was the very least I could do to repay her.

The court, which had been seemingly held hostage by Maren's childish outburst, suddenly sprung to action with royals rising from their thrones to verbally assault me.

"How dare you!"

"In our throne room, of all places!"

"She must be out of her mind!"

"Unbelievable that Earwyn stooped so low as to—"

Meanwhile, the old man chuckled a little as if to say "I've been waiting for someone to do that."

"I don't care who she says she is, take her away!"

"GUARDS!"

I rolled my eyes yet again, submitting as two guards grabbed me roughly by the arms with no care in the world; I was out of magick and energy and grit and whatever else it would've taken to fend off several grown Ulmosi men who were equipped with far more power than I had access to. Regardless of what happened next, I'd stood my ground for myself, my husband, our unborn child, and our friends on land. I looked up at Earwyn and winked at him as I was unceremoniously dragged from the throne room. It was kind of nice to be carried away after exerting so much of my waning strength; I even let my boots drag on the floor without protest.

Just as they were about to pull me from the room, however, the doors burst open with guards hauling someone in the opposite way. They tossed their captive onto the floor in front of the thrones, and when the person lifted their head, it was hard for me to hold back a gasp.

"You," Maren hissed, stomping toward the slumped-over prisoner. "Don't you think it would've been useful to mention we were dealing with a royal here? Not to mention a *pregnant* one?"

Anala glanced back at me and then looked at Maren with a blaze I was shocked she had the energy to maintain. She set her jaw hard, in typical Anala fashion, and I was admittedly impressed by her absolute devotion to herself. "Now what good would that have done *me*?" she asked honestly, glaring at the royal before her. "Besides, I didn't think she would make it back here!" Even from where I barely stood, it was obvious that they'd roughed her up as well and that she was talking through, at best, a busted lip. "I helped you get your stupid prince back! And at worst, Mycel should've been dead from her people withdrawing her magick – that was the deal. I did my part!" The room buzzed as everyone realized that she'd been playing each and every one of them, myself included, to try to climb her way to power. It was sad, really; I wondered for a moment what her history was like, that she was so desperate to control something... desperate enough to risk the lives of so many, including her own. She'd wanted to get rid of me to open up access to Yannava: access only she'd known about until that day. Then she could leverage her ties with the humans and Ulmos to create some sort of alliance at the top of which she'd triumphantly sit. I couldn't suss out the details in that moment, but at a glance the pieces fit together. "Who cares if she's pregnant? You're telling me that the Ulmosi have never killed a kid?" she spat angrily.

Maren snapped at the guards now holding me up just as they were about to escort me from the room. "Keep her here for a moment, I'd like her to see how we handle traitors in Ulmos." The court elders watched on with satisfaction in their expressions; it was clear that they liked Maren's vision for their kingdom.

My eyes widened as I realized that Anala's execution, for lack of a better word, would not be swift or painless. Somewhere, someone triggered a mechanism that opened a hole in the floor of the throne room; through the hole, there was a bubble that looked penetrable by hand and that clearly led deep into the ocean. Perhaps this was an easy exit for the royals if needed; maybe they'd use it if under siege. It seemed out of the way enough. But when one of the guards extended a twisted, magickal hand toward Anala, much like they had to Earwyn in the forest, I crushed my eyes shut. She protested as her borrowed gills sealed themselves closed. I couldn't bring myself to watch another person's throat be torn to bits or revealed or whatever hell the creation and destruction of gills had come to be.

"No, no, don't do this!" she screeched, both from the pain and the knowledge of what was coming next. The fire in her voice was unmistakably Anala, but the sheer terror, which I'd never heard from her before, was new. It made my stomach turn. "You need me, you need a connection like me! I can help you! You really think *water* is going to help you overtake Yannava? The humans? You need *fire!*"

No one acknowledged her pleas, but when I forced my eyes open, I noticed that Earwyn's were glazed over with tears. He was more merciful than that, even to those who had harmed him or his loved ones. Perhaps he'd have found a way to imprison or exile her instead. I wondered briefly if any of his sadness came from the realization that he or I could be next up for this fate. There was a brief moment where his gaze met mine at the same time that Anala glanced back to look at me, as if I had any power in that moment... or as if attempting to muster an apology that would never come. Any apology would've been an attempt at self-preservation; we all knew that she longed to see me burn along with everyone else.

It took only a swift moment for one of the guards to shove her through the bubble despite her clawing and begging, where the royals watched her struggle to swim and breathe until she eventually drowned. Her body thudded against the underside of the throne room floor as it was pulled away by the current. Suddenly a gush of red filled the water in the bubble, and I saw a massive white-tip shark swim by with one of Anala's manicured hands hanging from his mouth.

This in itself felt savage, disturbing, and unnecessary, but not much could have prepared me for the reappearance of the white tip, which stalled under the glass dome and began twitching oddly. Seconds later it had shifted into a grown man who was then hoisting himself out of the port in the floor, causing a splash of water to follow him through the bubble. When he stood fully, he towered over nearly everyone in the hall: a massive, naked beast of a man who was heavily muscled aside from his protruding midsection where he had the physique of a strongman. He thoughtlessly shook his head, causing droplets of water to splatter on the marble floor beneath him, where puddles were pooling from the liquid dripping off his body. When he lifted his gaze, I had to stifle a gasp. I knew that face; in fact, it was the stunning copy of Firth's own wholesome, handsome mug, but somehow made brutal and violent. I snuck a glance at Earwyn, who was cringing as he looked away from the massive man. Was this a twin? Not only that, but was Firth's twin a varispirit? We had some shapeshifters in my realm, but they were highly valued and treated like royalty. Something about his role in disposing of a traitor made me think this wasn't the case for varispirits in Ulmos. The sea-based kingdom continued to surprise me with its harshness.

"Rhodes," the king addressed the giant man, nodding in his direction.

"My lord," he responded, bowing his head submissively. He wiped his mouth with the back of his hand, smearing the last droplets of Anala's remains across his cheek. It was quite the sight, seeing this man who could devour the room in an instant submit to the cruel hierarchy of the kingdom. I wondered if this had always been the man's role or if this had something to do with his twin's betrayal of the kingdom; perhaps it was punishment. When I surveyed the varispirit's stance I couldn't help but question if he knew that his brother was alive. Again, the stark nakedness of his presentation also suggested some sort of punishment given that the rest of the court was dressed so fully and elegantly. There wasn't anything wrong with his form, but it certainly looked out of place in that setting. It seemed cruel and unusual to force this man to dispose of traitors as a reminder of what may have happened to his brother on land. I swallowed hard as I watched the interaction, desperate to instill some hope in him with the news of his brother's health and safety.

"You're dismissed."

Rhodes nodded again in acknowledgment and turned to leave, meeting my gaze briefly as he did so.

I was escorted from the hall.

CHAPTER TWENTY-FIVE

*T*he dungeon of the Ulmosian kingdom was ancient, and the stone of its walls looked as though it had been flooded many times; the porous rock was rounded and worn from the constant beating of sea salt and water. Upon my entry, I had to resist the urge to run my fingers over the walls. Somehow, the chamber was dry at the time I happened to be inhabiting it, though. The general odor of the space was briny, and it made me miss the fresh air of the forest even more. Fatigued beyond belief from my journey and holding myself up in front of the Court, I immediately let myself lean back against a wall and close my eyes.

The being in my belly tumbled or kicked in response, as if he'd been tired of all the back-and-forth as well. "I know," I murmured, commiserating with the only living creature I seemed to have left. Time ticked by and nothing changed; I didn't even hear the bustle of other prisoners in other cells. Would they feed me? Or let me starve to death in this place that surely none of my kind would ever venture to? I felt unbearably trapped because despite my surroundings seeming like any other jail cell, I knew that I was deep in the ocean, and that thought was endlessly unnerving. If I could muster the strength to escape, there would surely be none left to get Earwyn and then swim all the way to the surface without being apprehended; the Ulmosi were faster underwater and undoubtedly stronger than I was at that point. And as Anala's demise had demonstrated, the creatures of the deep ocean were not gentle with non-Ulmosi.

I slid down the wall so that I could sit and rested my head on the tops of my knees. It felt like surrender, but I lied to myself and said I was just resting, recouping my strength for when my next brilliant escape plan struck me.

No plans ever came.

The next time the door to the cell opened, someone was being shoved inside along with me. I really wasn't in the mood to deal with some random Ulmosi prisoner who'd been caught going too close to shore or looking at Maren the wrong way, so I kept to myself in the corner, trying to control my breathing, until I realized that the person hadn't moved once they'd been let in.

I looked up cautiously to see the outline of the only person that mattered in that stinking hellhole: Earwyn.

"Goddess," he breathed, the mask finally falling from his tortured face. He seemed afraid to touch me, but he did anyway, closing the gap between us in quick strides and gently pulling me to my feet. Every muscle in my body screamed with fatigue. I needed rest desperately but knew it wouldn't be coming any time soon unless my execution was right around the corner.

"Wonder." I reached for my husband and let myself be pulled into his arms, tired and weak, but grateful that if this was how it ended, at least I'd made true my promise to come back to him. When I tilted my chin up to look him in the eyes, I could see just how drained he was, could feel just how tortured he'd been. But in true Earwyn fashion, he made nothing about himself.

"You're alright?" he asked, running a soft hand against the side of my cheek to brush stray locks from my face where they'd been plastered by sweat and tears and saltwater. When I nodded, he continued, "And Firth? Zara?"

"They're okay," I breathed, pressing my forehead to his. "Safe, at least for now, and they're together." Despite all he'd been through, he wanted to ensure his people, his real people, were okay. It was a small reminder of how much I loved him and why.

"How…?" It seemed that he couldn't even begin to ask how I'd gotten myself into Ulmos, let alone jailed for sneaking in and attempting to free him. He brushed my hair with his fingers again, this time pulling it away from one side of my neck to expose my gills. I knew how brutal they looked; last I'd checked in the mirror, they were still bruised and barely healing.

"It's okay," I assured him, taking his hand in mine so that I could press my lips to his palm. I felt slightly relieved when my hair fell over my neck again. Hadn't he been tortured enough without having to see my wounds? I tried to change the subject for whatever it was worth. "Is Rhodes Firth's…"

"Twin, yes." He nodded absentmindedly.

When he stepped back to hold me at arm's length and look me up and down, though, I must've shot him a confused glance. I'd already told him I was okay. Tired, worn, unsure of how much longer I could fight this fight on unfamiliar grounds, but okay for the time being. I was upright, at least. "I'm okay, Wyn, I promise."

"And the baby…" he breathed, reaching a trembling hand to my midsection but struggling to actually make contact. "Our baby…"

I couldn't help the hearty laughter that overtook me as tears pricked my vision. "Our baby is fine," I told him to the best of my knowledge; my body had been through a lot in the months prior to our reunion, and while I wouldn't have been shocked if that had made it uninhabitable for the time being, I could feel that this little creature was as strong and resilient as the both of us were. "I thought I'd lost you," I confessed suddenly, tears pricking at my eyes. I pressed my forehead into his head, desperate to reconnect after so much time apart but terrified at the idea that we were likely about to be separated again. I didn't care, though, if this was just a tease; I intended to fully absorb whatever time I could with my husband.

"Never," he told me seriously. Apparently no longer fearful of breaking me, Earwyn closed the gap again, one hand pressed lovingly against my belly and the other tangled in my sweat-matted hair. He kissed me again and again, tenderly at first, then with a hint of desperation.

When we pulled apart, I couldn't help the tears that wet my cheeks. "Wonder," I breathed, pressing my forehead to his again and taking in the warming comfort of our closeness. "Forgive me."

"Whatever for?"

"I sent you back here," I acknowledged, choking back a trembling sob. I was disgusted with myself. "I practically handed you over, and look what they've done to you." I traced his hollow cheeks and then brought one of his bruised hands up to my face so I could kiss it in apology. I knew there had been no other option if I ever wanted to see Earwyn again, and still the guilt weighed on me heavily. "I'm responsible for this."

"You're responsible for my still being alive, Mycel," he stated firmly. "Don't tell yourself anything otherwise."

"How can you say that?"

He took my hands in his, kissed them tenderly and then looked me in the eyes. God, I'd missed his gaze, missed lying in bed with him in silence as we drank each other in. "You had no choice but to turn me over that day in the forest. In your heart, you must know that there was no other way out of that situation; we would have both ended up dead. You had to—"

"But—"

"Listen to me, Mycel. As powerful as you are, we didn't stand a chance. But now you're here. You're with me again... and it was the thought of you, the thought of this moment, that kept me fighting each day. I won't allow you to think otherwise because it wouldn't be the truth." We looked into each other's eyes, the sound of our shallow breathing echoing in the small dungeon cell. "You're the reason I still draw breath." He kissed me hard and deep, making our time apart and its effect on his insatiable hunger for me very clear. I returned the gesture with equal vigor despite my exhaustion.

Moments later found us stripping each other bare with no regard for our surroundings.

Immediately ravenous for him, I bit and kissed him roughly along his bare shoulders as he made quick work of my clothing. When I had a moment to examine him closer, I realized the extent of his imprisonment in Ulmos; he was much thinner than I'd last seen him and had ample bruising along his normally golden skin. I doubted that they'd physically beat him, but knew that his strong will had likely led him to refuse food and fight back whenever he was cornered or forced into something. I halted my passionate touch to trace my fingertips over the lines of his now-thin abdomen, and when our eyes met again, his sunken in with exhaustion, and mine bleary with tears, I told him honestly, "I'll kill them." I would. I'd make them pay for how much they'd hurt this man, not only recently but throughout his life.

"I know, Your Highness." He didn't mock me, no, instead he acknowledged the power of my position and the foolishness of his people to question it. There was something undeniably sexy about that power, too, and though I had felt powerless up until that moment, in seconds, we were on each other again.

Breathless, I pulled back for a moment. "Wait." I shoved a hand frantically into my hair, searching for a particular tangled knot, then grinned when I found the right one. It took me only seconds to slip Earwyn's ring back onto his finger, and I crushed my mouth to his before he could comment. My ring, of course, had never left me. "That's never leaving your finger again. Take me now," I begged him as he dragged his teeth along the flesh of my throat. We were desperate, ravenous, careless. He pinned me forward up against the bars of the cell door so that my breasts mashed themselves between each section of the cage and pushed himself against me. He was hot and hard as stone, his erection firmly against my ass. I needed him. "Now," I pleaded, and to my immediate pleasure, he bent me forward and plunged himself into me with no regard for foreplay. The way he stretched me was exquisitely painful, and I leaned into the pressure; he was my missing piece in every sense.

"Goddess," he growled, showing a rough, domineering, and almost frantic side of himself that I hadn't seen before. He was claiming me in a place we had both grown to despise, and as his balls slapped heavily against my throbbing clit, it felt like a huge middle finger to the kingdom of Ulmos. I held back nothing, letting my absolute delight be known through moans and whimpers and enthusiastic encouragement as my man, my husband, and my king, fucked me hard and deep. "So good," Earwyn growled, gripping my hips with sweat-slicked palms as he rammed into me. Hyper-aware of the situation and our surroundings, I could feel the cool metal of his wedding band pressed against my flesh. It wouldn't leave his finger ever again, or there'd be hell to pay.

I was approaching the crest of what was sure to be one of many orgasms when footsteps caught my attention. Earwyn slowed, but I reached to my side to grab his ass and urge him into me harder, faster. "Don't." That way, when Maren, who had likely come to spit some hateful venom at us, walked by our cell, she saw her fiancé happily engaging in what she could never get him to do willingly. She even made eye contact with me as she approached the cell and realized what was happening, and I couldn't control the lust-filled "God, Wyn, just like that" that burst from my panting lips as I threw my head back. She scoffed and hurried away before I could look at her again. "Ugh, you're so deep," I gasped, reaching back to dig my nails into one of his thighs as he brought us both to the edge quickly.

He placed a large hand on my lower belly, using his fingers to expertly massage between my thighs and his palm to squeeze himself as he plunged into me. "Do you feel me all the way in here?" he asked, knowing full well that his size meant I could practically feel him in my ribcage. He was truly claiming me inside and out, and I couldn't have loved it more.

"Yes! Yes... yes..."

I forgot about Maren almost immediately following her departure, though in the moment I may have snickered a little bit.

Despite his weight loss and exhaustion, Earwyn still had strength to hoist me up into his arms without pulling out of me, and hammered up into me as I wrapped my legs around his waist. He kissed me with the hunger of a man imprisoned, and I returned the gesture, licking the sweat from his upper lip as I reminded him, "I love you, I love you..." between rough, biting kisses. It'd been so long since I was able to say that to him face-to-face.

He almost looked pained when he finally unleashed himself into me, pumping hard and frantic as his blue-green eyes locked on me; his expression was animalistic, uncontrolled, and beautiful. I realized then that he'd never let me see him so vulnerable before.

At this point, though, we had nothing left to lose. "Ah, goddess, take it all," he groaned as his pace slowed with each brutal spurt.

"Mine," I declared, loving the heat of him filling me so intimately. I could already feel his come dripping back down out of me and heating both of our bare thighs. If I had to go this long without him ever again, there'd be hell to pay.

We were parched and panting and sweat-slicked when we finally surrendered to our exhaustion and lay down on the pitiful excuse for a bed in the cell. It creaked under our weight, and part of me wanted to leave it broken as another insult to the kingdom it belonged to. I rested my head on Earwyn's bare chest, acutely aware of how much I'd missed him, and breathed him in. I tried to stifle thoughts of being the next to meet their fate under the bubble in the throne room when it struck me that, in my excitement, I'd left a question unasked. I looked up at my husband without removing my head from his chest and tangled my fingers in what was left of his sandy locks. "How did you get down here?" I asked, feeling a bit ridiculous for not having pried earlier; it seemed like an important question. "Did you sneak away or... no, you wouldn't have." I knew enough to know that if the Ulmosi didn't want him to do something, they'd make it so.

"They've finally given up on me."

"What does that mean?"

"It means I'm no longer worth the effort to them. I'm not getting them what they want with the humans or with Maren, so they have no use for me."

I swallowed hard, searching his face for any indication of how he felt. I wanted to know what had happened while we were apart; it was clear that whatever had happened had hardened him. Was the Earwyn I knew still in there somewhere, or had his hatred for his family taken over? Unfortunately there wasn't time to figure that out, but I hoped that there would be sometime, somehow...

Before I could comment, he continued. "I couldn't care less what happens to Ulmos now, but we aren't going down with it."

"How can you be so certain? We're both imprisoned and powerless in a kingdom full of people who hate us... if we're going anywhere right now, it's deeper into this hellhole."

A deep, booming voice interrupted our conversation and caused me to sit upright immediately. "This is... not what I'd expected to find down here," commented Rhodes, who was standing at the door to the cell, finally clothed. Well, mostly; he at least had pants on this time, but his thick, muscular upper body remained bare. I imagined clothes were difficult to navigate if you were constantly switching between animal and human form. The comment felt humorous, but his expression indicated nothing of the sort; he was stoic and reserved and clearly less warm than his brother. As I looked him over, I recalled my interaction with the shark that had stopped me from floating out to sea in my despair. Had that been Rhodes? Had this gruff, angry man actually saved my life once already? "You two have really thrown all your cares out, haven't you? Are you just waiting to die down here? I'm sure Maren is cooking up some special plan for you both."

"Now we're even," I told him, referring to his fully nude introduction in the throne room. I could feel Earwyn's embarrassment radiating off of him, but didn't bother to cover myself. Maybe I *had* given up.

"Not *all* of our cares," Earwyn murmured, jerking his chin toward the other man. "Do you have it?"

Without responding, Rhodes unlocked the cell, then pocketed the key again before tossing us a fistful of clothing each. Earwyn caught his gracefully. Mine hit me directly in the face, then flopped onto my lap in a fully appropriate level of clumsiness. I sat looking a bit dumbstruck as Earwyn stood and began dressing himself in the new attire without any commentary. Admittedly, I found myself a bit shocked at how comfortable he was naked, but then again, modesty seemed rather unimportant when certain death was in the forecast. Certainly Rhodes would agree with that given how freely he let it all hang loose in the throne room.

"My lord?"

"Rhodes, that's enough." Earwyn rolled his eyes at the title. "Come on."

"Fine, Earwyn." The large man sighed and then nodded before switching to sign language. I immediately registered his brother's name, but tried to avert my gaze, intimating that their use of sign language was intended to keep me out of the conversation.

I sorted through the clothing in my lap and began dressing, slightly surprised when Earwyn answered him aloud. "He's alive."

"You're joking."

"Seems like a cruel thing to joke about," Earwyn told him, pulling a skin-tight shirt over his head. The fabric hugged his torso snuggly and appeared to be made of some sort of water-resistant material. "Mycel left him before she came here. He's being cared for by one of her friends." He moved onto yanking similarly fashioned pants onto his legs.

"I haven't *heard him* since you came back, Earwyn."

I swallowed hard. "He almost died." I looked down at the clothing in my lap, a pang of guilt in my heart as I thought of Firth's injuries and the sacrifice he'd made because of our love for each other. But they were safe, thank gods, and it seemed like he would soon be reunited with his brother.

Almost as if he could hear my thoughts, Rhodes sneered at my comment before signing to Earwyn again. I couldn't blame him; I had become the source of so much pain for so many people. I only hoped that escaping Ulmos would give me the chance to make reparations.

Earwyn, still lacing up the front of his pants, spoke in return, "Big brother? Rhodes, you're twins."

"I was born first," Rhodes insisted. "By three minutes." My heart ached for the way he obviously cared for and wanted to protect his brother; it reminded me a lot of Firth's devotion to Earwyn. "I'm supposed to take care of him, just like he takes care of you. You know that."

"But he's okay now. Did you hear... or see... who hurt him before he went dark?" I knew the answer, but desperately wanted confirmation that it hadn't been one of my people pitted against me.

Rhodes barely spared me a grunt. "I took care of her. You saw." As the last word left his lips, I noticed a flash of red appear on his shoulder, then scurry down his arm and into his pocket; Ember had survived despite her person's fate. I wanted to ask about Rhodes's plan for the tiny lizard, but assumed he wouldn't bother to respond. Seeing the lizard did, however, make me wonder what would happen to Maz if I was hurt or killed. Would he be punished for my perceived crimes, or would he go free?

Clearly bored of my questioning and commentary, Rhodes resigned himself to waiting outside the cell for us under the guise of being a lookout. Again, I couldn't blame him for his distaste. What reason did he have to like me or owe me allegiance? As I pulled on my own clothing, I saw him inspecting an arsenal of blades that he'd tucked into his clothing and wondered how he kept hold of those when he was in his animal form. I pulled my own blade out of the boots that had been tossed aside during our passionate lovemaking and tucked it into my outfit, willing myself to use it if I needed to. I wondered if I had it in me to take a life if it came down to protecting my friends.

CHAPTER TWENTY-SIX

The clothing that Rhodes had brought us allowed us to swim without the weight of the water weighing our clothing down. I felt light and nimble – well, as much as I could – as I donned the seaweed fiber wetsuit. It would, hopefully, allow us to get back to shore faster, especially with him helping us in his shark form. As we snuck through the jail of the kingdom, I was surprised to see that most of the cells were empty. It was clear that the Ulmosi preferred not to keep prisoners for long and there was no doubt that our sentencing was set to happen soon. I noticed streaks of red across the walls of one cell as we passed and looked away quickly, trying not to imagine my own blood decorating the walls. It was time to go.

As a varispirit who had been enlisted – or enslaved – to serve the royal family, Rhodes had access to one of the exit portals which led directly out into the ocean and didn't require him to be let in or out by a kingdom guard. When we approached this portal, he slipped out, then we watched him shift into his shark form in the water. It was terrifying and awe-inspiring all at once. The idea that this man could snap his teeth and destroy someone was promising for his ability to protect us, but I reminded myself that I needed to stay on his good side. Once he'd shifted, Earwyn and I slipped out of the portal as well. It took me several practice breaths to reacclimate to the use of my gills and the sensation of freezing saltwater rushing through my lungs, but I nodded and grabbed on to one of Rhodes's fins while Earwyn took the other. The white-tip shark hovered for a moment before jetting off in what I assumed was the direction of the shore. Surely this method of travel would be much faster than my own sluggish attempts at traversing the deep.

At first, our journey home was uneventful. Almost boring. I even saw Genny swim by; Earwyn had assured me that she would meet us at the surface. I wondered if we'd arrive at the shore and return back to the apartment as if nothing happened. Perhaps we'd introduce Rhodes to our favorite Chinese place and eat it while watching old Western movies with the subtitles on. Earwyn even glanced over at me across Rhodes's massive back and winked. Easy-peasy, as the humans say.

But our leisurely cruise on the S.S. Rhodes was cut short when a blur shot through the water and slammed directly into him. It disappeared into the darkness of the sea, but not before jostling us all so much that we went soaring through the water in different directions. The taste of salty brine filling my throat caused me to attempt to cough in the water and fail. I was upside down for a few seconds before I turned myself and glanced around for both our attacker as well as my travel companions. I spotted Rhodes and Earwyn, mostly by the white tips of the shark's fins and Earwyn's flowing hair, but just as I swam toward them, the attacker blew past me and toward them again. It was another shark. Massive, hulking, and vicious looking in comparison to Rhodes; this was a Great White. I didn't have time to consider who else in the Ulmosi kingdom was a varispirit and how they'd discovered our escape plan. Instead, I swam. I trusted that Rhodes had been heading the right direction. Earwyn seemed to have the same idea. I glanced back to see Rhodes being circled by the Great White again.

I couldn't leave him. I'd left too many people.

Earwyn shook his head at me in the water and gestured the way we'd been going as if to say "Keep going!"

I shook my head "no."

My husband gestured to his belly, then pointed to me. But how could I live with myself if I'd let someone else die just to protect myself and my child? It wouldn't be right.

It took some maneuvering, but I was able to pull the blade from my boots, which I'd refused to leave behind, and swam toward the dueling sharks after attempting to steady my nerves for a second; that was all the time I could stand to waste. I tried to stay out of the Great White's line of vision, grateful that he was distracted by his pursuit of Rhodes, and swam up next to it as quickly as I could. I reached for his fin just for him to dodge me in his underwater fight.

I reached again and brushed my fingertips along the White's massive fin. My grip slipped.

It turned to look at me, its empty black eyes boring into mine. Its rows of teeth were so close to me I almost forgot what I had been doing and felt mesmerized by the gaping maw that was soon to destroy me.

A shadow approached from the side, and Rhodes rammed the other shark in the gills, causing it to lose its focus on me. Then, I swung. The blade cut through the water much more slowly than I was used to, but I managed to lodge it into the creature's other side, which caused it to halt its pursuit of Rhodes immediately.

The water exploded with a cloud of red, and I tasted the metallic tang of blood as I continued breathing. It was all I could do not to retch. Before I could think more or react, Earwyn had grabbed me by the sleeve, and we were being pulled through the water again as his other hand kept us attached to Rhodes. When Earwyn looked back at me, dragging me through the ocean by my clothing, the harshness of his expression startled me. I couldn't read his mind, but I could guess that he was thinking something along the lines of "I just got you back. Don't do that again, Mycel." My newfound strength told me I couldn't make that promise.

CHAPTER TWENTY-SEVEN

*W*hen we crawled onto shore, barely breathing, barely alive, I was shocked to see Firth and Zara waiting for us in the dark. The beach seemed empty of patrons, without a single bonfire or tipsy couple wandering its moonlit sand. There was no way for them to have known that we'd escaped and were returning home or when. I wiped my hair from my face and spat out a mouth of saltwater as I crawled ashore, searching their expressions for information on how they'd arrived there just in time. Had Rhodes somehow communicated to them? Was this a homecoming? Could we finally breathe a sigh of relief?

It was then that I noticed an Ulmosi guard standing behind them, very obviously pointing a blade at them in a threatening fashion. He had them waiting for us. He'd beaten us there, known we were coming. Dread filled me, leaving my frozen body feeling even more numb. This was all wrong.

I saw Mazus fly overhead and let out an alarming screech just as Firth's knees hit the sand; I didn't hear him, just saw his beak open in a silent scream.

"Firth…"

Rhodes's twitching, transforming figure crawled ashore next to me as his brother's shirt soaked with blood, a gash in his throat rapidly widening. The guard dropped his weapon, my weapon, my blade… and released Zara, shoving her forward on the sand next to her dying lover; she hit the ground hard, unable to catch herself with her hands and landing face down in the grit. I watched the light drain from Firth's eyes as if in slow motion. Rhodes had barely switched to his human form in time to catch his brother's body before it fell forward, lifeless.

Zara let out a wail that sliced through the air, shattering the fragile silence of the night, and snapped me back to reality. Sand stuck to her face, plastered by ocean water, tears, and snot.

I dropped to my knees in the water, unable to take another step toward the gruesome scene before me. Part of me lacked the energy, and the other was afraid to see the brutality up close for fear of it becoming a reality. My husband hauled himself out of the water and cried for the first time in our relationship as he cradled his dead best friend's head in his lap. He stroked his short hair so tenderly, so lovingly, that it brought tears to my own eyes. He must have known that losing Firth one day was a possibility with him as a royal bodyguard, but to love him and then lose him so brutally… there could be no preparation for such a heinous act.

Rhodes screamed at his brother as he shook him. Begged him to stay here, to stay with him, to look at him, damn it. Apologized for failing him, verbally cursed himself for letting him leave. Begged to trade places. Anything for his little brother. I'd never shake those sounds from my mind, but sharing them, immortalizing them in writing, would feel like the violation of a sacred union. The most brutally painful part of the scene was watching him sign each word as he spoke, something he'd always done when communicating with his little brother.

Zara was flung over her lover's large body, her fingers gripping the bloodied fibers of his shirt as if she could pull him back to earthside. She pulled so hard I thought her fingers might break; as mighty as she was, she barely budged his still figure. This was the end of their beautiful, but brief chapter. It felt cruel that Earwyn and I should have even a moment more together when she had Firth ripped from her so savagely. Would I lose Zara to this same tragedy? "Do something!" she screamed at Rhodes, the last of us who might have a whisper of magick left. I wondered if it made things worse to see his replica there, drawing breath when her copy was no longer. To meet under such circumstances, when the person they both loved most had been cut down in front of them, seemed an unusually cruel move from the universe. When her gaze met mine, she wailed, "You promised him! You said you'd keep us safe!" I had failed them.

This was our punishment for what the Ulmosi viewed as betrayal. Our love; our kinship with the humans; our refusal to submit to a system that thrived on greed, abuse, and murder; the reclamation of our power... it had all culminated here, in the loss of our most trusted and innocent ally.

This was a threat that said – no, screamed – "Submit or lose everything."

This meant war.

*Follow Mycel and Earwyn's journey in Seaborne,
book 2 of the Terrafolk trilogy.*

ABOUT THE AUTHOR

Francesca Crispo is an aspiring fantasy romance author living near Seattle, WA. She received her B.A. in English Literature from ASU in 2016 and her M.Ed. from ASU in 2018. When she isn't writing or running a business full-time, she enjoys spending time with her family and dogs!

facebook.com/francesca.crispo.author

instagram.com/francesca.crispo.author

tiktok.com/@francesca.crispo.author

Milton Keynes UK
Ingram Content Group UK Ltd.
UKHW041952031123
431812UK00001B/89